ISBN-13: 978-1-943443-02-4
ISBN-10: 1943443025

Dedication

For my children, Kaitlyn and Justin. You are the very lights of my life and I couldn't be more proud to be your mother.

Prologue

Five years earlier...

Livia

"Do you, Peter, take this woman, Livia, to be your lawfully wedded wife? To have and to hold from this day forward, for better, for worse, for richer, for poorer, in sickness and in health, to love and to cherish, till death us do part?"

"I do," he responds. Smugly.

"Do you, Livia, take this man, Peter, to be your lawfully wedded husband? To have and to hold...."

Every little girl dreams of her wedding day. That magical moment when you pledge your undying love to the man who makes your heart beat a little faster, who makes your panties a little wetter and who you think will make the most handsome salt-and-pepper-haired ninety year old ever to walk the earth. Your father will walk you down the aisle, arm in arm, in a wedding dress so beautiful, your childish vision couldn't do it justice and he'll struggle to hold back the tears of both happiness at giving you away and sadness that you're no longer his little girl.

Every young woman dreams of the honeymoon that will quickly follow. Will he whisk me away to Paris, where we'll live on wine and cheese and each other for two weeks solid? Or will we fly to a secluded island, sit on the beach, soak in the sun and drink pina coladas that our private

3

butler delivers every hour on the hour? Or maybe we'll decide to cruise the Mediterranean, visiting exotic stops such as Istanbul or Rome or Santorini. But at the end of the day, it really doesn't matter where you go, because you'll be together.

And every girl, young or old, dreams of being married to a man who worships the ground she walks on, puts her on a pedestal and would give his life for hers without thought or hesitation.

I was every girl. Except, instead of the fancy wedding, complete with tears of joy, I'm standing in a courthouse in front of a justice of the peace with tears of heartbreak welling in my eyes. Instead of the elaborate gown, complete with a long, beaded train that I picked out with my sister and my best friends, I'm wearing a simple black sheath and matching pumps, which fit my somber mood perfectly. And instead of marrying the man who I love to the depths of my very soul, who will love and cherish me all the days of our lives, I'm marrying a monster...

"You may now kiss the bride."

...who will make the next one thousand two hundred and twelve days of my existence a living nightmare from which I cannot wake.

Chapter 1

Livia

I see him across the room. I'm utterly breathless.

My heart races.

My stomach flutters.

My soul disintegrates into a pile of scattered ashes once again.

I'm a complete fucking mess. No muscle will obey my command to move, even my eyelids. They refuse to take away his image for even a second.

Why is he here?

I shouldn't be taking this risk. I shouldn't be openly ogling him, but I can't look away. Holy mother of perfection...he's everything I remember and more. As breathtaking as the very first time I laid eyes on him. He's every woman's fantasy, probably men too. I see other women watching him and I want to scratch their eyes out. Some blatantly stare, as I do. Some sneak sly glances so their spouses or dates won't notice.

Foolish.

Of course their dates notice a textbook male specimen such as him in the room. All other men are busy pissing in a circle around their women to ward him away.

As if sensing my weighty stare, his eyes lock with mine. Neither of us move.

The woman dripping off his arm, hanging on his every word, seems oblivious to our connection. Every sound fades away as we stare into each other's eyes from across the ballroom. Eyes I'm all too familiar with but haven't seen in what seems like a lifetime. Eyes that haunt me.

God, I miss him with a raw ache that intensifies daily.

"Wow, look at that fine piece of ass. He's fuckable," whispers one of my best friends, Kamryn, following my stare.

The best of my life.

He starts across the room in my direction, his date all but forgotten as he leaves her in his dust. She's calling after him, but he simply waves his hand in dismissal, not bothering to look back. His angry eyes never leave mine, his full lips drawn in a tight thin line.

Oh shit. Time to go.

"Kam, I'm not really feeling well, sweetie. I'll call you in the morning after my interview." I'm frantic to escape. I turn to leave, heels clicking as I quickly walk toward the exit. Kamryn practically runs to keep up.

"Let me call my driver for you, hon."

I call over my shoulder as I race toward my escape. "No, no. It's fine. There are plenty of cabs out front. I'll just hop in one and be home in no time. Really, it's fine."

Her grip is like an iron fist around my arm as she maneuvers me back to face her. Kam frowned, clearly not believing the blatant lie I threw her way. Whatever. Over her shoulder I estimate he's just fifty feet from where we now stand and moving at a clipped pace. As if by divine intervention, he's stopped by a buxom blond whose nipples are ready to fall out of her slutty dress any second. One deep breath and pop, they're free. He shakes her off, heading in my direction once again. Can't blame her for trying.

Crap Livia. Get. Out. Now.

"I think I may be sick, Kam. I'd really like to get home before I lose those little shrimp thingies I just ate." Not so much of a lie this time. My stomach *is* doing somersaults.

I turn and flee. I hear Kam call after me, but keep going this time. Making it to the safety of a cab before *he* reaches me is paramount.

Damn Kam and her insistence that I wear her four-inch Louboutin heels. So what if the fire engine red is a perfect complement to my also borrowed black leather strapless sheath. The shoes are still half a size too small and pinch my feet, making a hasty escape nearly impossible.

I should ditch the damn things like Cinderella. I bet she didn't even 'lose' her glass slipper. She was no doubt trying to escape this supposed Prince Charming because he was an arrogant asshole, and it fell off in her urgency to get away. In traditional antifeminism fashion, a man weaved an elegant story about how much better a girl's life would be with a boy in it. He would swoop in and save her from her persecuted life and they would live happily ever after.

Bullshit. All of it.

There is no happily ever after. Not for me anyway. That childish fantasy was ruthlessly shattered over five years ago.

I make it out of the ballroom, down the stairs and have the front hotel door halfway open when a strong hand clamps down on my shoulder, effectively stopping my forward movement. An electric current runs through my body and I feel him everywhere. His hand may as well be between my legs for all my body cares.

Damn you Louboutin and your impractical shoes.

"Hello Livia," a deep sensual voice drawls behind me. His voice and touch combined almost make my knees buckle. After all these years, he still has the same effect on all of my senses like the day we met. He sounds the same, albeit a bit more grown up. And a *lot* more sexy.

Jesus, I don't think I can do this.

You can do this Livia.

You have *to do this.*

Be cold.

Be unaffected.

Lie.

I take a deep breath, will the tears back, and steel myself before turning to face him.

"Hello Gray. Fancy seeing you here." *Holy...breathe, Livia, breathe.* I am almost taken aback by how utterly gorgeous he is. He had been stunning across the room and he was always beautiful, but up close he's like a golden angel sent directly from heaven—or hell—to tempt me. His face is no longer boyish, but all man, complete with

8

the sexiest scruffy whiskers I have ever seen. This is more than a five o'clock shadow, but not quite a full beard. I'm a sucker for scruff. Especially on Gray, but he's never worn it like this. It's downright sinful.

Double damn.

"What are you doing here Livvy?" *Livvy.* I haven't heard that name in over five years. It sounds so damn good I want to weep.

Dig deep, Livia...maintain the façade you've perfected so very well.

"I came for the same reason you probably did, the animals." Bravo for me. I sounded very confident...and very *stupid.* My internal head is shaking at me sadly.

He says nothing, remaining stoically silent, his eyes searching mine for the truth.

Subject change, before he asks too many more questions, for which I'll have to build lie on top of lie. I've told so many lies I need a cheat sheet to keep track of them all. "So, why are you in Chicago?"

His penetrating gaze makes me even more nervous than I already am, and I start to squirm. I never intended to run into anyone I knew here, let alone him. I would have never let Kam talk me into this stupid fundraiser otherwise.

Shit. Shit. Shit. This is so not good.

"I took over my father's company, and we moved the headquarters from Detroit to Chicago last year."

He lives here? In Chicago? My mind is spinning. I'm trying to process the fact that my ex-fiancé lives in the same city as I do, and that he took over his father's company already. I didn't remember Frank being that old. I shouldn't be engaging him in conversation, but I can't help but ask, "Did he retire?"

"No. He died." I gasp and my heart sinks.

"God, I'm sorry Gray, I had no idea. Your dad was a wonderful man." He was like a father to me, more so than my own, who'd essentially sold me to save his own life. I loved that family. They were like my own until they weren't anymore.

"Of course not, Livvy. How could you possibly when you fucking disappeared over five years ago, without a trace, without a call, without a forwarding goddamn phone number?" His retort was ripe with barbs, and it stung in the way it was meant to. I deserved some of his ire yes, but not all of it.

Gray has no clue the living nightmare I've endured. What I had done for my family or for him. And it would stay that way. I have to get away from him before I do something stupid, like spill my guts. He is my past, and as much as it deeply pains me, he has to stay that way. Too much has happened in the last five years that I simply can't overcome. I am damaged goods now, and Gray would never want me if he knew the truth. I need to get the hell out of here before I break down. I can't keep the tears back much longer.

"I have to go. It was nice to see you again, Gray." I need to get out of here before I throw myself at him and beg for his forgiveness. Because even though I don't quite deserve it, a small part of me desperately craves it. Gray is my first love. The only man I will ever love. And that young, naive woman now buried deep inside me will hold tightly to the memory of her first love with her last dying breath. It's all that has gotten me through the worst days of my life.

And it's all I have left.

I spin to leave when a strong hand pulls me back once again. Every time this man puts his hands on me, I bend to his will, and right now I feel like a torch has been set to my bones and they are far too pliable. My eyes flit between it and his ever so handsome face. He gets the gist and lets go.

Although his voice has softened, his annoyance clearly rings loud when uttering his next words. "How can I get ahold of you, angel? I'd like to have dinner. Catch up."

My heart skips a beat. I haven't heard that endearment in so long, I have to blink back the tears threatening to fall. I *want* to agree. I nearly do. But then common sense slams back into my frontal lobe at a hundred miles per hour. If I spend time with Gray, he'll pepper me with questions. Questions he has *every* right to have answered. But those are answers I won't give. I can't. He can never know.

Gone is the young, naïve, rosy-colored glasses woman he fell in love with. Gone is the carefree, idealistic woman he'd asked to be his wife. What stands in her place, instead, is a cynical, horribly used and hopeless one. Shattered beyond all repair.

"I can't," I whisper. Then I do turn and flee. Luckily, there are several cabs waiting out front and I hop in the first one, yelling at him just to drive. As I turn around, I see Gray standing on the sidewalk, breathing hard, watching me drive away. Deja vu cuts me like a sharp knife and I begin to sob silently.

11

These are the first tears I've allowed myself to shed in four and a half years.

Once again, I am leaving the only man to ever make my stomach flutter and my heart race. The man who pursued me relentlessly for that first date by returning for six straight nights to the pizzeria I worked at until I said yes. The man I'd dreamed of having children with. Growing old with. The only man I have, and ever will love.

All because of *him*. Always because of *him*. As with every day for the past five years, I curse the day Peter Wilder set foot into my life. And I curse my father for bringing him there.

Chapter 2

Livia

"Right this way ma'am," the petite, slightly overweight receptionist directs, as we walk the short distance to a small, but very nice, conference room. "You're rather early, so it will be a while before Mr. Nichols is ready to see you. Help yourself to water or soda in the fridge over there while you wait."

"Thank you," I murmur.

Yes, I am a good thirty-five minutes early. Without a car, you have to follow the train schedule. I pass on the drink. I'd already stopped at a Starbucks across the street from the tall downtown office building and had a double shot espresso hazelnut macchiato. I am buzzing from the copious amounts of caffeine I'd just ingested.

But the caffeine is an absolute requirement. I had been up half the night unable to stop thinking about Gray. Seeing him had been like picking an old scab. Now you have to treat it, disinfect it and bandage it again because it's bleeding. If you ignore it, blood leaks everywhere, leaving behind stains you can't get out. I can't afford any more stains. I already have too many.

I look out the window and wonder how, out of all the cities in the world, could we possibly be *living* in the same one? I'd moved to Chicago because no one knew me here, it is big and I could get lost in the millions of people.

So is it karma or fate that I'd ran into my former fiancé at an event that I should have never been at in the first place? If Kam's date hadn't bailed at the last minute, I never would have been there, and I'm not yet sure if I'm grateful or regretful that I was. It'd been crushing to see him with another woman, to see that he's moved on. But it was nice to add a new recollection of him to my well-used memory banks. My memories of him were all that got me through some very dark, very rough times.

Walking away from him last night flooded my heart with nearly unbearable pain, and I'd spent a good hour sobbing into my pillow, wallowing in self-pity. And that was a deep, black pit I couldn't allow myself to fall into again because God knows, I would *not* make it back to the top this time.

During the little sleep I did manage to get, it was as tortured as my consciousness. I dreamed of Gray, as I often did, but this was different. It seemed so very real, and I'd dreamed of Gray now versus the Gray I remembered. Of his scruff tickling the inside of my thigh before his mouth latched onto my aching sex. Of the way his thick fingers stretched me, readying me for his heavy cock. Of the way he'd grab my hair and use it as leverage while he pumped ruthlessly into me from behind until I shattered around him, screaming his name. But this was rougher. Raw. Fast and hard.

And I loved every minute of it. I only wish it were real.

When I woke, I was so achy and needy I exploded after just a few swirls on my soaking clit, and I was still in agony. Both physically and emotionally. That was a very bad place to be. I breathe through the familiar sadness that always shrouds me, willing it away.

Gray would surely not like the sad, cynical woman I've become underneath my crusty outer shell. Hell, *I* don't like her either. I know that façade slipped a little when I saw him last night. For a fleeting minute, I felt like the old Livvy that he'd known and loved. And I know he'd seen it.

I feel off kilter after seeing him. I need to call Dr. Howard and make an urgent appointment because my regularly scheduled one isn't until next week. I need to talk to someone, and she's only one of two people that know my entire story. The other I haven't seen since he helped me escape two years ago.

For the first year I lived in Chicago, I saw Dr. Howard three times a week, gradually weaning down to just every other week now. I'm a far cry from where I was when I stepped foot into this city for the very first time and there's no doubt I wouldn't be where I am today, both mentally and emotionally, without her. But I feel thrown for a giant loop after last night and I'm floundering. A balloon let loose in the gusty winds, unclear on where I'll end up.

"Ms. Kingsley?"

"Ah, yes, sorry." I wonder how long the fair-haired receptionist has been calling my name.

"Mr. Nichols will see you now."

15

"Yes, thank you." I glance at the clock on the wall as I exit the room.

8:55 a.m.

I have effectively wasted an entire half hour daydreaming instead of preparing for the job I so desperately need. And to what end? The past is what it is. It can't be changed or altered. *Or forgotten.*

I've been free of Peter Wilder for over two years now. I need to stay in the here and now and put on my best game face. I have my lies all neatly in order. Lies no one can really verify, but would garner me the sympathy I need to land the job all the same. The fact that Kamryn knows someone high up here will probably help too.

I smooth out my borrowed black pencil skirt and straighten the blood red sheer, long-sleeved shirt that I've paired with my own red camisole underneath. The outfit is complemented with three-inch black peep toe shoes and some light jewelry. It's edgy, but not slutty. If I do get the job, Addy graciously said I could borrow her clothes anytime until I can afford some nice ones of my own, since my wardrobe is made up almost entirely of Goodwill hand-me-downs. She is really a great roommate and friend.

Blondie shows me to the elevator, inserts a special card key, and instructs me to take the polished glass lift to the twenty-sixth floor where I will wait in the reception area until Connie, Mr. Nichols' current admin, collects me.

"Good luck," she whispers as the doors shut. I do my best to give her a genuine smile, but it's difficult with the butterflies churning in my stomach.

All too soon the elevator doors open. Quickly spotting a few chairs off to the left, I sit and scan the area.

Typical layout, with cubicles and offices lining the wall, a glass display case on the far wall houses the many awards HMT Enterprises has received. I know one of them is for an employee-friendly environment.

In preparation for today, I've done a lot of research about HMT Enterprises. They have quite a few technology patents and recently expanded into the residential space. Their main business, however, seems to be very high end, very sophisticated and very expensive commercial security systems.

Wesley Nichols, whom I'll be interviewing with, has been with the company for three years, quickly climbing his way up the corporate ladder. HMT is a privately-owned company, and I like that about them. They only have to answer to their board, not Wall Street. I'd read enough to know they are a very fair, very employee-friendly company to work for and offer a lot of free on-site benefits, such as a fitness center, a café and dry cleaning services.

With money being as tight as it is, free is good. Hopefully, I can land this job and I won't be so strapped. Maybe I can even think about going back to school to finish my education degree and I can eventually do what I've always dreamed of doing. Teach. It sure would be nice to fulfill one of the many dreams I had once upon a time.

A movement in my peripheral catches my attention. A very beautiful, very tall and very pregnant young woman is heading my way. "Ms. Kingsley, I'm Connie."

"Pleased to meet you," I say, rising from my plush chair.

As we walk—well, I walk, Connie waddles—down several long hallways, she chatters my ear off as if we're old friends. I like her instantly.

"As you can tell, I'm ready to pop any minute. My due date is in three weeks, but it could really be any day now, so we need to get my replacement hired ASAP. I'm going to be a stay-at-home mom since I just can't bear to leave my baby boy with anyone else. I told Wes to get on the stick earlier, but he dragged his feet, as usual. If you do get the job, you'll really have to stay on top of him. Deadlines, meetings, calendars, lunch. All that stuff. I like him, but he's pulled in so many directions and really is a bit of a scatterbrain, but he's a good boss. You'll like him too, I think."

We stop at a closed office door and Connie takes a big gulp of air, replenishing her lungs from her long tirade. "We're here."

She knocks and after a deep male voice gives her permission to enter, she opens the door and walks in, looking over her shoulder to ensure I'm following. The comforting smile she offers me eases my tension a bit.

My nerves must be visible. It took me several agonizing days to make my decision to apply for this position and finally get up the nerve to go to the DMV and get an official state ID. I've spent most of the last two years trying to keep a low profile, taking on relatively menial jobs where they didn't check your background or care that you didn't have a driver's license, but I'm tired of living paycheck to paycheck. So much time has passed that I feel it should be safe now to have a real job.

"Wes, this is your nine o'clock interview, Livia Kingsley."

A very handsome, thirty-something looking man stands and walks around the front of his desk holding his hand out to mine, which I take. "Ms. Kingsley, pleased to meet you."

"Pleased to meet you too, Mr. Nichols."

Glancing at Connie, he says, "Thanks, Connie. Now go get off your feet and take it easy."

"Gladly. Good luck," she murmurs excitedly as she walks by, closing the door behind her.

"Take a seat." Mr. Nichols gestures as he rounds his desk, sitting in his fancy leather, rolling desk chair. "Now, where did I put your resume?" he mumbles scanning his desk, which is in complete disarray with papers scattered everywhere. Connie may have understated the situation. It appears that Wesley Nichols is very disorganized. As Vice President of Research and Development, I'm not sure how he can afford to be.

"Here," I offer, handing over another copy I'd brought with me.

"Thank you." He smiles. "Point for you already."

I study him while he studies my resume. He really is quite handsome, with wavy light brown locks and long lashes framing his dark blue eyes. He's wearing smart-looking dark-framed glasses that make him look older than he probably is. His

19

trim, athletic build makes it obvious he takes good care of himself. I also notice he's not wearing a wedding ring. Too bad he doesn't stir a thing down south. No one does anymore. I wish I could just move on and let a man fuck my brains out, but I can't. The only man that's stirred those feelings is a man I can never have again.

After a few quiet minutes of reviewing my skills and experience, which he had clearly *not* done before our meeting, he raises his eyes to mine. In a very unexpected and unprofessional move, he rakes them over my body, stopping too long on the swell of my breasts, which are clearly visible through the scant blouse. Suddenly I wish I'd worn something a little less...sheer.

"So, Livia...may I call you Livia?" I nod, and he continues. "There seems to be quite a gap in work experience here. Three years, to be exact. I don't see where you were attending college during that time period either."

It wasn't really a question, but a statement that demanded an answer nonetheless. One I'd been fully expecting.

"Yes, Mr. Nichols. I had to take some time off work. My father was diagnosed with pancreatic cancer and we didn't have the means to really afford home health or hospice care, so I had to quit my job to take care of him."

Number one rule when weaving your precarious web of lies...always sprinkle as much of the truth with it as possible. My father *had* gotten pancreatic cancer and we *couldn't* afford any care because he'd spent every penny he earned gambling, but that had been after I'd married Peter Wilder. I hadn't quit my job to take care of my father; instead I'd been sold to pay a debt to the mobster that my father owed hundreds of thousands of dollars to and couldn't pay, except with one of his daughters. Alyse, my younger sister, had been saddled with caring for our poor excuse of a father as he died a slow, painful death. For her sake, I'm glad he's gone. But if I had it my way, he'd still be alive, suffering, which is the least he deserves for the torture he put me through.

"I'm so sorry, Livia. I hope he's better."

"No, he passed last year." Also true. *And his selfish soul is rotting six feet under where he belongs.* My shrink would be none too happy to hear me think like that, but I can't help the way I feel. No amount of therapy will ever allow me to let go of my hatred for him and what his actions did to our family and so many others.

A sympathetic smile turns his mouth. "I'm very sorry for your loss. I lost my mother six years ago to lung cancer, so I can empathize."

"It gets better each day," I reply, trying to inject a little sadness into my voice when that's the last thing I feel.

A half hour later, I'm being escorted out of Wes's office—he insisted I call him Wes—with his hand at the small of my back, and I am told he'll be in touch shortly. The interview went well. I was sure I'd gotten the job, even though I didn't have much executive assistant experience. It helped that I could start right away. Dundee's, where I currently waitress, didn't need much notice. It wouldn't be a hardship to replace me.

An hour later, I walk into my quiet apartment and strip out of the borrowed attire, returning it to Addy's closet. I call Dr. Howard's office. Luckily she had a cancellation and can get me in tomorrow afternoon.

I have to work the late shift starting at five, and it wasn't quite noon, so I throw on a pair of sweats and crawl back into bed, hoping to get at least a couple hours of shut eye before I have to get ready.

Snuggling under the covers, I try to clear my thoughts of Gray, of Peter, of my father, of my fucked up life. Like every single day for the past five years, I try *not* to remember that I should be happily married to Gray Colloway and teaching third graders. I try *not* to imagine how beautiful our children would look with Gray's piercing hazel eyes and my dark hair and full lips. I repeat Dr. Howard's words: *One day at a time.* I try *not* to fall into that empty pit of lonely, murky, desolate despair when life hands you a shit deal and you're helpless to change it.

Instead, I try to be strong as sleep's fingers pull at my consciousness. Only I know my dreams will once again be filled with what could have been but will never be.

Happiness.

I'd thrown that chance away when I gave myself to the devil to save my sister from the same fate.

Chapter 3

Gray

"What the hell is up with you, man?" Asher asks.

Plenty.

"Nothing," I grumble.

Apparently not listening to a word I've said, he continues, "Bullshit. You haven't been acting like yourself for weeks. I've had to repeat myself three times already, and the Board of Director's meeting is in just two weeks. Did you even hear what I told you about a possible accounting discrepancy in the CFC business?"

"No, sorry. Go on."

Sighing and scratching my stubbly chin, I lean back in my chair and stare at my younger brother, Ash. He starts talking again, but I'm unable to focus, my attention elsewhere entirely. I watch his mouth move, but don't hear the words.

When our father, Frank Colloway, died several years ago, I took over his consulting business, which we now call Colloway Financial Consultants, CFC for short. Asher and Connelly, my younger twin brothers by a year, followed in my footsteps, both graduating with an undergrad and MBA in business and, together, we not only run my father's successful financial consulting business, we have substantially expanded it in a very short period of time. CFC was the initial company, but we've purchased two more in the last three years.

Asher is now CEO of CFC and Conn took over as CEO of Wynn Consulting, a Human Resources consulting firm that we acquired last year. A new security company we bought six months ago rounds out our three current companies under GRASCO Holdings, where I now act as Chairman of the Board.

At just thirty years old, there was no doubt I was young for my position, but there was also no one as driven to succeed as I am. I threw myself into my career, sometimes working eighteen hours a day, only to get up early the next day and do it all over again. One of the reasons I offered as many of the on-site amenities to my employees as I did is because *I* needed them. I eat, breathe and sleep this company, and I expect my employees to do the same. If you give them everything they need at work, free food, free gym, free dry cleaning, free on-site clinic, then they work harder and longer and are more loyal. It's a win-win for all, really.

In some strange way, I owe my success to Livia Kingsley. After the woman I loved more than life itself crushed my soul by disappearing the day after I proposed, never to hear from her again, I threw myself into my father's company and climbed the ladder quickly. When my father died of a heart attack three years ago, the board easily named me CEO.

But my brother isn't wrong for questioning me. Ever since I laid eyes on Livia Kingsley two weeks ago at the Shedd Aquarium fundraiser, I've been a fucking emotional mess. She is all I can think about and it *is* affecting my attention at work. Truth be told, she has never been far from my thoughts and, in part, the reason I work as hard as I do is to eradicate her from my brain. And most of the time it works...until I lay in bed at night.

I went through all the gut-wrenching stages of grief and loss when she up and left me. At first, I simply didn't believe it was true. I repeatedly called her cell, her father, her sister, her friends, her work. I was relentless. Livvy loved me, she'd agreed to be my wife, there was no way she would simply desert me the very next day with no explanation. The note she left said she'd be back soon. She wasn't.

It didn't take me long to move onto anger, and fuck, was I ever. I told myself that if I ever saw her face again, I wouldn't be responsible for the vile and cruel things that would involuntarily spew forth. I was a sleeping volcano, seething with fury and rage and hate just below the surface and it was actively seeking an outlet.

I eventually hired a private detective to see if he could turn her up because I'd convinced myself something must have happened to her. I was sincerely worried about her safety, and I didn't believe the bullshit her father was trying to cram down my throat about her leaving of her own accord, that she'd changed her mind about marrying me. But it was like she was a fucking ghost. She was gone, with absolutely no trace. I constantly scanned the obits, convinced I would come across her name because the only way she would possibly leave me was through death.

25

After a bout of brief depression where I drank everything and fucked anyone I could get my hands on in a desperate, but failed, attempt to forget, I finally moved onto acceptance. That was, by far, the hardest part. I had to finally accept that it was *me*. That *I* wasn't good enough for Livvy, and she thought her only recourse was to flee. That was a very bitter, and ego-bruising pill to swallow.

"For the love of Christ, come find me when you get your head out of your ass," Ash complains as he slams my office door.

I ignore his outburst, turning my chair toward the glass windows that overlook the Chicago Loop, lost in thoughts of my angel. Every day of the past five years without Livvy in my life has been bleak and dark. The pain has lessened, but only marginally.

Over the past few years, I've tried not to think of the days that I was once happy. But since I saw Livvy a couple weeks ago, I've done nothing else *but* remember. As I stare out into the crystal blue sky, I let myself drift back to the first time I saw her.

Conn, Ash and I walk into Rocky's, in my opinion one of the best pizza joints in Detroit. We're all home from college for the holidays and I'm happy to spend some time with them.

We're shown to a table and take a seat, looking over the menus that the hostess left with us, but I already know what I want. It's the same thing I get every single time I come here. Deep-dish pepperoni with black olives and green peppers. I may not be creative, but I certainly know what I like.

26

I hear her laugh first. It's deep and sensual and enthralls me like a siren's song. I look around to find the source that's stirring my dick. When my eyes settle on a waitress two tables down that I've never seen here before, I feel this strange buzzing in my chest. My God in heaven, she's stunning and I can only see her profile.

Then she leaves their table, turning our way. My breath catches and my dick hardens painfully when our eyes connect. This magnificent green-eyed, chocolate haired beauty is a siren and I will gladly follow her to the depths of the ocean, even if that means my certain death.

I'm not one of those guys that believes in love at first sight, but I guess even I can be proven wrong. There is something special about this creature. I don't know her name, I don't know her age, I don't know her hopes and dreams, I don't know if she's already spoken for, but I do know this. I want to. I have to know every single thing about her. I've dated a lot of women. Fucked a lot of women. But I have never felt like this about any of them without even a word uttered between us.

Her steps slow briefly as she heads our way and I know she's also feeling the heat that's running hot between us right now. I feel like my skin is on fire and if anyone touches me, they'll get scorched.

My brothers quiet, following my gaze until the curvaceous vixen stops right in front of me. Her eyes leave mine and land on my brother Conn and my temper flares. Conn could charm the panties off of a woman with a simple scan of her body and a crook of his finger. I don't want her looking at my brothers. I only want her eyes on me.

"Hi. I'm Livia and I'll be taking care of you boys tonight. Can I start you with a round of beers, maybe?"

I can't help but notice she's avoiding all eye contact with me now as I continue to stare. I hear Conn and Ash talking, but I have no idea what they're saying or what the question was because I'm stuck back on her name. Livia. Sounds like the perfect name for my wife.

She walks away without another word in my direction and I follow her with my eyes until she rounds a corner and I can't see her anymore.

"Careful there, lover boy. You're going to scare her away if you keep looking at her like you want to eat her," Ash says while laughing.

"I do." I don't laugh, because I'm dead serious. I want to consume her.

Livia spends the rest of the evening trying to ignore me, but much to my brothers' chagrin, I ask her out repeatedly. And she repeatedly, but politely, declines. I know when a woman is playing hard-to-get, but Livvy isn't just playing. She is hard-to-get, which only makes me try harder.

What she doesn't understand though is that she snared my soul the second she stared into my eyes. If I didn't think she was interested, I would leave it alone, but I know she is. I see it with every shy stolen glance. I see it in the flush of her skin. I see it in the flutter of her pulse when she's standing next to me.

I want her. Desperately. And my desperation makes me relentless.

I smile remembering my feeble attempts to impress Livvy that first night backfired when I boasted that I would be finishing my undergrad in business at MIT that spring and would be applying at Wharton for my MBA. She told me I was arrogant and 'accidentally' spilled a glass of water on my lap when she was clearing the table, to which she barely apologized. My brothers laughed their asses off and told me I was losing my touch.

I was. She had me so flustered that night, so completely infatuated, that I was acting like a sixteen-year old trying to ask a girl out for the first time. It was embarrassing.

That evening, I left her a tip that was double the price of our meal, which I paid for the next night when I returned and asked for a seat in her area.

When she sees me, she stops dead in her tracks for a moment or two, a slight blush creeping adoringly up her neck. She is not as unaffected by me as she'd like me to believe. Her mouth lied, but her eyes and body did not. And I would absolutely use that to my advantage.

"I don't need your charity," she says caustically as she approaches my table.

I can have any girl I want. I am young, smart, good-looking and rich, and someday destined to take over my father's business, along with my two brothers. But I don't want just anyone. I want her. I want this girl beyond any rational reason and I will not let up until I have her. In my bed and in my life.

"It's a good thing I'm not a charitable person, then," I reply, drinking in her essence as if it's the only thing keeping me alive. I'd gone twenty-four hours

without looking into her mesmerizing eyes and I was starved for her. How I would go back to Massachusetts for my final semester after the holidays were over, I didn't have a clue.

"Go out with me," I state plainly.

"Are you really that conceited or are you just stupid? I thought MIT was a college for smart people?"

I laugh, shaking my head. My God, I love her wit. "I'm that confident."

"I already told you I didn't want to go out with you," she huffs, but once again I call bullshit.

"I don't give up that easily, Livvy."

Anger causes her face to redden. "My name is Livia. Not Livvy."

"Tomorrow night. Just one date." My voice remains stoic and calm, but inside I am begging.

"I have to work tomorrow night."

"Then the night after that."

"Sorry. I have to work every night for the next six nights. Some of us need to make a living."

The rest of the meal she conducts her obligatory waitressing duties, asking if I'd like another beer, asking if I'm ready for the check, but refuses to make any more small talk or answer my question about when she would be free.

But she'd unknowingly given me a piece of information, which she'd regret the rest of the week. She'd given me her schedule. And it didn't matter how much pizza I had to eat or how many parties I had to miss, my ass would be planted in her section every night until she relented.

Every day I came in she softened a little more, gave up a little more information about herself and when she saw me there on the sixth night, I knew I finally had her.

"Aren't you getting sick of pizza yet?" she sighs, a small smile turning her gorgeous lips. Lips I desperately wanted wrapped around my cock.

"To tell you the truth, I'm really starting to fucking hate it," I tease, drawing a laugh from her. I will never forget it. My very first laugh.

"Then why do you keep coming back?"

"You."

She looks at me thoughtfully, like she's trying to work out a puzzle. "What are you really after, Gray?" she sighs.

Wow. A smile, a laugh and the use of my name. I got a triple tonight. I'm hoping for a homerun and a "yes" to going out with me would get me there.

"You," I tell her sincerely.

She shakes her head. "You're a good-looking guy. You could have anyone you want. Why me?"

I'm a little taken aback at that question and her lack of confidence in herself. I try for humor but she just cocks a brow at my joke. "You think I'm good-looking?"

I try again, going with the blatant truth this time. "Why not you, Livvy? I find you extremely attractive, but there's something more about you, unique, different. And I have this visceral need to figure it out. There's white hot chemistry between us and I know you feel it too."

She hesitates before answering. "You're going back to school soon."

31

Excuses, excuses. "What are you really afraid of, angel?"

Her gaze drops momentarily to the floor before sweeping back up to mine. "We're very different, you and I."

If she means social status, I couldn't give a fuck. I don't care that I'm going to MIT and she's going to a community college. I don't care that she's a waitress and I'm being positioned to run a multi-million dollar company. I don't care about her address or the clothes she has on her back or what kind of fucking car she drives. I don't care about any of that. I care about her, but I can't tell her that without sounding like some crazy asshole that's just trying to get into her pants.

"I've heard opposites attract," I say instead.

She smiles and chuckles lightly, eyeing me shyly. "I don't sleep with a guy on the first date, so if that's what you're after then you might as well not come back."

I smile back. "Good. Neither do I." *That's a lie, but I find that even if she wanted to end our first night together in bed, I'm not sure I would. It would demean the evening and her and I want far more from her than just sex. She just doesn't know it yet.*

"Okay," she says quietly.

"Okay? Okay you'll go on a date with me?"

Her lips curl. "You've worked pretty hard for it so I guess I'll throw you a bone."

I lean back in my booth and grin. She stands there for long seconds smiling back at me before pulling out her little notepad and writing on it. She

32

rips off the paper, handing it to me. Glancing down I see it's a phone number.

"This real?" I ask, shaking it in the air.

She laughs. God I'm already addicted to it. To her. "Yes. It's real. Well, ah, I guess I should get back to work."

"Okay. I'm going to call you later."

She nods and turns to leave, taking care of her other stations. For the next hour I watch her work, barely touching my pizza, barely drinking the beer sitting in front of me, because I can barely take my eyes from her. Whenever she catches me, she beams and it makes my heart soar.

Later when she brings me the check, I finally ask her what I've been dying to know all night. "So, ah...what date do you sleep with a guy on, then?"

Smiling, she answers, "I guess you'll know if you get there."

After finally convincing Livvy to go on a date with me, the rest, as they say, is history. We clicked, like I knew we would, and spent every free minute together until I had to return to school three weeks later. I loved school, but being away from Livvy was excruciating and the last few months dragged by slowly. We talked and skyped daily. I came home as much as I could and she came to see me when her class and work scheduled allowed, although that was infrequent because she couldn't afford the plane tickets and was too prideful to let me pay. I hated it, but loved her all the more for it at the same time.

That's one of things that I ended up loving about Livia the most. She was extremely proud. Her mother left her when she was young. Her father was a gambling addict and they had to struggle for everything they had. She was a born fighter. Livia worked hard to put herself through school because all she ever wanted to be was a teacher. I wonder if she's doing that now. Teaching somewhere. I hope so. She was always suited for that calling.

Once I moved back to Detroit that May, Livia and I were inseparable. We spent most nights at my apartment, because she still lived at home with her father and younger sister. I remember feeling insanely jealous when she insisted on sleeping at home, because I wanted her always with me where she belonged. But I also understood her need to spend time with Alyse, her younger sister, because her father did a piss poor job taking care of her.

Livia was the first serious relationship I ever had and I haven't had a serious relationship with any woman since because I am not whole and I never will be. I can't offer something of myself that isn't available. I am irreversibly damaged, a part of me dead and gone with her. I've done my fair share of dating recently—if you want to call it that—but with each slide between a woman's legs, I can still only imagine Livvy. I have base needs to sate, but I don't want the women I fuck. The only thing I really want is *her*.

When I felt the weight of a stare across the ballroom, the hair on the back of my neck prickled, and when our eyes connected, my breath stopped. She was alive. And seeing her in that tight, short black dress and those red fuck-me shoes gave me an instant hard-on.

Throughout the years, I'd often imagined I've seen Livvy. At a bar, at a restaurant, walking down the street. But it was never her. Having no choice, I left my date, Lena, in the dust and chased after her to see if *this* Livvy was real, but she ran. Just like she'd done so many years before. And once again, I was ruined.

The day after the fundraiser, I tried unsuccessfully to find her. If she has a phone number, it's unlisted. I've been struggling ever since on what my next step will be. I have this gut-wrenching, burning, instinctive need to find her. Now that I've seen her again, now that I know she's alive, I will not let Livia Kingsley off the hook that easily. She owes me some fucking answers and I aim to get them. I don't know if she's living in the city, but when I told her I had moved to Chicago, she could not hide her surprise, so I have to believe she's here. Somewhere.

And since I can't find her on my own, I'm doing the only thing I can.

Bonnie, my admin's nasally voice, rang through the speaker. "Mr. Colloway, I'm sorry to bother you, but a Burt Jaffrey is on line one. He insists it's important."

"It's fine, Bonnie. I'll take it." Pressing the flashing light, I answer the call I'd been anxiously waiting for. "Burt, I have a job for you."

"Of course, Mr. Colloway."

"I need you to find a woman. Livia Kingsley. She doesn't appear to have a listed phone number and I can't find any type of account on social media. No Facebook, no Twitter, no LinkedIn accounts, but I do believe she's living in Chicago, or the burbs somewhere."

"Any other pertinent information?"

I relay her description, date of birth and give Burt Livvy's father's address as I last knew it.

As I place the phone back into the receiver, Bonnie's voice fills my office yet again. "Mr. Colloway, Ms. Ramsey's on line two."

Christ, I am in no mood to deal with Lena today. Or *ever*. Sensing I've been pulling away, she's been a stage five clinger these past two weeks, and it's time to cut her loose. I should have never have taken her to the fundraiser after she'd casually mentioned going to her parents for the holidays, which are still *months* away yet, but I loathe attending those events alone.

But I do with Lena what I've done with every other woman since Livvy. I use her. Judge me if you want, but she's just a warm body and a tight pussy, nothing else. I'm not serious about her in the slightest and it appears she's starting to hear the Wedding March, so it's time. Lena's just another stand-in for the woman that my mind pathetically won't let go.

They all are.

"Tell Ms. Ramsey that I'm busy for the remainder of the day. In fact, tell her I'll be out of the country on business for the next week."

"Of course, Mr. Colloway." Gotta love Bonnie. She does whatever I ask. No questions.

I don't really know what I'll do when I finally find Livvy. Because I *will* find her. I'll use every resource at my now extensive disposal to do so. I've pined after her memory for years and seeing her now, healthy and alive, my anger and hurt came back with renewed vengeance.

So when I sit down across from Livvy and force her to tell me why she left, will I finally be able to forgive her and get the closure I long for? Or will I strip her down and fuck her raw, like the visceral need inside clawed at me to do?

I despise myself for wanting her so much. Despite the fact that she ripped the beating heart out of my chest, after seeing her again...fucking her until she screams for me is all I can think about. All I want with a desperation that borders on obsession.

So...maybe I'll do both. Maybe I'll fuck her one more time so I can finally forget about the woman who ruined me so long ago. Maybe then I can finally stop seeing her face in every other woman I take.

Then I can walk away. *Will* walk away. My heart will remain unscathed because it's already dead. Mangled beyond all repair. *By her.*

But even as I think it, I know I can't do it. I know I'm lying to myself.

Fuck her? Absolutely.

Walk away from her? Not a hot chance in hell.

I already know that once I find her again, no matter the reason, I can't walk away from the one woman who, whether she knows it or not, whether she *wants* me or not, still owns every part of me. Regardless of why she left, regardless of the pain she's caused me, and regardless of if she's over me...I am *not* over her.

And I never will be.

The moment I set eyes on Livia Kingsley, my heart started beating again and I felt like I could take a full breath for the first time since she disappeared. I felt alive. The only way I can continue feeling that way is to make her mine again.

If she thought I was relentless pursuing her the first time, watch out Livia Kingsley. "Because you ain't seen nothing yet, angel," I whisper.

Chapter 4

Livia

"How's your first week going?" Emma asks, approaching my desk.

Just fucking jolly.

"It's been a little stressful," I reply, holding up a finger as I answer the incessantly ringing phone, telling the caller Mr. Nichols is in a meeting for the day and patching them through to his voice mail.

"Shit luck that Connie went into labor early, isn't it?" Emma said.

"You're telling me," I mumble, answering another call.

Blowing a long strand of dark hair out of my eyes that had fallen out of my ponytail, I look back up at Emma. At a petite five foot two inches, Emma is another executive assistant on this floor and is as stunning as she is tiny. She can't weigh a hundred pounds wet, but she has the biggest boobs I have ever seen on someone that small. And she must have been born without a filter because the things that come out of her mouth would embarrass a sailor. I'm no prude, but I'm not nearly as crude as Emma. On the first day we met, she made a point to tell me her boobs were not fake and even told me to feel them.

Um...I passed and I may have been awkwardly, covertly glancing at them ever since, wondering...

But despite, or maybe even because of her directness, I like Emma, and she's been my godsend this week.

After only two days of training, Connie's water broke at work and just three hours later she had a happy, healthy baby boy, whom they'd named Roberto, after her husband's side of the family. He was like the tenth Roberto or something like that. And what woman has their first baby in three hours? I would never get that lucky. Not that I'll get the chance.

"Did you see the pictures of little Roberto? Isn't he so adorable? And all that black hair! It's so thick, it looks like he needs a haircut already."

"Yeah, he's very beautiful." A little pang of sadness and envy rushes hot through my veins. Sadness at what was taken from me. Envy for what I'll never have. Because of a monster. My face must have fallen, because I feel a hand on my shoulder and when I focus back on Emma, hers is etched with concern.

"Are you okay, Livia?"

"Yes. Yes, I'm fine."

She smiles, but it's one of sympathy. "How about lunch today?"

I sigh. "I can't, Emma. I have to get the status on a few patents, file Mr. Nichols' expense reports, which are late, and try to duplicate last quarter's presentation for the board meeting next week. Connie was trying to finish all of that before she had the baby, but never got a chance to show me what to do or where to pull the information from." And on top of all that, PowerPoint isn't my best skill.

Carrying three plates on each arm? Piece of cake.

Selecting a nice bottle of Sangiovese or Chenin Blanc to complement your mahi mahi? Bring it on.

Importing a document, making graphs and ensuring all fonts are nicey-nice and lined up properly? Not so much. And for some reason, I am reluctant to admit I need help.

"Okay, but if you need anything, please let me know. Don't try to take it all on yourself. I'm here if you need me."

"Thanks, Emma. You've been great."

Emma starts to walk away when she spins back around and says "Oh!" so loud, I thought she'd hurt herself. "I forgot, it's thirsty Thursday at Gil's. One-dollar pitchers with a ten-dollar cover. All night long. A few of us usually go after work for dinner and a few pitchers. Join us. You can get to know some of the others."

I internally sigh. I don't drink much *or* make many friends. Friends just ask too many personal questions. While I've somewhat perfected my story, every once in a while a question comes up that I don't have a pre-formulated answer to, and I'll have to add another lie on top of the already hefty pile. And remember it. I'm something of a subject matter expert at winging it now. But it's easier to just stick to my short story and stay to myself. Kamryn and Addy know I have secrets, but neither of them pry. Most others don't take a hint so well.

"I'm going to have to work late on this Emma. It's the first big meeting I've been involved in, and I

41

don't want to make Mr. Nichols look bad. But ask me again." Or not. If I turn people down enough, they simply stop asking. It's a lonely life, but one I've accepted. Even embraced.

"Okay. But I'm going to hold you to that, girlie."

I simply smile as she bounces away, her girls practically slapping her in the chin.

Then I get back to work. Because if I don't figure this shit out, and fast, I'll not only be working late tonight, I'll be here every single night until next Friday's board meeting.

Then I may just end up saying yes to Gil's thirsty Thursday dollar pitchers.

Chapter 5

Gray

"Well, fucking look harder. She's *here*. I saw her with my own goddamned eyes." I'm about ready to go through the phone and strangle this incompetent asshole.

"I'll keep trying," Burt sputters.

"She has to have a goddamned driver's license, Burt."

"No, sir. She has an expired license from Michigan."

Fuck.

"Did you try the guest list from the fundraiser? She was there, so she had to have purchased a ticket." Once again, she'd just vanished. Like fog. One minute, there and the next...gone.

"I already did that. There was no Livia Kingsley on the guest list. Is it possible she changed her last name?"

Was that possible? I'd been so struck with both shock and relief at seeing her alive that I didn't even check her left hand for a ring. The thought of another man touching what was mine made me feel murderous. The thought that she would *let* another man touch her made me violently ill.

Yes, I know I'm a goddamn hypocrite.

"I don't know. I suppose it's possible. Get me the security footage of the fundraiser. She was with a woman that night. If we can identify her, then we can track Livvy down." I should have cornered that woman after Livvy ran, but she spent the rest of the night attached at the hip to a wealthy man I'd recognized from other events. And he looked like he'd take out anyone who came near the beautiful blonde.

"On it. It will take a few days and probably some Benjamins."

"I don't fucking care what it costs. You get me that goddamn tape and you track down this blonde friend of hers or I assure you, you will never work in this city again. It cannot be that hard to find one woman. Jesus!"

"Yes, sir."

I slam down the phone just as Ash walks through my door, but my thoughts are distracted by the news that Livvy's father died three years ago from pancreatic cancer, and the house that was once his now belongs to a young married couple with a baby on the way. I've tried Livvy's sister, Alyse, twice with no return phone call. I'm about ready to get into my car and drive to Detroit to track her down and make her tell me where Livvy is.

"Looks like a week hasn't improved your mood any," he says as he saunters in uninvited and flops in the chair across from my desk.

"Did we have a meeting?" I snip.

"Are you going to tell me what the fuck is going on with you, Gray? You've been a class A prick for the last three weeks."

I lean back in my black leather desk chair just as Conn pops his head in. "Am I late?" he asks. He glides in and shuts the door behind him.

I take a quick look at my daily calendar and see I have a meeting scheduled with Jake Campbell, the CEO of HMT Enterprises right now. "As much as I'd love to sit and gossip about my feelings and shit, I have a meeting with Jake right now."

Conn grabs the other free chair across from my desk and takes a seat, getting comfortable like it's a fucking barbecue and I should hand him a beer. "No, you don't. I had Bonnie put that on there because I knew you wouldn't take a meeting with us since you've been avoiding both of us all week."

Fuckers. He was right, but still. My temper flares.

"What is this? Some sort of goddamn intervention?" I spit. I love my younger brothers deeply, but they can be a pain in the ass sometimes. They constantly stick their noses in my personal business.

When Livvy first disappeared, my brothers were my rocks. Hell, Ash nearly single-handedly pulled me back from the brink of self-destruction when I was drinking myself to death. Or *trying* to.

After a year dragged by, they each tried their hand at setting me up on blind dates in hopes that I would move on, but I shut that shit down right quick. Ash's taste in women runs a little edgier than I like, and Conn runs through them faster than a high-speed paper shredder. God knows his dick had probably been in half the women he tried setting me up with. After the countless women I'd fucked in my

45

drunken stupor that I didn't even remember, I was now more selective about who I spent my limited time with.

"See what I mean?" I heard Ash say. "You talk to him and he just zones out, like there's a fucking carnival going on in his head. If he does that at the board meeting next week; that will not be good."

"Nothing is wrong," I pipe up. "Jesus, stop being so damn melodramatic, Ash. I thought you gave up acting in like the ninth grade."

"Hey, I told you that was just a phase, asshole. Jesus, let it go already."

"Not a chance in hell," I chuckle. Asher hated it when we brought up his "theatre days." He played Putzie, one of the lesser—or should I say *unknown*—members of the T-Birds in the ninth grade musical *Grease*. To this day, we'll still randomly plant pictures of birds, or crudely cut "T's" in his car or his apartment or a meeting folder. But we stopped calling him Putz a few years ago when he planted me on my ass with a wicked right hook.

"Ash is right, brother," Conn interrupted, veering us back to their misguided path. "You've been moody, short-tempered and very distracted. You're usually nose-to-the-grindstone non-stop. Camille told me you've missed two meetings with her over the last three weeks."

Shit. Camille is my head of Human Resources. Bonnie is retiring in only a few short weeks and I need to find a new assistant. Fast. Half of me is in denial. Bonnie has been with me since I started working at my father's company over six years ago. She knows me inside and out. She knows my style

46

and she anticipates my needs. She's simply a treasure and will be impossible to replace. I even tried bribing her with a huge pay increase to stay, but her husband retired last year and has been pestering her to do the same so they can travel and spend more time with their kids and grandkids.

"I've been busy."

"Well, you're going to be admin-less if you don't get your shit together. And you can't have mine," Conn quipped. Conn's assistant is a young, voluptuous hottie that I'm quite sure my brother only hired because she has a healthy set of DD's that she readily puts on display. I warned him against tapping that, but I highly doubt he took my advice. Conn has a hard time keeping the one-eyed snake in his pants around any beautiful woman. And with his rough, magazine-cover good looks, he has no issues landing them.

"What gives, Gray? If you can't talk to *us*, who can you talk to?" Conn asks me softly, genuine concern creasing his forehead.

I silently stand and walk the short distance to the window, putting my back to them. For some reason, I'm unable to look at their faces when I tell them that I've found her again, and this time I'm not going to give her up. They will *not* be happy and they will *not* be supportive. Livvy not only broke my heart, she broke my spirit, and my brothers were left behind to pick up the bloody, shattered pieces as best as they could. She changed me. Not for the better. I can't bear to see their disapproval when I tell them I plan to hunt her down and make her mine again.

47

"I saw Livvy at a fundraiser a few weeks ago. I think she's living in Chicago. I've hired a private detective to find her."

Ash stood up so fast, the chair he was sitting on went flying behind him. "What the fuck, Gray! That bitch ruined your life!"

Now I do turn back around, and the look of rage on my face makes my little brother freeze, but my calm, icy voice is even more menacing. "If you call her that again, I can assure you that your pretty face won't look so fucking pretty after I get through beating the shit out of you. Try explaining *that* at the board meeting, brother."

At six feet two inches, both of my brothers are the same height, but I tower above them by a good two inches and at least twenty pounds of solid muscle, thanks to the time I put in with my personal trainer three times a week. I can take Ash down easily and he knows it. Over the last couple of years, Conn has put on quite a bit more muscle, but I still think I could take him if he pushes me.

And they know I'm not blowing smoke up their asses with my threat.

Ash laughs, and some of the tension fizzles. "Is this going to be another repeat of Penny James?"

Penny James was the last girl we got into physical blows over. When I was a freshman in college, unbeknownst to either Asher or I, Penny started dating us both. But while the cat is away, the mice will play. Turns out it didn't matter which Colloway brother she was fucking, as long as she wormed her way into one of our hearts...and our wallets.

It all came to a head when I came home for Christmas break. Penny said she had some family obligation and Ash was out on a date. Let's just say things got pretty heated on Vincent and DuPaul streets when I saw them walking out, hand in hand, on my way into Rizz's Tavern across from the diner they were leaving. Ash ended up with a broken nose and a cracked tooth and pretty healthy shiner for about two weeks. Last I heard, Penny had filed for her third divorce.

"You're not fucking Livvy are you?" Of course, I knew he wasn't, but if I thought another man's hands on my woman had my vision turning a hazy, violent red, the thought of one of my *brothers'* hands on her made me homicidal.

"Jesus Christ, Gray. You need to get ahold of yourself, man. After what she did to you, if I ever see her again, fucking her is the *last* thing I'll do," Ash bellowed.

"We're just worried about you, Gray. She destroyed you before," Conn said.

"I know," I sigh, sitting back down. "There is no possible way I can make either of you understand." Conn had a thing for a girl way back in high school, but nothing serious since then, and Ash had his heart stomped on by the woman he was about to propose to, so he's pretty cynical about relationships in general. I'm not sure either of them could possibly understand the bone-deep love I have for this woman. She's part of me, surely as if she's been woven into my own flesh. Neither of them had yet met the woman who breathed the very life into their lungs. I had.

49

"Did you talk to her at the fundraiser?" Conn asked cautiously. I knew where this was going.

"Briefly."

Ash and Conn looked at each other knowingly, and I knew exactly what they were thinking. *I* was thinking the same thing, which is why I agonized over calling Burt. If she wanted to talk to me, she would have given me her phone number. She wouldn't have run. I wouldn't have had to hire a private detective to track her ass down. And if she really wanted me, *she* would have found *me*. Hell, she never would have left me to begin with.

I know this. I know it all. And I don't give a shit. There is something bigger going on here. I *feel* it seething in my gut. Even more deeply than the day she left me. I'm going to find out what the hell it is, because while Livvy's lips told me she wouldn't see me, her body, and more importantly, her eyes, didn't relay that same lie.

The moment I touched her, I heard her breath hitch. I saw the flush of desire on her fair skin, and there was no mistaking the lust and longing in her expressive emerald eyes. I know, because she had the same effect on me. Her feeble attempt at cool and aloof fell flat on its face.

"I hope you know what you're doing, Gray," Ash sighed as he stood to leave.

"I do." What I don't add is *too*. Thankfully they both depart without another word. I understand their concern because if the roles were reversed, I'm pretty sure I would react the same way. The Colloway brothers are enormously protective of one another.

My cell rings. It's Lena. I roll my eyes, not answering. I normally didn't keep women around as long as I had Lena. I never should have let this thing with her go on as long as it did, but quite frankly, I've gotten lazy. I'm tired of trying to find new women to sate my needs. It's not particularly easy finding a mentally stable, somewhat intelligent, attractive woman who wants a no-strings relationship.

But now that Livvy was back, I wasn't going to have to go through that process anymore. Because, unbeknownst to her, that woman would be *her*. But there would be so many fucking strings attached, she'd never get untangled this time. Just as soon as that incompetent PI finds her.

Livvy is hiding something, or behind something, but come hell or high water, I will find out what it is. I will incinerate it. I will obliterate any and every barrier that stands between us and the happiness we deserve.

Because out of everything that I saw that night at the fundraiser, I know, without a shadow of a doubt, that I saw *love* still swimming in her teary eyes as she turned and fled.

Chapter 6

Livia

He's on one knee in front of me and I can't breathe. I can't hear anything through the roar of blood rushing like Niagara Falls in my ears. I watch his mouth move. I watch him pull out a fancy jewelry box from his coat pocket and open it. I watch a lone tear slowly streak down his cheek.

Then I'm on the ground with him, throwing my arms around his neck, whispering yes, yes, yes and kissing him everywhere my mouth can reach.

I don't care that we're in public, kneeling on the dingy, greasy floor of Rocky's. The only thing I see is the man I love with every fiber of my being. The only thing I hear is him murmuring words of undying love in my ear. The only thing I feel is his strong, comforting arms cradling me tightly to his hard, sinewy body. A body that I want more than anything else at the moment.

"Take me home and make love to me," I beg. I don't want to be here anymore and I don't know if I can wait the half hour drive to his apartment before he sinks inside of me. In fact, I know I can't.

Standing, I take his hand and drag him from the floor, quickly walking through the restaurant to the Employees Only area, which I can easily access because I work here. Pushing the door open and pulling him through with me, I shut and lock it and pull his mouth to mine on a groan, turning our bodies so his back presses against the door. I fumble with his belt buckle as I break our kiss and trail my lips eagerly down his neck.

"What are you doing, angel?" he rasps, his breathing erratic.

"I need you in my mouth. Right now." I now had his jeans pulled down his thighs and was already on my knees in front of him, sinking his throbbing cock impatiently between my lips. The taste of his pre-come had me moaning, taking him deep.

"Christ, Livvy. You suck me so good." His hips push forward, and his hand threads tightly through my hair. I look up to snare his hooded, desire-filled eyes with mine. "Harder, angel," he demands. When I increase my pressure, his eyes break contact with mine and roll back as his head falls against the wood. "Fuck, yes. Just like that."

I know every single thing my man loves. I know how to strum his body expertly, as he does mine, so I lightly fondle his balls, reaching back with a finger to gently stroke his perineum. His cock swells, his thrusts increase violently, and my scalp stings from how hard he grips my hair. "I'm gonna come, baby."

Seconds later, loud bellows that can't be mistaken for anything other than one in the throes of an orgasm, echo off the four thin walls of the lounge. I swallow every drop of his salty goodness and continue licking him until he softens.

Strong arms reach under mine and he pulls me to him, grabbing my lips in a bruising kiss. "Let's go home. I want to fuck my new fiancée properly in private. Only my ears will hear you moan and scream

53

for me." His silky voice feathers in my ear, causing goose bumps to blanket every inch of flesh.

"I love you Gray Colloway."

"Not half as much as I love you, my soon-to-be wife."

I wake from my dream with tears streaming down my face. I haven't dreamed about the night Gray asked me to marry him in years. It shreds my already butchered heart to microscopic pieces. I was deliriously happy that night. We went back to his place and made love until the sun rose.

After only four hours of sleep, my father called, begging me to come home. He sounded scared. I thought something had happened to Alyse. It wouldn't have been the first time. I left my sleeping fiancé a note that I'd be back soon, but when I got home, Alyse was nowhere to be found. Instead, standing in my father's living room was a wolf in sheep's clothing. And he was surrounded by his gun-toting, roughneck pack mates. I'm here to tell you, a loaded gun in your face by someone who isn't afraid to use it will make you do just about anything.

The next choked words out of my father's bleeding mouth changed my life. *"They're here for Alyse."*

My father. I had missed so much of my life because of my father, because of his weaknesses. Peter Wilder may be the monster that literally held my life, and that of my family's, in his hands, but my father was the catalyst. The decisions he made led us all to where we all are today. His greed, his lack of integrity and his selfishness had far reaching effects on so many lives.

Even in death, I'll never forgive him.

They didn't want my father's life to pay his debt. No, that would serve them no purpose, so they took his daughter instead. While Peter wanted Alyse, he settled for me. But I would selflessly do it again. With Alyse's fragile state at the time, she would not have survived a man like Peter Wilder; he would have broken her within a week. It took him far longer with me.

I did the only thing I could to save her. I threw myself on the proverbial sword. I married a man I did not know, a man I did not love...a man who turned out to be the vilest, most ruthless and cruel of men to ever walk the planet.

It's over. It's behind you, Livia. After over three years of tortured hell, I'm free from both my literal and invisible chains, and my sister, Alyse, is safe and successful and happy and healthy. In love. *That's* what matters. She has no idea the fate she escaped, and it will stay that. My single regret is that I crushed the man I loved in the process of saving my sister.

My phone rings, pulling me out of my reverie. I quickly wipe my eyes and silently curse the fact that I had to run into Gray again. Now I feel like I've taken several steps back in my ability to cope with the circumstances the universe decided to hand me. I may not be living, but I was at least surviving until I laid eyes on the man I am still in love with. The man I'd constantly thought about seeking out over the last two years but couldn't as I was no longer good enough for him.

I grab my cell and looking down, I see it's Alyse. "Hi Lysee," I answer, trying to sound upbeat, when I'm breaking apart inside.

"Hey, Libs. I haven't heard from you in a while. Just wanted to see how you're doing. Did you get that job?"

The one concession I'd gotten from Peter was to keep in touch with Alyse, but only sporadically. He'd let me have supervised phone discussions, so I didn't reveal anything I shouldn't, but I was never allowed to see her. I didn't lay eyes on my sister for three long years. When my father got ill and passed away, she couldn't understand why I refused to come home. I told her I was in Europe and couldn't afford the ticket back. Lame excuse, but it was all I could offer. Of course the truth was, Peter wouldn't let me, but I couldn't tell her that because she didn't know about Peter. It definitely put a strain on our relationship, but we're finally bouncing back, slowly.

"Yes, I did. I started on Monday, but the girl I'm replacing went into labor early, so now I'm trying to get by on my own." It was Saturday, and it had been a hell of a long week. I foresaw many long evenings next week too. I would be glad when this board meeting was over because next week that was my sole job. Making my boss look good. I did not want to get fired and have to go back to waitressing again.

"That stinks."

"Yes, it does. But I'll get by. I'm lucky to have gotten the job." I was just hoping Wes wasn't regretting hiring me.

"When are you coming home? I want you to meet Finn."

Finn was the man that Alyse had fallen in love with. She started dating him a just a few months ago, right after we sold our father's house, and I haven't been able to set foot again in Detroit. The idea of going back there, where there are memories of Gray everywhere I look makes my stomach lurch. So I haven't met Alyse's boy-toy yet, but by the way she talks, the guy could give Jesus a run for his money. He is *"perfect in every single way"*.

Gag.

And call me a bad sister, but even though I am over-the-moon happy for her, I just don't want to witness it first-hand. I may be better, but I'm still human. And far from perfect.

"I can't really afford a bus ticket right now, Alyse, but as soon as I get my first couple of paychecks under my belt, I promise I'll come back for a weekend." I didn't own a car. I lived close enough to the train and bus stations that public transportation worked out just fine for me, so never saw the need to invest in a car. I didn't even have a driver's license, anyway.

When I moved here, Grant, the man who literally saved my life, thought it best to keep as low of a profile as possible, so no license and the lease agreement was in his name, along with my cell phone. *Grant...God I miss you.*

"Great. You can stay with us. Finn really wants to meet you. He keeps asking me when you're coming." I thought it was way too early, but they moved in together a couple of months ago.

"I'll come as soon as I can, okay?"

"Thanks, Libs." I smile at the nickname she's had for me since we were kids.

We talk for a few minutes about mundane, irrelevant things before we hang up. I promised I would call her next week.

Deciding it was time to get my ass moving and be productive, I got up and threw on my workout clothes. Because I was so busy at work, I hadn't had time to take advantage of the gym, but Addy had recently joined a gym a just a few blocks away and was able to get me a free six month pass, so I'd been enjoying running and taking some classes. I'd slept in too late for the spinning class this morning, but I'd enjoy a good run on the treadmill instead.

An hour later, I was sweaty and felt marginally better. I went about the rest of the day running errands and cleaning our small apartment, which didn't take long. By 6:00 I had laundry done and put away, I had a cupboard stocked with my soup for the week and I was just settling down on the couch to watch *Dirty Dancing* when I heard the key rattle in the door.

"Hey, chicky," Addy chirped. Striding through the door, her hands full of grocery bags, she slams it shut with her foot.

"Hey, Addy." I take a spoonful of my hot chicken noodle soup and blow on it before shoveling it in my mouth. When she gets her groceries put away, she stands at the counter with a hand on one hip, just staring at me. "What?" I finally ask. I look down to see if I'd spilled something on me or if there was a spider crawling on my leg like last week. Just thinking about it makes my heart pound.

Yeah, that wasn't my finest moment. Even the smallest of spiders scare the shit of out of me. The glass of milk I had in my hand wound up dripping down my face, and I let out a scream so loud, we had Mrs. Ruffalo, the resident busybody, knocking on our door asking if everything was okay. We never did find that spider. I'd been on the lookout for it ever since.

"What the hell are you wearing?" Addy asked with a disgusting sneer on her face.

"Um, they're called pajamas."

"Yes, I know what they're called. The question is...why is a twenty-eight-year-old single woman wearing pajamas at six o'clock on a Saturday night?"

"Addy..."

"Livia..." she replies mockingly. She comes over, takes the soup out of my hands, carries it back to the kitchen and dumps it down the drain.

"Hey!" I yell, jumping up from the couch, stalking after her. "That was my dinner!"

"That was an appetizer, for fuck's sake, Livia. That wasn't dinner. I'm taking you out to celebrate your new job. My treat." She walks around me, but not before grabbing my hand and dragging me behind her down the hall to her bedroom.

"Addy, no. You don't need to do that," I argue. I hate feeling like a charity case that my friends think they need to take care of. And while I won't be buying a brand new BMW anytime soon, with this new job, at least I shouldn't have to feel like I constantly need a handout.

She stops ruffling through her closet long enough to shoot me a death glare. "I know I don't *have* to. I *want* to. Besides, it's really Kamryn's treat. She's meeting us at Finnegan's for dinner at eight, and then we're going to Firefly for some after-dinner drinks and dancing. If you're lucky, maybe we'll find you a nice, tatted bad boy to oil your lady bits. God knows they need it."

"Addy, no."

"Livia, yes. No arguments. Now go jump in the shower, slut up your makeup and put your hair in a sexy twist. And put on this hot little number." She throws a royal blue scrap of fabric at me that's supposed to be a dress, along with some strappy silver heels. I've seen this dress on Addy. It barely covers her ass, and hers is much smaller than mine. "Kam's sending a car to pick us up at seven fifteen, so chop-chop."

Fuck me. *Really?*

My friends don't do this very often, but every once in a while they find it incumbent upon themselves to try to get me laid. They think I can't find a man and that's the farthest thing from the truth.

At five feet seven inches, I'm no skinny Minnie, but I'm in very good physical shape. I have curves and look like a woman should. My bright green eyes stand out against my fair skin, especially with my chocolate brown hair. I may not be runway model gorgeous, but I know I'm attractive enough to bed a man, should I choose to do so. I just don't. Hell, my boss has hit on me enough this week, that if I went into his office, lifted my skirt and bent over his desk, he'd gladly fuck my brains out.

But there is only one man I want between my legs and I can't have him. I simply can't stomach the thought of anyone else there.

"Addy, I really don't think I'm up to it."

My best friend stops what she's doing and looks at me pointedly. "Livia, I know things have been rough for you. I may not know who, what, or why, but I see your sorrow. Whatever happened in the past, you're here now. You're alive, you're young, you're beautiful, and you have a lot inside you to give. You need to live life, not be holed up in a shitty two-bedroom apartment eating chicken noodle soup for supper. And besides, *I* need this as much as you do."

"I know," I tell her quietly. "Fine. Okay. I'll agree to dinner and dancing, but. Do. *Not.* Try. To. Hook. Me. Up. Understood?"

"Yeah, yeah," she waived, turning back to her closet to pick out her own slutty attire.

I turn and stomp out of her room like a five-year old who was told she couldn't have a cookie before dinner.

Ugh. What have I let my friends talk me into?

Chapter 7

Livia

The music is deafening, the dance floor is packed and I've already turned down two offers to take me home and one to "get nasty" in the bathroom. I've only been here an hour. It must be a full moon and mating season because the werewolves have clearly descended onto the unsuspecting humans.

Kamryn called ahead and reserved us a booth, so at least we have someplace to escape the throngs of people milling about, and for that I'm relieved.

Addy went to the bar to get some more drinks. Our waitress has been slammed tonight, complaining that someone just quit this morning and another called in sick. I feel bad for her. She's working her ass off. I can relate.

My eyes roll as I see Addy approach our table with a tray of shot glasses filled to the brim with a clear liquid. Addy is a very beautiful woman, both inside and out, and as she makes her way back through the crowd to our table, I watch men watch her. At five feet eight inches, she's only an inch taller than I am, but her legs go on for miles. The blood red dress she's wearing tonight shows them off to the nines. Her mahogany hair and large, expressive hazel eyes round out a package that is every guy's wet dream.

"Oh no," I say, as Addy sets a hangover waiting to happen on the table. "I've already had one martini." It was dirty and one hundred percent alcohol. My head is already swimming.

"Oh yes," she quips. "It's my mission to get you drunk tonight, Livia Kingsley. No excuses."

"I'm half way there," I complain.

"You've had one drink. Stop your whiny bitching and take a shot."

Kam nudges me. "Come on, Liv. You deserve a fun night out."

You know what? They're right. I do. "What the hell," I say, taking one of the tiny glasses. "What kind of poison did you bring me anyway?" My nose wrinkles when the fumes hit me.

"What else, babe? Tequila."

"Ugh. Anything but tequila," I whine.

"Breakfast of champions," Addy laughs as she holds up her own glass. "To Livia. Congrats, babe. Things are finally looking up for you."

"Here, here," Kam adds before we unceremoniously shoot them back. My face scrunches when I suck on the sour lime. I hate tequila, and the only way I can take a shot of it is with training wheels. My friends know me so well.

"Addy, how are you doing?" I ask, concerned about my friend. Her boyfriend of over a year just broke it off with her recently and while she appears to be holding things together pretty well, she does the same thing I generally do. Hold the pain in and push it way down.

63

"Couldn't be better," she retorts. My brows rise in challenge. "Really. I'm better off without him. I don't think he ever loved me anyway."

I reach across the table, squeezing her hand. "That's his loss then."

"Damn straight it is." I watch my friend take another shot, drowning the sorrow in mind-numbing liquid. I can relate all too well.

Two hours, three shots and two more dirty martinis later, I'm on the dance floor laughing and shaking my ass with my two best friends. Two hotties that look a lot like brothers saunter up behind Kam and Addy, who have now drifted away from me. Looks like maybe one of them will be getting their lady bits oiled instead of me.

My head feels numb and fuzzy, and I'm having a hard time focusing on any one thing in particular, so I shut my eyes and let my body instinctually take over, swaying to the booming rhythm. I'm so lost in the thrum of the bass as it beats through my body, that I don't immediately register the strong hands that grip my hips from behind. But I do register the thick erection that's now prodding my backside. And I feel the hot breath that's tickling my neck. The music has now slowed to something sultry, and I open my eyes to see that the dance floor is even more packed, if possible.

Soft lips graze my bare flesh and, even though, my body is slick with sweat from the hours of dancing, it chills at this stranger's touch. Dr. Howard's words play through my head. *"It's alright to let yourself live again, Livia."* I should pull away, but I don't. Maybe she's right. Maybe it's time I try

64

living again. So I close my lids and lean my head back on his shoulder, moaning.

But instead of enjoying the moment with someone new, I imagine the hands tightly gripping my hips are Gray's. I pretend the mouth nibbling my sensitive skin is his. I wish that the hand now sneaking around my stomach pulling me tighter as he grinds us to the slow beat of the music belonged to the man I still loved with my whole being.

"I want to fuck you," a deep masculine voice whispers in my ear. And then he surprises me by brazenly cupping my mound and caressing my clit in full view of anyone who cares to watch. My borrowed dress is short, and with his hand where it is, I'm almost indecently exposed.

I meant to say no, but in my poison-induced fog, *yes* tumbled out of my mouth instead. If I keep my eyes closed the whole time, I can stay lost in my fantasy that it's Gray who's caressing me. That it's Gray's fingers that will make me come. That it's Gray who will fill my empty body instead of this unknown man.

The stranger grabs my hand, dragging me quickly through the swarm of damp, grinding bodies to a darkened hallway on the other side of the club. Even with my heels, he's several inches taller than me, with a broad build and short dark hair. His jeans mold his tight ass perfectly. He takes a turn down another hallway which offshoots to the left and is even darker than the one we'd just left. It seems like he knows where he's going.

When we near the end, he pushes me back against the wall and plunders my mouth. He tastes like beer and tobacco. His hand snakes under the front of my dress, quickly finding my drenched core beneath my tiny black thong, but at the first brush of his fingers against my sex, my stomach rolls. *I don't want this. I can't do this. I'll never be able to do this with anyone but Gray.*

"Stop," I pant against his mouth. I break the kiss and try pushing him away, but he thrusts two fingers inside me instead. "Stop," I say more forcefully this time.

"You want this baby. You're dripping for me." His lust-laden voice reverberates through me as he continues to painfully pump his hand into me.

"No, I don't." I squirm to get free, but he's tightened his grip on me and has me pinned in place with his strong body. A familiar panic overtakes me, and I start to fight in earnest. I will *not* be a victim again. Never again. I raise my knee toward his boys, ready to strike, when suddenly he's pulled off me and thrown violently into the opposite wall.

"I believe the lady said no, fuckhead." It's so dark in here I can't make out the face of the man who's now come to my rescue, but he's even bigger and bulkier than the guy who just had me pinned to the wall and I suddenly have a very bad feeling. I don't wait see what happens next. I turn and flee.

Shaking, I walk as fast as I can in these god-forsaken four-inch heels. I'm on the edge of a full-on panic attack now and I haven't had one of those in almost a year. I'm halfway to the door, intent on just getting the hell out of here, but as I near the exit, my skin prickles and I dare a glance back.

Watching my every move is the man I just know is my rescuer. His hot gaze bores into me, and he looks pissed. He gives me the same creepy feeling as he did in the hallway. I quickly turn around and push my way through the doors that lead to both silence and freedom.

With deep, slow breaths, I work to keep the panic from overtaking me as I hop in the yellow cab I can't afford and give the foreign driver my address. I shoot Kam and Addy a quick text so they won't worry when they can't find me and sit back on the cracked vinyl-covered seat. One, two, three, four, five. I close my eyes and count methodically as I breathe slowly in and out.

Peter is dead. Peter is dead. Peter is dead. I keep repeating that to myself. *There is no reason anyone having anything to do him would be looking for you, Livia.* I've been fine. I've been safe for the last two years. *You're free.*

I know this, but then why do I suddenly feel like the past has come back to haunt me? In more ways than one?

And why now?

Chapter 8

Gray

It's late in the afternoon and I'm only half way through reviewing the second of three one-hundred-page reports when my phone rings. I almost let it go to voicemail, but decide to glance at the caller ID.

"Hi, Mom," I answer just in time.

"Gray, sweetie, how are you?"

"I'm doing good, Mom. How are you?" My mother is the best mother on the planet, hands down. She's feisty and bull-headed, but she would give the clothes off her back for her children and anyone else for that matter.

She tried to be strong when my dad died three years ago, but it's been hard on her to lose her husband at the young age of fifty-five. College sweethearts, they'd been together for thirty-five years, married thirty-four of them. And it's been even harder since her three boys up and moved from Detroit to Chicago, although Ash spends a fair amount of time in Detroit at our CFC branch that we still maintain there.

We tried convincing her to move here with us, but she refused. *"I grew up here. My life is here. I've already lost your father. I don't want to move away from my friends and start a whole new life, Gray. I'm far too old for that. Besides, you don't need your mother hanging around in your apartment when you bring a woman home. No woman wants to marry a man that still lives with his mother."* That was laughable. I rarely brought a woman to my apartment. And I'd prefer the company of my mother to that of almost any woman, quite frankly. *Almost.*

"I hope you're not working, Gray. It is Sunday, you know. You need a day off." Doesn't matter how old you are, your mother will always mother.

Of course I'm working. I work seven days a week. "Not too hard, Mom," I reply. I don't even try lying to her. She would know.

"You're going to burn out if you keep up this pace. I don't want you to end up in an early grave." Her voice choked on the last couple of words. My father had a heart attack at the age of fifty-seven. My mother was convinced it's because he worked too much and didn't take care of himself physically. That's one of the reasons I work so hard to stay in shape and eat healthy. I can't help the instinctual drive to succeed, but I do try hard to manage the stress of it all, so I don't end up like my father.

"Mom." My voice is soft and consoling. "I'm fine. There's no need to worry."

"Okay, sweet boy. I actually called because I was wondering if you and your brothers could come home this Saturday for a family dinner? It's been a while since I've seen my boys."

Shit. Guilt eats at me for not making more time to spend with my mother. I've been so focused on the upcoming board meeting and the new acquisition I'm vetting, that I've been neglecting her.

"This weekend won't work, Mom. We have a big board meeting on Friday afternoon, and I'm afraid I have a dinner on Saturday evening that can't be changed."

"Oh." Her disappointment guts me.

"But I'll see if next weekend works. Let me talk with Ash and Conn."

The pep in her voice returned. "That would be wonderful. Maybe you would even have enough time to spend the night on Saturday?"

"I think we could probably make that work, Mom." I don't care what my brothers have on their agendas; they'll have to change it. We've all been too neglectful of our mother and I can tell she misses us terribly, but she would *never* guilt us into coming home. "I'll call you early next week to confirm, okay?"

"Yes, yes. But only if it works. Don't go changing your plans because of me." I smile. I would do anything for my mother. "Oh, and Gray...if you have anyone special to bring home, that would be just fine too."

Oh, I have someone special all right. I just need to find her.

Chapter 9

Livia

"Well, Livia, I think we're pretty close. Can you pull the Winston report and print fifteen copies?" As I turn to find this elusive report he's referring to I notice Wes running his eyes frantically over his desk, mumbling to himself and scratching his head, as if he's forgotten something else. Which he undoubtedly has. How this guy even has a job, I'll never know. I've never seen someone so disorganized in my entire life.

As I find the report on the server and start to print copies, I fume. It's now eight o'clock on Thursday night and not only am I tired...I'm just plain pissed. We probably still have a good two hours of work ahead of us. At least. Wes has a meeting with Jake Campbell, the CEO of HMT Enterprises, in the morning at 9:00 to review all of the materials for the board meeting. We will hand them off and Mr. Campbell will present to the board, so we have to be ready with every piece of information before that morning meeting.

The presentation isn't yet done, and I'm quite sure Wes has forgotten a dozen other things that he'll remember as they slowly filter through that muddy thing he calls a brain. For fuck's sake, I could be here all night.

What a useless twat. The guy must be fucking brilliant to have kept his job. More and more I think that Connie ran things around here. Not him.

I have worked until eight or nine o'clock every night this week. I had to call Addy to pick me up one night because I'd missed the last train. And it's not that I mind working hard. I *don't*. I just don't like working my ass off for a gropey, egotistical, unorganized airhead who can't even remember what he ate for lunch today.

Umm...tuna on rye, with a side of potato salad, you douche. I could still smell the stinky fish on his breath every time he breathed on me. Next time I order that for him, I'll make sure to ask for a handful of mints. A giant fistful. Maybe he'll get the hint. Or not. He's pretty dense.

Speaking of Addy, my cell rings. "Hey," I answer tiredly.

"That good, huh?"

I have to refrain from saying what I really want for fear I'll be overheard and then promptly fired. "Yep." I pop my "p" for effect.

"Call me no matter how late. I'll come pick you up."

"I'll take a cab, Addy. You don't have to do that again." Not only is Wes's ineptitude affecting *my* life, it's affecting my roommate's.

Asshat.

"Absolutely not. I'm not going to let you spend that kind of money. Or ride with some sketchy cabbie that far. Call me. No matter how late."

I'm silent, weighing my options until she adds, "Livia. Call. Me."

72

"Fine. Okay. Thanks, Addy."

"See you later."

We say our goodbyes and hang up just as Wes yells for me from his office. I sigh and roll my eyes as I stand and walk to his door.

"I have the presentation up, Livia. Let's sit down and go through each slide together to see what I'm missing. Bring Connie's files from the last meeting."

Two hours later, we're finally done and I'm exhausted. Mentally and physically. I'm printing and binding the last of the materials in the copy room when I feel someone watching me. I turn my head and find Wes staring hungrily.

At my ass.

Today I'm wearing an off-white pencil skirt that hugs my curves and a navy sleeveless blouse that I've tucked into the high waist. I've complemented it with matching navy pumps. I'm proud to say this entire outfit is mine. I may have borrowed Addy's sparkling dangly earrings, but everything else is one hundred percent mine, thanks to a Sunday afternoon shopping trip we took where we hit some really great season end sales at Macy's.

"Did you forget something else?" I ask, as I turn back around to the task at hand. I suck in a sharp breath at my snippy remark. One stupid word can change an entire sentence. I hope he's too distracted that he doesn't realize that's what I really meant.

"No. No." He walks forward until he's right behind me. I don't turn, but I can feel his body heat and since my hair is up today, his warm breath tickles my neck. It makes me cringe. It makes me think of not only what a fool I made of myself on Saturday night, but how I put myself in danger. Had big and bulky not found me, I could have been…

I shudder. I don't even want to think about it.

Wes reaches out and grazes my exposed skin with his fingertip. My disgust is rapidly morphing to anger. I have done nothing to lead this man on and he's my boss, for God's sake. For the umpteenth time this week, I wonder how I'll ever be able to keep this job. I've caught on quick, I like the few work friends I've made and I love the salary, but I don't know if I can handle Wes's advances without kicking him so hard in the balls he chokes on them. And his advances are becoming more blatant with each passing day.

"You were really great this week, Livvy," he says softly. My anger spikes. I won't let any man call me that. That name is reserved only for Gray. And I know I'll never hear it again.

"I prefer Livia and thank you." I snap the last binder closed, spin and step around him, but not before he gently grabs my wrist, stopping me. I know the look on my face is purely lethal because he lets go like he's just been burned.

"Would you like to get a drink?"

Hmmm…would I like to have a root canal?

"No, but thank you."

"At least let me give you a ride home. It's the least I can do since I've made you stay so late. I'm sure you've missed your train."

I try my level best to smile, but I'm quite sure it comes across as more of a sneer. "Thank you, but

74

my boyfriend is picking me up. In fact, he's already on his way."

"I didn't realize you had a boyfriend," he replied, unable to hide his disappointment.

Why the hell didn't I think of this earlier?

"You didn't ask. I'll see you tomorrow," I say with false sweetness as I walk out of the copy room and quickly make my way to my desk where I grab my purse and head toward the elevator.

"See you tomorrow, Livia," he calls after me.

I don't reply, but I do throw my hand in the air acknowledging his pathetic attempt to right things between us.

As I step into the elevator, I mentally pat myself on the back. I have a good feeling that tomorrow will be the start of a new working relationship between my boss and myself. A more professional one. The boyfriend ruse will surely get him to back off and if it doesn't, I'll just have to unleash my inner bitch. She's been dying to take someone out.

Once the doors close, I text Addy that I'm ready for a ride and make my way down to the first floor to wait the thirty minutes it will take for her to get here. I then head to the bathroom to avoid Wes in case he catches me waiting.

Even though I vowed to stay away from alcohol for a while after last Saturday, I think one celebratory glass of wine when I get home won't hurt. After less than two weeks on the job, I single-handedly got the sorriest excuse for a Vice President I've ever seen ready for one of the biggest meetings of the year. And it feels good. *More* than good.

Cheers to me.

Chapter 10

Gray

"You'd better have good news for me," I snap when I answer my phone and stand to pace. I've been on fucking pins and needles all week. My patience is stretched so goddamned thin, God help the person who's standing next to me when it snaps, which is bound to happen any minute. Even Bonnie's smartly kept her distance.

"I do, sir. The woman accompanying Ms. Kingsley to the fundraiser is Kamryn Winthrop. She owns her own clothing design company. She's been out of town on business this week, so I haven't been able to talk to her yet."

"And *that's* your good news?" I can feel the tenuously tight grip I have on my patience slip a little more. My blood pressure is so high right now I wouldn't be surprised if Bonnie walks in here at the end of the day to find me dead and stiff in my chair from a stroke.

"No. A background check popped up," Burt replied.

I freeze. "For what?"

"A job. A company called HMT Enterprises on—" I hear papers shuffling before he continues, but I already know what he's going to say. I make my way back to my chair and blindly sit.

"Ah, the loop. At the corner of West Randolph and—"

"West LaSalle," I mumble, nearly unable to process what I'm hearing.

"Yes, that's it. Are you familiar with them?"

"You could say that." Burt's never been to my office, so he doesn't have a clue where I work. He knows my position at GRASCO Holdings, that's it. "When was the background check?"

"Two and a half weeks ago, sir. And with that, I do have a home address for her as well." Burt rattled it off, but I'm almost too stunned by this news to write it down. She's been right under my nose, in *my* very building, working for one of *my* companies for the last two weeks? And I didn't have a fucking clue.

"Thanks, Burt. I'll mail you a check today."

I immediately pick up the phone and call Camille. The board meeting starts in less than ten minutes and I don't have time for this shit, but there is no way I'm going to wait another single second not knowing where to find Livvy.

"Gray, how can I help you today?" Camille's sugary voice oozes through the speaker. Camille is a very beautiful woman, with legs that go on for miles and tits that a guy would love to sink his cock between. And if she had it her way, it would be mine doing the sinking. But I don't fraternize with my employees. Ever. It's not good business.

Except now I'm about to break my one cardinal rule because Livvy is apparently my employee. *Shit.*

"Livia Kingsley. Look her up and tell me her position within HMT."

"Uh...of course. Just a minute."

I hear her fingers click on the computer keys, but otherwise we remain quiet. The silence is deafening. I wonder what Livvy's doing and whom she's working for. I watch the clock and realize that I'll be late to my own meeting. I've not been late to a board meeting once in the two years since we've formed GRASCO Holdings. Every single person attending that meeting knows how I feel about lateness.

"Camille," I growl. "I'm in a bit of a hurry here."

"Of course, sir. It's pulling up now. I'm sorry, the system is running slow today."

After several more beats of silence, she finally gives me the information I've been dying to hear. "Livia Kingsley. She just started a week ago last Monday as an executive assistant to Wesley Nichols."

Nichols. VP of Research & Development.

Brilliant, but a bit flighty.

Handsome.

And very fucking single.

"Thank you." I hang up as she starts to speak, not caring that I'm cutting her off.

I grab my folder and my cell phone and dash out the door, heading quickly to the stairs, but not before Bonnie stops me to hand me a couple of messages. The boardroom is on the thirty-fifth floor and my office is on the thirty-fourth. I take the stairs quickly, two by two, but my mind is not on the

79

meeting ahead. It's not on the sales or marketing or financial review that I'll spend all afternoon listening to. It's not on the agenda that I painstakingly put together and the business decisions that need made today.

No. It's on the one woman I've longed to set my hungry eyes on again for the past three weeks. Hell, the past five years. And the fact that, in a few short hours when this meeting wraps up, I'm headed to the twenty-sixth floor to finally get the answers that I fucking deserve.

And to finally reclaim the one thing I'd thought lost to me forever.

My fiancée.

Chapter 11

Livia

My hands are sweaty, my stomach is in knots and my head is spinning.

Jake Campbell didn't show up for the 9:00 meeting this morning because there must be a contagion of pregnancies at this place. His wife went into labor early with their first child and he was at the hospital with her. Where he should be.

But Jake then told Wes *he* would have to give the quarterly update to the board in his place and Wes freaked, promptly telling me that I would be attending the meeting with him since I'd put all of the materials together. And he needed someone to run the presentation while he talked.

Umm...didn't they have those clicker things for that?

But that's not why my body's revolting against me. No. It's not the fact that I'm not capable of hitting the little forward arrow on the computer when Wes is ready to go to the next slide. It's not the fact that I'm sitting in a room of very powerful, very good-looking men, where I am completely out of place, because not only am I the only female, I'm also the only assistant in attendance. And it's not the fact that this is the very first important business meeting I've ever attended.

Nope. It's none of those things.

It's the fact that Gray Colloway's two brothers, Asher and Connelly, now sit across from me at this long table, staring. Fire's blazing out of Asher's sockets so hot, I wouldn't be surprised if I spontaneously combust. And Connelly's sitting stock still, concern and confusion wrinkling his forehead. The tension in the room is so thick it hangs like a dark, menacing raincloud, threatening to blast me with ten thousand volts of death wielding electricity any second.

When Asher and Connelly walked in together a few minutes ago, they were laughing and bantering, as I'd always fondly remembered, but the minute they saw me, they both froze. As did I. Asher's loud voice made me jump when he yelled, "What the fuck is *she* doing here?" Um...ditto.

Connelly, always the more laid back of the two, quickly calmed him down. I heard him quietly tell Asher this wasn't the time or place.

So while all of this was nightmarishly bad, what had me feeling like I could spew the bowl of Wheaties I had this morning for breakfast was that if Asher and Connelly were here, the chances were high that Gray wasn't far behind. And why *were* they here to begin with? In my research, I knew HMT was recently acquired by a holding company. And then suddenly it hit me. Gray, Asher, Connelly, GRASCO Holdings. *Holy Jesus.*

"Where's Gray? He's never late to these meetings," Asher asks, accusing eyes never leaving mine. Everyone senses that something is wrong between the three of us, but no one dares ask, including Wes.

Connelly pulls out a cell phone and dials quickly. "Bonnie, where's Gray? He's late." After a short pause, he adds, "Okay." He shoves the phone back into his pocket. "He's finishing up a call, then he'll be here."

Holy hell.

I break Asher's stare and look down at the table, but I can still feel all eyes upon me. I can hardly breathe. This cannot be happening. This is both everything I've wished for and my worst possible nightmare all at the same time. I've thought of nothing else but Gray's heated stare and the warmth of his hand on my bare skin since I saw him at the fundraiser. And any second now he's going to walk through that door.

I have to quit. Or I'll be fired. Either way, this is my last day at HMT Enterprises because after Gray walks in and sees me here, there is no way he'll let me stay. Or that I *can* stay. I can't possibly work in the same building as he is every single day and wonder each time I walk around the corner if he'll be there. Or every time I walk into the gym, if he'll be shirtless, pumping iron. Or when I step into the elevator, if he'll be waiting inside.

Gray is the most persistent man I've ever known. My defenses will hopelessly crumble at my feet, and I'll do something foolish, like tell him everything. And I can't do that. He can't know.

Oh God. Blood thumps loudly in my ears, and it's hard to pull enough oxygen into my lungs. My life was finally looking up and suddenly it's crashing down around me into a million shattered pieces again. Reluctant tears sting my eyes. I fight with everything in me to hold my shit together.

"Livia, are you okay?" Wes asks softly, placing a hand over mine. "You look white as a ghost."

I swallow hard, unable to answer through my constricted airway. Just then, the light chatter in the room completely stops and, feeling his eyes pierce me, I look up.

But Gray isn't looking at me. At least not my face.

He's looking at my boss's hand, which is still covering mine. And when his fiery eyes connect with Wes's, Wes pulls it back like a snake has bitten him. A mean one.

Then his heated hazel eyes finally connect with my watery ones and all oxygen is depleted from the room like a backdraft. I want to simultaneously run into his arms for the protection and affection I so crave, and bolt so fast and so far he can never find me. I want him on top of me, inside me, taking every bad memory and replacing it with love and goodness.

I want to cry for all the things I can't have.

We stare helplessly at each other. I feel the volley of eyes on us, back and forth, back and forth, waiting to see what will happen next.

The pressure in the room has increased tenfold, but instead of animosity, all I feel now is the sexual tension rolling thickly between us. It's palpable. It always was. He looks absolutely edible in his charcoal, fitted suit. The mint green button down he's wearing underneath makes his hazel eyes take on a shimmery hue.

"Livvy," he finally says, breaking the silence as he walks in, taking the empty seat next to me. He opens his folder like this is the most normal thing to happen in the world. I don't respond. I can't.

As the meeting starts, I realize that Gray didn't look surprised in the slightest to see me when he walked into the room.

I have no idea what that means.

Chapter 12

Gray

When this meeting is over, I am going to kill Wesley Nichols. I don't care how fucking brilliant he is or the fact that he graduated summa cum laude from Penn State. As soon as I stepped foot into the room and got over my initial shock at seeing Livvy sitting here, in the flesh, I zeroed in on that fuckers hand on hers. And I just about lost it. He got the message quick, however, and that's the only thing that kept me from flying across the table to choke the life out of him right then and there.

I knew Wesley Nichols would be here. That was one of the messages I quickly read on the climb to the meeting. Jake's wife delivered early and he sent Nichols in his stead. But I was very shocked to see he'd dragged along his assistant to a board meeting. The fact that he had his hands on my woman, and can't run a fucking computer and talk at the same time has steam rolling out of my ears. The guy is a blathering, nervous mess.

So at the end of his presentation, I do the only thing any other man in my position would. I put him on the hook and watch him squirm.

"Mr. Nichols, where are we at with the latest optical detection design patent?" I have no choice but to look over at Livvy as I ask my question because he's sitting on her opposite side. But instead of watching him, I watch her.

"Umm, let me check my file here." He opens several folders and shuffles papers around nervously for long, indeterminable minutes. As I watch her, watching him, I can tell she knows the answer but is afraid to speak up.

"Livvy, would you happen to have a status update for me?"

The look on her face is priceless, and I almost feel bad putting her on the spot. *Almost.* But I wouldn't do it if I weren't certain she knew. I would never intentionally embarrass her that way in front of my peers. Or my brothers.

Nichols has now looked up and his eyes flit uneasily between Livvy and me, as do hers.

"Ah, yes," she says reluctantly. "It was rejected and an appeal was filed three weeks ago."

That surprised me. That patent was filed before we even acquired HMT and why the fuck didn't I know this before now? This was supposed to be cutting edge security monitoring technology created by HMT's own renowned developers that would not only revolutionize the security industry, but make GRASCO Holdings a hell of a lot of money. That's one of the main reasons we decided to purchase HMT Enterprises to begin with.

"What was the reason for the denial?"

"A patent for similar technology has already been obtained," she replies, chewing anxiously on her lip.

I snap my eyes to Nichols, who looks like a deer caught in the headlights. He should fucking

87

know this and the fact that he doesn't means his days here are numbered. Since we only acquired HMT Enterprises just several short months ago, I've only had the opportunity to meet with him a handful of times, and I was so wrong when I pegged him as flighty. He's a fucking incompetent moron who's going to be standing in the unemployment line come Monday. And by the look on his face, he knows it.

The rest of the meeting goes by slowly. I feel every single one of Livvy's quiet sighs, as if they are connected directly to my cock. I'm attuned to her every breath, every tap of her finger, every cross and uncross of her sexy legs, which I have the utmost pleasure to view in my peripheral vision, courtesy of the tight black skirt now rising with every movement she makes.

I want to pull her into my lap and hold her. I want to strip her clothes and fuck her raw on this table until neither of us can breathe without the other. I want to own and worship every creamy inch of her, like I once did.

"Gray?" Ash grates impatiently.

"What?" I huff.

"I said, Willis is reviewing the CFC books, but initial reports indicate we may need to hire a forensic auditor."

Shit. Ash had tried telling me about this financial discrepancy a couple of weeks ago and I had my head so far in the clouds, I never followed up. And by the irritated look on my brother's face, he's thinking the same thing.

"How much is the discrepancy?"

"Over half a mil, but it's not confirmed yet."

"Shit," I mutter under my breath.

"I should have a report in a few weeks. We'll go from there."

I nod. I trust my brother implicitly.

"Is there any other business to discuss?" I ask. I'm impatient as hell to adjourn this meeting so I can talk to Livvy in private. I want to spank her ass so she can't sit down for days. Or fuck her blind. Sitting next to her for these last three hours without being able to touch her has been excruciating.

"Good," I say when my question is met with silence. I rise, as does Livvy, who is quickly pulling her papers together in hopes to make a hasty escape. *Too bad, angel. You aren't going anywhere.*

As she steps back from the table and turns away, I gently grab her elbow, pulling her into me. "Not so fast," I whisper. I lean down and take a deep whiff of her intoxicating scent. I can't help myself. Jesus, I've missed her so damn much.

Her eyes flick to mine and I see them pleading with me not to do this here, but there is no way in hell I am letting her out of my sight. For all I know, she'll run again and hide so deep I'll never be able to find her.

"Gray, please." Her soft voice is as beseeching as her green eyes are beguiling. I am entranced.

"Gray, don't forget dinner at seven-thirty."

My eyes never leave hers when I answer Asher. "Change of plans. I can't make it."

Her sparkling emeralds widen slightly before her face falls in resigned acceptance. Her eyes shift from mine and I want them back. I want to stare into her now broken soul and fix whatever happened between us. But I have no fucking clue what that is.

And she's going to tell me come hell or high water.

"Gray—" Ash starts, but stops the second I whip my head around. I'm sure the look on my face is feral and he simply throws up his hands in frustration, shaking his head before turning to leave. Conn is watching silently from the door, a slight smirk on his face.

Fuckers. Both of them.

"Uh, Livia. Is everything okay?"

I now turn my death glare to Wesley Nichols, who will soon be pounding the pavement for a new job.

"That will be all," I grit, punctuating every word.

"Of course, Mr. Colloway. Uh, Livia, I'll see you later." He turns and scurries out of the room like a mouse that's been kicked. It's a blow I wish I could have physically delivered instead of verbally.

Like fuck you will, Nichols. You will never lay eyes on my Livvy again.

I didn't miss the heated way he glanced at Livvy several times throughout the meeting or the fact that he had just as good of view at her sleek, creamy thighs as I did. My jaw now aches from gritting my teeth for the last several hours.

With everyone now gone, I release her elbow and silently walk to the open door, closing it softly and locking it for good measure. We shouldn't be disturbed, but still. I walk to the wall and press a button that starts the descent of dark blinds over the glass windows that overlook the hallway. We'll need completely privacy for what I have in mind.

When I turn back toward her, she's nervously watching my every move, rooted to the spot where I left her. I slowly walk back toward her, stopping with only inches separating our bodies.

Her eyes lock on mine. Her heat seeps into me and I want to wrap myself in it and forget every day of the last five years ever happened. I want to lean down and kiss her pink, glossy lips. I want to back her up against the closest wall, reach under that tease of a skirt, rip her panties violently from her hips and find her slick heat with my fingers. With my cock.

I want to get lost in her.

But I can't. I need answers. I *deserve* some fucking answers.

"Start talking," I rasp.

Chapter 13

Livia

I silently watch him as he glides to the door and closes it. My traitorous eyes fall on his toned, tight ass when he turns to the wall and punches a button that shrouds us in complete privacy from the outside world. Our hot gazes collide when he turns and stalks back to me, stopping a hairsbreadth away.

There are very few men that exuded complete confidence, if not a bit of arrogance, like they were born with it. They wear it. They own it. They make no excuses for it. They couldn't help it if they tried. There's a very fine line between cocky and confident, and Gray is one of the few men I've met that can pull that off successfully. You are simply drawn to the man. It's inevitable. He's magnetic.

And over the last five years, he's mastered that skill to smooth perfection.

"Start talking," he demands. I shudder when I feel his warm breath scatter over my flushed face.

This is it. This is the inevitable moment I knew would always happen, although I prayed it wouldn't. I knew the minute I saw Asher and Connelly walk into this room that I was screwed. For a second time, I would have to ruin the man I love. The man, who for some unknown reason, still cares about me. I can see it in the scorching way he burns me with his gaze. I'd felt the heat every time he'd looked my way for the past three hours.

But not only did I not want to say the words, I was a chicken shit. I *couldn't* say them. My entire body was shaking uncontrollably and I felt a little light-headed. I could really use a few shots of tequila about now. Or the whole damn bottle, which is a testament to the state I'm in because I loathe tequila.

"What do you want to know," I ask, stalling for time, desperately wracking my brain for an excuse better than the one I'd come up with. Because I knew Gray would see right through it for the lie it was. He was always too good at reading me, from the moment our eyes connected so very long ago and I tried unsuccessfully to deny my attraction to him. He *knew* I wanted him back then. He was so right.

His jaw clenches. Anger clouds his mesmerizing hazel eyes. "Oh, no you don't, Livvy. Don't you fucking play games with me. The very *least* I deserve is an explanation for what you did to me. To *us.*"

"You're right," I whisper, barely audible. He does deserve that. I wish I could give it to him. I spin away, unable to look him in the eye as I try to push the bitter-tasting lie past my lips, the one that will deliver the final crushing blow, but he grabs my elbow, turning me back around to face his wrath.

"No. You don't get to run away. You did that once already. I want you to look me in the eyes as you try to lie your way out of this one, Livvy. Because I know whatever's about to come out of that pretty little mouth of yours is nothing but a pile of shit."

I open my mouth and close it again, speechless. He pulls me into him, so our bodies meld together from knee to chest. One hand holds my arm, while his other snakes around my waist, holding on for dear life. His face is mere inches from mine, and his ragged breaths wash over me like a hot summer breeze.

Jesus, how I've missed him.

His touch. His kiss. His love.

"You forget how well I know you, Livvy," he murmurs. "I can see the wheels spinning behind those gorgeous eyes of yours, just trying to come up with something plausible to appease me. Something that won't rip my fucking heart out of my chest and leave me bleeding out for a second time."

I'm snared in his fiery gaze, unable to look away. Unable to deny his words or catch my breath. He leans in closer, running his nose erotically along my cheek. I inhale sharply.

His anger is justified.

His lust just confuses me.

"You ruined me, Livvy," he croaks. The pain and agony I've caused him laces thickly through every syllable and I don't have to see his face to know he speaks the truth. His confession guts me and tears spring into my eyes. *I've ruined myself too, Gray.*

"I'm sorry," I choke out. There are no words I can utter that will ever be good enough. No words that will erase the pain and suffering I've caused Gray. The truth would only cause him more pain.

Even if he could forgive me, *I* don't deserve *him*. Not anymore.

"Sorry's not fucking good enough," he bellows, releasing me like a hot coal, pacing to the other side of the large conference room. "I need to understand, Livvy. Jesus, I deserve to know why the woman I love more than the air I breathe deserted me less than twenty-four fucking hours after she agreed to be my wife!"

I try to hold it in. I try, but I can't. He's the one that's suffered because of my actions. Well, we both have, but how dare I make this about me. I *know* what I did; he doesn't. He just thinks I abandoned him.

The moisture in my eyes involuntarily spills over, streaking my makeup. Standing in the presence of the best thing to ever happen to me, and the man who apparently still loves me, I've never felt as alone in my entire life as I do at this moment. And the last five years have been some of the hardest and loneliest I think any human being could ever endure.

When I'm silent for too long, he barks, "Say something, Livvy. Say *anything*, for Christ's sake."

I shake my head. I won't. I simply refuse to destroy the love of my life any more than I already have. I can't lie. I can't tell the truth. I don't know what to do. I feel like an animal trapped in a corner with no way to escape. "I can't."

He pushes off the wall he's been leaning against and in five long strides is standing in front of me. Grabbing my shoulders, he shakes me. Fury rolls off him in potent waves, but I know he won't hurt me. "Can't or won't?" he demands through gritted teeth.

I hold his angry eyes with watery ones, pleading for him to understand. Silently begging him to simply accept my apology and move on with his life. Without me. "Both," I answer, my voice involuntarily cracking under the burdensome weight of my own emotional anguish.

His hard eyes soften. *He knows*. He knows I'm hiding something big, life altering. The knowledge swirls as he gauges my reaction. And his next quietly spoken question undoes me completely. "What happened to you, angel?"

I can't help what follows next. The tenuous emotional thread I've been balancing on for years finally breaks, and the one person I need to catch me when I fall does. I bury my face in his expensive, undoubtedly custom-made suit, and uncontrollably sob, clinging tightly to him like a child. Clinging like he's a dream that will be ripped away from me any second.

Like it has so many times before.

I don't deserve comfort from the man I destroyed, but he gives it. I don't deserve his soft-spoken words of warmth, but he whispers them. I don't deserve to be held in his arms again after the suffering I have put him through, but that doesn't stop him from sitting and pulling me onto his lap, cocooning me in his strength.

After unknown minutes tick by and the worst of my meltdown passes, his finger slides under my chin, tipping it up so our eyes meet. His are full of torment, but I also see love and, God help me, forgiveness swirling in the mix. Mine are full of regret and brokenness and sorrow. I try to hide the multitude of other emotions bubbling to the surface. I guess I fail miserably.

"You still love me."

My breath hitches. No truer words have ever been spoken. *I do*. I want to scream it until my throat is hoarse. I want to tell him I've never stopped. I want to make him understand I would never have *voluntarily* left him. To protect us both, I have to deny him, but my mouth refuses to form the words.

"I—"

I try to look away, but he grabs my chin firmly between his fingers and forces my eyes back to his.

"Convince me you don't love me, Livvy and I'll walk. You can run and this time, I won't try to find you. But if I don't believe the bullshit you're about to try to shove down my throat, fair warning, angel. I will be relentless in my pursuit of you. Last time was *nothing* compared to the lengths I will go to in order to make you mine again."

I can't think straight. There were so many things said in those few sentences that have my head reeling. But the unspoken words I heard are the most profound.

I can't wrap my head around how I could have hurt him so deeply, but still earn his forgiveness. Is he playing a sadistic game with my damaged heart and my fragile trust? Is he trying to lure me into thinking he can possibly absolve me for an unforgivable wrong and then crush me under his boot, like I did him? Would I blame him if he tried?

Sadly, no.

I was unable to keep the question rolling around on my tongue from spilling out. "How can you still want me after what I did to you?"

He grabs my face between his strong hands. His eyes shine with pure, unadulterated love and my stomach goes into a free-fall. "I've never stopped. And I'm a fool's fool, because, God help me, I never will." His hungry, lust-filled eyes flit between mine and my lips, which I unconsciously wet. My breathing is out of control. "Tell me you don't love me, Livvy," he rasps. His control is razor thin. One wrong word and it will slice him in half, mutilating him beyond repair.

I shake my head. I should be pushing him away, not drawing him in. I should tell him to run as far and as fast as he can, but I can't force myself to do it. My love for him is too powerful. My willpower too weak. "I can't," I sob. Fresh tears balance precariously on my eyelashes.

His lips crash to mine and I let them. He takes and I silently beg him with my body to take more. I know I'm making the biggest mistake of my life because I can't keep Gray. No matter whether he can forgive me or not, I can't forgive myself. He will never be mine again. So I'll take this one stolen moment I've been granted and I will revel in it. I will lose myself in it. And I will store it away as my last blissful memory of him, erasing the painful ones from the past few years.

If he wants my body, I'll freely give it. He already has my heart. He always has and he always will. But what I can't give him is the last piece of my soul, and I'm barely holding onto it. It pleads with me to be released into his soul-sucking kiss. He's trying to take it, but I need to keep that buried deep within me in order to survive the agonizingly lonely, bleak days ahead of me without him.

Because this is the last time I'll step foot in HMT Enterprises. And this is the last time I can let myself see or feel or touch Gray Colloway.

Chapter 14

Gray

Livvy's lips taste exactly as I remember. Warm, sweet and uniquely her. She's intoxicating. She's breathing life back into my broken heart, and I want nothing more at this moment than to be buried balls deep in her sweet, slick pussy so I can finally feel whole again. She couldn't lie to me. She couldn't tell me that she didn't love me because I know the truth. I knew it the moment we looked into each other's eyes three weeks ago.

She still *does. Then why did she leave you?*

I was lying when I told her I'd let her run. Now that I know she loves me, I'll never let her leave me again.

No matter what.

Pain and darkness churn in her soul like witch's brew, dulling her once bright eyes. I want to take it away. I want to tell her that absolutely *nothing* can make me stop loving her. Something happened, something she's afraid to tell me, and I'm filled with regret that I gave up. I'm filled with self-loathing that I simply gave into the lies that were being fed to me. I failed her.

But right now I push all that to the back of my mind because, at this very moment, it's irrelevant. Livvy's here and she still loves me, which means she *will* be mine again.

And I aim to have a taste of what's mine right fucking now.

I force myself to free her swollen lips from mine and lift her off my lap, setting her on the hard maple table. Smoky gazes locked on each other, I pull the blouse from her skirt and slowly draw it up over her head, waiting for her to protest. She doesn't. I unhook her black lacy bra that cups her ample breasts like a fitted glove, letting it fall to the floor, expecting her to stop me. She won't.

Neither of us speaks with our mouths, but we don't have to. Everything that needs to be said flows between us, unspoken. We both want this with a desperation that's almost burning out of control, belying the slow, reverent way I'm stripping her.

Physically.

Emotionally.

I break our connection and rake my gaze down every inch of her exposed skin. Her torso is bare and her skirt has ridden up almost to the top of her toned, snow-driven thighs. The darkness at the juncture of them calls my name. Chills rise on her flesh. Her berry-ripened nipples are as hard as erasers and my mouth waters for a taste, which I don't deny myself.

She moans at the first flick of my tongue, her hands flying to my hair, pulling me closer. *Fuck, yes*. After only moments of teasing, I take her hardened nub in my mouth completely, sucking hard. I pluck the other between my thumb and forefinger.

"Gray," she breathes. She remembers how hot we used to burn, just like I do.

Fuck, I'm as hard as a rock. I shouldn't do this in my boardroom, but I'm unable to stop. The second my flesh touched hers I was a total goner.

I kiss and lave my way over to her other nipple because it's begging for my attention too. *Jesus Christ, she tastes good.* No matter how many women I've been with, no one has, or ever will, compare to her. I'm like a starved man, unable to get enough. Unable to stop gorging. I have to be inside of her right now.

I reach behind to undo the zipper on her skirt when she stops me.

"Leave it," she rasps.

I pull back to see what she's really saying, knowing desperation is written all over my face. My cock pulses and my balls ache. "I need to fuck you, Livvy. Christ, I need to be inside of you right now." *I need to make you mine again.*

Without a word, Livvy hops off the table, reaches under her skirt and removes matching black lace panties. Holding my eyes, she turns toward the table, leans over and shimmies up the offending fabric.

Fuck. Me. Her round, smooth ass is begging for my hand. Her glistening, bare dark pink lips are parted and my mouth hurts at the thought of tasting her.

"Sweet Jesus, angel," I murmur, drawing a finger through her wetness, back to her puckered hole. I circle and tease, drawing a low moan from her now parted mouth.

"Fuck me, Gray. *Please.* I need you so much." She sounds as frantic as I feel.

102

I want that too, but I'm not going to miss this opportunity to taste what's mine either. I sit back in the chair. Rolling it close, I place her legs on either side of mine so they are now resting on the leather instead of the floor. I spread her silky thighs as far apart as they'll go and lean in for my first lick.

And see fucking stars.

"Gray..." she groans, heavy head falling to the table.

"I'm going to eat this pussy, Livvy. *My* pussy. I've been denied it far too long."

I grab her cheeks and spread them, using my thumbs to pull her nether lips apart and start to feast. I lick and suck until she's moving frantically against my mouth, trying to reach the peak and fall over. I thrust my tongue into her soaking channel and feel her walls tighten around me. *Jesus, how I've missed this.*

"Gray, please, please," she begs.

Dragging my wet thumb up to the place I know she craves it, I ease in, pulling a wail from her throat, causing her to writhe faster. I move another digit to her clit and start to circle deliberately, applying just the right amount of pressure.

She immediately detonates, crying my and God's name over and over. It's music to my deaf ears. I will never get enough of the way my Livvy sounds when she comes undone by my hand, or my mouth, or my cock. I let her ride my face and my fingers until she slows and her body sags.

Standing, I reach for her hips, gently turning over her boneless form. The only position that I've ever taken another woman in the last few years is

103

from behind, so I don't have to look at their faces. It made it easier to pretend they're Livvy. So, the first time I take her after being apart for so long, I intend to look into her eyes as she bares her soul to me.

I want it.

I need it.

I *crave* it.

And I will have it as I sink my cock deep inside her.

"You're so beautiful, Livvy," my thick voice rasps. With her dark hair fanning out on the table, her fair skin radiating like starlight and the blissfully sated look on her face, she looks like an ethereal goddess spread out on an altar. My altar. Mine to take. I almost want to weep at the sight of her, and I have to keep telling myself repeatedly this is not a dream. This is real. She's right before me, in the flesh. Her innate beauty makes me breathless.

Her lust-laden eyes hold mine as I quickly undress, my clothes joining hers in the pile on the floor beside me. With one push down of my navy boxer briefs, my straining, heavy cock springs free and it's throbbing to finally be home. My hands slowly travel up her trembling legs as I ask the questions I'm burning to know before I fuck my fiancée for the first time in over five years. And I still think of her that way. She's *mine*.

I know I should use a condom, but I can't. It's not like I carry them around in my pants pockets at work anyway, and I'm not waiting a minute longer to be inside her. And I don't give a shit if she ends up pregnant. I *want* her to. I want to tie her to me for fucking ever so the thought of leaving me again causes her physical pain, like it did when she left me.

"Tell me you're clean, Livvy." I haven't been raw with another women since her.

She nods and whispers yes.

"Tell me there's no one else," I choke, now running my dick up her wet slit, readying it for the hot plunge. I don't know what I'll do if she says yes.

"There's no one else," she whispers, no hesitation. I see the truth in her eyes.

I release a breath I didn't realize I was holding. I cover her and link her hands with mine, so we're skin to skin, except for the fabric that's still bunched around her waist and thrust into her tight pussy. Five years simply melt away like shadows in the light.

Our eyes lock. "Tell me you're mine, angel."

"Ahhhh, Gray," she breathes, her eyes closing in pleasure.

I pull out slowly and drive again. It takes three times to seat myself to the hilt of her tight channel. Her smooth walls grip me like a boa constrictor and I know that no other man has been inside her sweetness in some time. And that pleases the fuck out of me, more than it should.

"Tell me."

"Gray." She turns her head away. Releasing one hand, I cup her face, turning it back, never losing my slow, methodical rhythm.

"Look into my soul and know that it belongs to only you."

She closes her eyes. If the clenching of her inner muscles is any indication, she's close to a second orgasm, so I stop. I deny her. Her eyes fly open.

"You own me, Livvy. You own all of me, so. Tell. Me. You. Are. Mine."

Her eyes mist, she swallows hard. I move my hips, slowly withdrawing nearly all the way and thrust so hard she expels a harsh breath. "Say it." I repeat my deliberate movements and start to feel the telltale tingling in the base of my spine. She's so tight, so hot, so Livvy. I know I won't last long. I rain kisses on her jaw, her eyelids, her parted mouth. I need her to admit she's mine before I let us fall.

"Say it, baby. Tell me you're mine," I beg quietly in her ear. Her body tightens. It already knows it's mine. Now I need the words.

Her soft reply makes my heart swell. "I've always been yours, Gray. Always."

Thank Jesus.

Her legs quiver and her snug pussy has become even more so. Her climax is almost upon her. I'm unable to hold back any longer and with her admission, I have one sole goal. To fuck her hard, sending her over the edge one more time before I follow.

Peeling myself from her sweat-soaked skin, I grab her legs, tilt her pelvis higher and pound into her with a fierce, rough pace. Our gazes lock until the rush of rapture forces her head back, her body convulsing. I swiftly follow with the most intense, most euphoric orgasm I've had since the night I asked Livvy to marry me.

My legs are liquid, but I manage to scoop her up and sit in the cushioned leather chair behind me, still tucked inside her wet heat. She clings to me, her head on my shoulder.

We're quiet, only our harsh breaths filling the room. I honestly couldn't be more content than I am right now. I love this woman to the deep recesses of my soul and as our breathing stabilizes and our bodies cool, I realize that while it's eating me up inside to not know what caused her to leave me so long ago, I'm willing to simply take what I can get.

Her.

She's it for me. She bewitched me the second our eyes met and while I thought I'd done a decent job at moving on, I realize that I've been a shadow of myself without her in my life. I feel like I can see in color for the first time in years.

It's funny how the mind can so easily fool itself. With the loss of someone you love, you trick yourself into thinking you're managing, coping, living. But you're not. You're simply existing.

If the sun is suddenly stripped away, eventually you'd get used to darkness. You have to. It's your new normal and you can't escape. It becomes part of your daily life. And after so long in the blackness you fool yourself into thinking you've adjusted. You think you can live. Thrive, even. But then the sunshine returns and it's bright and warm and comforting.

It's joy.

It's life.

It's your salvation. And you realize how very wrong you were. You weren't living at all. You were in a cold, lonely hell without those life-giving rays and you can finally see things clearly for the first time since you were plunged into that dark, bleak space.

Sitting here, quietly stroking Livvy's hair in comfortable silence, I'm hit with the realization that I've really been living in darkness this whole time and my sunshine has finally returned. My purpose in life finally restored. My blackness vanished. And I'll be damned if I'll let anyone, or anything, throw me into that dark void ever again.

Chapter 15

Livia

I didn't once think of the many times sex was forced on me during those long, interminable days with Peter. I didn't think of the beatings that would always follow, or the broken bones that would need time to mend before he started all over again. Instead, making love with Gray was always as I thought it would be. *Healing.* It helped that he held my gaze so I could stay in the moment. I let Gray have me, and I did nothing but enjoy every single second of it. The peacefulness that settled over me was deep and surreal.

But I've also never been more confused.

I shouldn't have let him in. In either my heart, or my body, but I can't bring myself to regret a single solitary second of what happened tonight. And I don't know how I can face Gray again while keeping this ugly, dirty secret bottled up inside me, where it belongs. He didn't push me for answers again, but there's only so long that can last. Even if we were to try to make a go of this, he would eventually press me. And I'd refuse him. The bitterness of my lie of omission would fester like an open wound, ultimately becoming so infected its toxicity would spread and become untreatable. And fatal to our relationship.

Gray thinks he loves me, he thinks he can forgive me, but, so help me God, if he knew my shameful secrets, he wouldn't. He *couldn't*. He'd turn and walk away with hate and contempt in his heart. And I simply can't bear that. But the thought of letting him go almost sends my body into complete shutdown.

I'm so screwed.

"Livia, what are you doing sitting here alone in the dark?"

The overhead light turns on. I squint my eyes at the hurt it inflicts on my retinas. I've been sitting on the couch in the dark, in complete silence, ever since Gray dropped me off hours ago. Against my protests, he insisted on bringing me home and walking me to the door. He wanted to stay, but I wouldn't let him. I needed time and space to think. He wasn't happy but respected my wishes. I told him I'd talk to him in a few days, but I fully expect he'll just show up on my doorstep tomorrow, uninvited.

"Livia, are you okay?" Addy asks, taking a seat beside me. Concern is clearly written all over her face and I'm glad my friend is here but want her gone at the same time.

I can't even speak. I simply shake my head and she wraps her arms around me, comforting me. Then she must spot what I'm holding because she grabs the small, velvet box from my hand. When she opens it, it makes that lovely little clicky noise that jewelry boxes do. You know, the one that makes your heart pitter-patter the first time you lift the lid. I hear her gasp at the beautiful, sparkling piece sitting in the cushioned middle.

110

"What the hell is this, Liv?"

"My engagement ring," I state flatly, not looking at her.

"Your engagement ring? Shut up. *Who* the fuck are you engaged to?" she shrieks. I haven't been on a single date since we've lived together, so of course this shocks her. I've never spoken of Gray or Peter. I've never shared my painful past with anyone, except my shrink. I've kept the fucking lid on that nightmare superglued shut. It's the only way I can cope.

Taking the box back, I shut it and climb off the couch. My hips are stiff and my right leg is slightly asleep. I walk to the living room window, gazing at the dark night outside from our third-floor apartment.

The day I offered my life for my sister's I briefly let myself break. But the second I walked out the door of my father's house, my resolve to survive was strong and fortified. I was given ten minutes and allowed to pack a small bag, taking only a few personal items with me, minus my phone. I was told I'd be provided everything else I needed. Lies, all of it.

I look down, turning the black box over and over in my hand and reminisce. While the details of the few minutes I'd spent packing are fuzzy and hazy because of the shock I was in, I distinctly remember taking my two-carat, emerald cut diamond engagement ring off my finger and hiding it under the loose floorboard in my bedroom. I retrieved it when we cleaned and sold our father's house, but I've not looked at again...until tonight. It felt too much like breaking the seal on that closed box. A seal that, once broken, could never fully be repaired.

Addy waits patiently for my reply to her question. She senses I'm on the precipice of a steep ledge and if she pushes me too hard, I'll simply tumble over and just be...gone.

I feel like a champagne bottle that's been shaken. Bubbles fizz and demand release. The pressure to be contained in their glassy, corked prison becomes too great. And eventually the top will blow; spewing its sickly sweet contents everywhere, creating a huge fucking mess, the champagne now ruined, the bottle an empty vessel to be discarded. Left behind.

I need to release some pressure, to tell someone *something* so I can lighten this heavy burden I carry around with me daily. Spinning, I lean against the ledge, opening the small square container in my hand. I don't look at her. I can't. Instead, I stare at that tiny, size six and a half platinum circle of trust that Gray gave me...which I broke.

"A little over five years ago I was engaged to a man named Gray Colloway." I smile as I let myself remember our whirlwind love affair and how very much I wanted to marry him. I still do. "He was the love of my life." *He still is,* a quiet voice reminds me. As if I need reminded of that.

"What happened?" she asks tentatively.

Then I do look up at her. "Betrayal," I answer simply. Not Gray's of course, but my father's. But I know my one-word reply has her thinking otherwise, and I feel bad for letting her believe a lie. *Add it to the pile.*

But if I talk about my father, I won't be able to help but mention Peter. And I'm just not ready to do that yet. I'm not sure I ever will be. Voicing it to someone who I care about makes it all too real.

"I'm sorry, Livia. I didn't know." She comes and gives me a much-needed hug.

"It's been too painful to talk about," I murmur.

Truth.

"Why are you thinking about it now? Something happened, I can tell."

How much to tell her? If Gray shows up on our doorstep tomorrow, she'll know that we've reconnected and I won't be able to keep the fact hidden that I now work for his company.

"If you can believe it, he owns the company I work for. How's that for that spiteful karma bitch?" Or *fate*, I wonder. I laugh, but it's bitter and threaded with anguish instead of humor.

Addy heads into the kitchen, returning with two large wine glasses filled to the brim. "Here," she demands, holding one out to me.

"Thanks," I mumble. I'd purposely not drank while I'd been sitting here, contemplating and reminiscing. My mood was already too dark. I felt like I was on the cusp of falling into a bottomless pit. Pulling me to the couch, we both sit.

"What are you going to do?" She studies me intently and I suddenly feel like a bug under a microscope.

"I don't know."

113

That's the truth. When I first saw Gray walk into that conference room, I'd already decided that I wasn't going to go to work on Monday. In fact, I intended to call Dundee's the second I walked through my apartment door, begging for my job back. But on the way home, Gray pleaded with me not to quit. He made me promise. And I've broken so many promises to him already; I don't know how I can stand to break another one. Me and my stupid mouth. I was never good at telling him no.

He knows me so very well. I never mentioned quitting, but he knew. He knew what my intentions were the second I stepped foot into his sleek black Bentley.

He reaches across console, turning my face to his. "You're not quitting, Livvy."

"Gray—" I protest.

"No, Livvy. I'll pick you up myself on Monday morning if I have to, but you're not quitting. HMT needs you."

I laugh. "I just started. They don't need me. I'm easily replaceable."

He cups my cheeks and leans so close our breaths mingle. "Fine. I need you and you're so wrong, Livia Kingsley. You're unique. A one of a kind rarity and there's no woman on the face of this earth that could possibly replace you."

I melt as our lips touch. I groan into his soft, reverent, worshiping kiss, lost once again.

"Promise me you won't quit," he urges between pecks.

"Gray—"

114

"Promise, Livvy." Our foreheads pressed together, his beseeching eyes find mine. I can't deny him.

"Fine."

The broad smile that spreads across his handsome, stubbly face sets my blood on fire. That time I initiate the kiss, unable to stop myself. We make out passionately in the front seat of his expensive car for several minutes before we finally break apart and I convince him to take me home.

"You're still in love with him. It's written all over your goofy face, Livia. Now everything makes so much sense. Why you never date or bump uglies with any other guys. You're still hung up on this one."

I scoff. "Even if it's true, it doesn't matter, Addy. There's too much water under the bridge for this to ever work." And too many lies. Secrets.

Her eyes challenge mine over the top of her wine glass as she takes a drink. "You know what I think?"

"No, but I'm sure you can't keep yourself from spouting your infinite wisdom, *Abby*," I say, referring to her alter ego.

"True," she laughs. Then her face turns serious and I know I'm in for a little *Abby* relationship advice. My best friend thinks she's *Dear Abby*, and during these talks, I always revert to the nickname. "I think that sometimes people have a second chance to right their wrongs. I think that sometimes the past simply needs to remain there and if you spend your life looking in the rear view mirror, reliving your mistakes, you'll never let

115

yourself be happy. Look forward, Livia, not backward."

My eyes prick. Sometimes she's so profound and makes so much sense, I feel like she's missed her calling. She should be counseling other fuck-ups like me, instead of teaching people to paint.

"I don't know if I can do that, Addy," I confess softly. "What if the past fuck-ups are so vast they simply can't be overcome? Or forgiven?"

"Have you tried?" she challenges again. My very intuitive friend knows we're talking about me now.

"No," I reluctantly admit.

"Well then, there you have it. The most forgiving people in the world are the ones who love us unconditionally, Livia. You just have to give them a chance to do it."

For some reason, although I still have so many secrets I'm hiding, I feel like a huge weight has been lifted. Maybe there is a tiny glimmer of hope shining at the end of this very deep, very dark, and very lonely place that I've been hiding in for so long.

The question is, do I let that hope grow or do I snuff it out. Do I let Gray Colloway back into my life or do I cut him loose? Would he still want me if he knew the whole truth about where I've been and the new person those awful experiences have turned me into?

I wish I knew the right answer, but my fear is...it's no.

Chapter 16

Livia

"Be a good girl, do as I say, and I won't hurt you this time...much." His hateful voice washes over me and sticks to me like a spider web that I can't shake off. He's the poisonous eight-legged insect waiting in the middle and I'm his prey. I'm helplessly caught and at his mercy. Except he doesn't inject enough of his life-stealing venom to kill me all at once. Oh no. That would be too easy. Too kind. Too merciful. And he's the furthest thing from merciful. He's a sadistic bastard who delivers the toxin ever so slowly, breaking me piece by piece.

He commands me to remove my clothes, which I do. I quickly discovered it's easier to obey, and denying him doesn't change the outcome. It only makes it more painful.

"You're getting fat," he sneers.

Oh shit. There is no way I can hide the subtle changes to my body.

"And your tits look bigger," he grits. Seconds later his face clouds over and I can tell he's put two and two together. And by the volcanic fire swirling hotly in his eyes, I know I'm in big trouble.

"Are you fucking pregnant?" he screams loud enough for the whole house to hear. I shake my head in denial, but he knows. He knows I'm lying. He viciously grabs my arm, painfully digging his fingers into my sensitive flesh. "How the fuck are you pregnant?"

"It's yours," I gasp, trying unsuccessfully to free myself from his iron grip. As long as I live, I will never forget the cruel jeer on his face as he brutally shoves me up against the bedpost, the unforgiving maple digging painfully into my back.

"See, now I know you're lying, little girl."

It's at this very moment I know my ruse is up. I know this baby is not his, and so does he.

"And do you know how I know?" he asks, deceptively quiet.

I shake my head, unable to speak.

"Because I've been firing blanks for over thirty years, you whore."

I remember the swift punch to the gut that had me doubling over in an effort to catch my breath. I remember the backhand to my jaw, which felt like a wrecking ball had just connected with my head. But what I remember most were the repeated kicks to my stomach as I lay on the floor, helpless, trying unsuccessfully to protect the only thing in the world that mattered to me.

And as the beating continues and I eventually begin to blessedly fall into unconsciousness, I remember Peter's orders to "take care of it and make sure she can't get pregnant again."

"Livia, Livia, baby. Oh my God." Grant's soft voice fades in and out. When I succumb again to the place where the pain can't touch me, I know I'll be okay. If anyone else had come, they might have finished me off, but I'd quickly come to find out Grant *was my only protector here. He just couldn't save me. No one could.*

A single tear slides into my hair, and I angrily wipe it away. It's early on Saturday morning, but I won't be going back to sleep. I stare at my ceiling, trying to shake off the dream I just woke from. It's a heart-shattering one that I can never seem to escape, no matter now long ago it's been.

Lying quietly, I think of the profound loss I'd endured that day. I mourned the loss of my baby every single day, and although it seems like yesterday, it also seems like a lifetime ago, too. Sometimes it feels as if it was somebody else's life and not my own, but the stabbing pain I feel quickly reminds me that's not the case. I've accepted my fate because I have no choice. I just try not to remember it too often.

When Gray and I had sex without protection, I knew I didn't have to worry about getting pregnant, because I no longer could. Peter made sure to take care of that after he took the most precious thing I had away from me. I never understood why he would do that if he couldn't have children, but of course, I didn't have to. It was just one of the many sick and twisted things he did simply to show me he owned me.

And, as always, when I thought about that day, it made me incredibly angry and devastatingly sad. Of everything Peter could have taken away from me, the loss of my baby, and the ability to have any more, were the greatest ones.

The beating when Peter found out about the baby was the worst, and it took me months to recover. I'd be six feet under had Grant not saved me. At the time, I would have welcomed it. I begged Grant to just let me die, but he wouldn't. He visited me every single day during my recovery and we became very close. It was six months after that incident before I saw Peter again.

As one of Peter's right-hand men, Grant was a constant in my life for the three years I was with that monster. He was often the only thing that stood between me and certain death. He saved me, literally. Grant continually told me I was strong, and eventually he made me believe it, but I wouldn't have been without him. My strength came *from* him.

But I never understood him, because underneath his rough exterior, which made him *seem* like he fitted in, Grant had a heart of gold, one he revealed only to me when we were alone. He was nothing like the monsters he played with, and the one time I dared ask him about it, he simply told me he had his reasons.

After Peter had died of a stroke, I had nothing. Peter and I may have been legally wed, but he used his great clout and vast resources to keep me, and our marriage, hidden from the public. Wouldn't do well for people to find out he'd essentially bought me. Besides, if he kept me secreted away, he wouldn't have to explain the physical injuries he regularly inflicted upon me.

Once Peter was gone, Grant got me out of that house of horrors and into this new life. He gave me enough money to make it through the first year. He helped me get back my maiden name on legal documents, trying his best to erase my ugly past. I owe him my life. I owe him everything.

He's the only other man I've ever been attracted to besides Gray, which is odd because Grant is the polar opposite of Gray. The only thing they have in common other than their striking hazel eyes is their height, both well over six feet. But where Gray's dark hair is always kept short and neat, Grant's black hair is long and unruly. He used to tie it on the back of his neck, which I always thought was sexy as hell.

Gray doesn't have a stitch of ink on him, but Grant's honed body is decorated with tats and piercings. Gray can rock a suit like no one I've seen, while I never saw Grant in anything other than well-worn jeans and tight, fitted t-shirts. Gray is the quintessential, sexy-as-hell successful businessman, and Grant is the quintessential drop-dead gorgeous bad boy. He drives a bike, wears a gun like it's part of him, likes his beer ice cold.

I'm surprised to find myself missing him. I haven't seen or heard from him since the day he dropped me off in Chicago a little more than two years ago. I touch my lips remembering the heated goodbye kiss he gave me and my stomach flutters a little.

I never wanted to be attracted to Grant, but God help me, I'm only human. We spent three years together and he saw me at my lowest and darkest times. He's an amazing man, inside and out. He was the only reason I was able to *physically* make it through those dark days and memories of Gray were the only reason I made it through *emotionally*. But I know even if I could have been with Grant, he would never have had all of me, and that's just not fair to any man.

That's one of the main reasons I haven't even considered starting another relationship. I meant the words that tumbled out of my mouth last night. I have always belonged to Gray. I always will. He owns me. He stole my heart eight years ago in Rocky's Pizza and I'll never get it back.

How I wish things could have been different for us. But if wishes were horses, beggars would ride. In the light of day I realize that even though Gray has my heart, and I apparently have his, a relationship between us could never work. Too much has happened. So I guess we're both screwed. Doomed to live sad, lonely lives full of regrets and what-ifs and unfulfilled wishes.

I sigh, throwing the covers back. I could lie in bed all day and moon about how different my life could have been. *Should* have been. But that won't change a goddamned thing. I'll still be Livia Kingsley, formerly secret wife to a mob boss, sold by her father to pay a debt. I'll still be barren and I'll still be without Gray.

Fuck it. *Enough wallowing, Livia Kingsley.*

I get out of bed, throw on my workout clothes and head out the door to the gym. Addy's still sleeping and probably still will be when I get home. She usually doesn't emerge from her darkened room until well after noon on a Saturday, unless she has a class to teach at *All Things Painting*, the painting business Addy owns.

After my four-mile run, I feel better, as usual. My head feels clearer, my energy level high. I run a few errands, as I usually do on Saturdays. With every step this morning, I can't help but notice the delicious soreness between my legs, a reminder of my afternoon romp with Gray yesterday, and the fact that I haven't had sex in close to three years. A small smile turns my lips.

After I get home and put my groceries away, it's still only ten thirty in the morning and it's a pretty nice September day, so I decide to walk the six blocks over to the quaint little coffee shop I've come to love.

I've gotten to know the owner, Carly, a young, pretty thirty-three-year-old single mother of the cutest little girl I have ever laid eyes on. Abigail is eleven and has long, wild ringlets of mahogany hair that cascade down her back. She's almost always at the coffeehouse on the weekends. She makes the most adorable beaded bracelets, which her mom sells for her and for the last two years I've bought way too many boxes of Girl Scout cookies from her. She's quite the little entrepreneur, just like her mother.

I put my ear buds in and head down the stairs, pushing my way outdoors into the cool morning air. I turn left and start making my way down the street. I've gone just a couple of blocks when I feel the hair on my neck prickle. I slow my gait and pull the headphones out. The foot traffic is rather light and as I look around, the only thing I see is a mother pushing a stroller about a block behind me and a group of teenage boys on the other side of the street that look pretty harmless.

I shake my head, laughing at myself. I'm being ridiculous and I know it, but I've been on edge ever since last weekend when I almost made the biggest mistake of my life with that stranger. But the thing that had me more rattled was the one that saved me. I can still feel his angry gaze boring into me.

"Hi Carly," I chirp when I enter the little shop a few minutes later. The bell dings, letting her know a new customer has arrived.

"Hey, Livia. How are you today?"

"Good. Where's Abigail?" I peruse the menu. I don't know why I do this every time since I always order the same thing. I'm a huge creature of habit.

"She spent the night with her grandma last night. I needed a break."

I try not to let the disappointment show. I really enjoy talking to that little squirt. She reminds me of innocence and dreams and I need reminded of the good in people occasionally. Ten minutes later and a promise that Abigail will be there next weekend, I leave with a large sugar-free caramel latte, extra foam, in hand and that's when I see him across the street, watching me intently. The man from the bar. My rescuer.

I panic and briefly turn toward the shop before spinning back around so I can get a better look at what he's wearing to describe him to the police if I need to. But when I turn, he's gone. Vanished. I scan both sides of the sidewalk, but he's nowhere to be found. It's like he was never there, except I know better. The way his eyes drilled into me gave me the same feeling as I had walking here, and I know this man has been following me. I've felt eyes on me several times this week but thought I was just paranoid because I never saw anyone or anything out of place.

I know for sure I'm being followed now, but the question is...why and by whom? And if this man meant harm, would he have saved me from certain rape in that bar last weekend? *Maybe, if he wants you for himself, or someone else.*

Panic paralyzes me and I'm truly terrified for the first time since Peter died. He had many enemies but did they know about me? Grant told me they didn't. There was only a handful of people who knew about my existence, outside of Peter and Grant. Grant told me I'd be safe, especially with returning to my maiden name and moving far away from Boston. He said I could be anonymous in a city of millions, like Chicago. Could he have been wrong? Could this be someone totally unrelated to my past? Could my father have owed someone else money and they're now here to collect? I honestly didn't know, but I felt in my gut it couldn't be that easy.

My past was back to haunt me.

My throat starts to close up. I feel my breaths getting shallow. My vision goes fuzzy and I faintly hear Carly calling my name as I lean back against the building, letting myself slide down to the sidewalk.

I thought I'd escaped. I thought I'd served my father's penance. I thought I was finally free.

I guess I was wrong.

Chapter 17

Gray

"Mr. Colloway, thank you for calling me," he says, rising from the corner table to shake my hand.

"Thank you for coming on such short notice," I reply, taking a seat across from him. I order a plain black coffee from the waitress before turning my attentions back to him.

"How can my organization be of service?" His sharp, grey, fitted Armani suit drapes perfectly over his broad, fit form. Dark, thick glasses sit on a nose that's clearly been broken several times, and a dusting of white hair rests around his temples. He's leaning back in his chair, arms draped casually across his lap, legs crossed. The confidence emanating from him could be confused as arrogance, but I knew better. And even if there was a bit of arrogance there, it was well earned. Robert Townley was the most sought after private consultant in the Midwest. His specialty was missing persons. His price tag, steep. And his client list, selective.

He'd refused my case before. But he wouldn't this time. I'd made sure of it.

"I need to find out some information about a woman."

The corner of his mouth turned up and his eyes glinted with mirth. "A Livia Kingsley, perhaps?"

"Yes."

"I thought I turned this case down five years ago?"

"You did." And I'm still fucking pissed about it.

"Then why am I here?"

"She turned up. Here in Chicago."

Robert reached forward, taking a small sip of his own hot coffee, after first blowing on it. "Then you have me very confused, Mr. Colloway. What exactly is it you think I can help you with if you've already found her?"

Everything, I think. *Anything*, I pray.

"Something happened to her." I pause, remembering the look she gave me yesterday. I saw the hollowness in her eyes. I saw the agony in her soul. And then I remembered what Burt told me. No driver's license. No cell phone or lease in her name? Something smells very fishy. "She's running. I need to find out what, or who, she's running from." And I need to bury them.

Robert sighed heavily, quietly contemplating me. "I'm afraid I can't help you, Mr. Colloway. I specialize in missing persons, and clearly your woman isn't missing any longer. Sometimes the simplest answer is the truth, which is often hardest for us to accept. In this case, maybe the simple answer is she left you and you just need to accept it. That's the sad reality in a large percentage of my domestic missing persons cases. I'm sorry, but anything that happened during that time you'll either need to hear from her or put behind you."

He rises to leave when my next question stops him cold, causing his eyes to rain fire down on me. "How's your daughter, Melody? She's what, about six now?"

He slowly sits back down, his angry gaze locked with mine. "Blackmail, Mr. Colloway? I'm impressed."

"It's not blackmail, Robert. Call it...incentive."

He resumes his relaxed position when he is anything but. "This will cost you a pretty penny," he says, his calm, cool demeanor contradicting the irritation slithering underneath. A small part of me hated to use the illegitimate daughter as leverage, whom he clearly tried to hide from the world, along with his mistress, Heidi, but truth be told, had I known about her five years ago, I would have done the same damn thing.

It turned out good old Burt may not be a great detective, but he was good for something, because that little factoid came up purely by chance during our last conversation when I casually inquired whether Robert Townley was still in business. Burt was about as loose-lipped as a two-bit hooker.

"I assumed it would." I will pay anything to rid Livvy of whatever or whomever she's running from. But first I have to know what it is and I know she'll never tell me. I didn't miss the pleading in her eyes yesterday when she basically told me to let it go. But I won't. I *can't*.

Livvy is different now than she was when we first met. She's still the same in so many ways, but she's more reserved and quiet and has a sadness deep inside her that she can't possibly hide no matter how hard she tries. She never finished her teaching degree and I want to know why. Teaching little kids was all she ever really wanted to do. I have to find out what happened to her during our time apart because I know in my gut something's not right. My fear is the unknown will poison us and I simply won't allow that to happen. I love her too much.

After I part ways with a very unhappy, but reluctantly agreeable Robert Townley, I head into the office to get some work done, but my mind keeps wandering to Livvy. I can't get out of my head the way her soft lips felt on mine. I can't stop feeling her smooth, silky skin underneath my fingertips. I'll never forget how her hot, wet pussy felt around my throbbing dick when I was seated fully inside her. It felt like coming home after a long absence. It felt like Eden. I crave her. I'm addicted to her. I always was. She's like my own personal heroin, and like any drug addict, I'd do absolutely anything to continue getting my fix of her.

Shaking my head, I try to focus. I need to get a few things in order if I plan on spending the rest of the weekend with Livvy, which I do. Hours later, I am knee deep in acquisition paperwork when I hear a soft knock on my door. I look up to find Camille walking in, a purple folder in hand.

"Thanks for coming in on a Saturday, Camille," I say, setting my paperwork aside.

"Oh, my pleasure, Gray," she purred. I had to admit that she looked very attractive today in her tight dark jeans and fitted, low-cut short-sleeve white shirt. Red heels raised her height at least another four inches. But my heart didn't pound and my dick didn't stir once. I didn't think either would again for another woman besides Livvy.

"So, where should we start?" she asks, taking a seat in the plush brown leather chair across from my desk. She perches right on the end of her seat and leans forward, elbows on the wood. The move pushes her impressive rack up and out and it was painfully obvious she knew exactly what she was doing.

I sit back in my chair, making sure to keep my eyes above sea level. "I need to see all of the personnel files for HMT's Vice President level and above for the last twenty-four months as well as every single technology developer. Both active and terminated. I want them all on my desk first thing Monday morning. And I need to know what type of employment contract we have with Wesley Nichols. I also want the personnel files of any direct report of Nichols as well for the same time period."

As much as I want to fire Nichols' ass, I know we executed employment contracts with all of the senior leaders at HMT when we acquired them, but the terms varied based on the position. I also have a bad feeling something fishy is going down with that optical detection patent, so I'm not about to cut him loose until I figure that shit out, because where there's smoke, there's usually fire. And Wesley Nichols reeked like smoldering brush.

"Yes, absolutely. I also have several resumes for Bonnie's replacement. There are two in particular on the top here that look very strong." She pulls out several pieces of paper, setting them in front of me. I don't look. I already know who's getting that job.

"No," I say, pushing them back toward her.

"No? But you didn't even look at them, sir. Bonnie's retiring in less than two weeks. You're already really behind. I mean, we could always get someone from the temp agency, I guess, but—"

"I already have a replacement," I interrupt.

Fifteen minutes later we have all the particulars hammered out, any opposition to my decision Camille kept smartly to herself. As she gets up to leave, instead of walking to the door, she edged around my desk. She looked nervous, running her index finger in quick circles across the shiny surface and I knew exactly what was coming.

When she cleared her throat, I decided to put her out of her misery, softly telling her, "Camille, I'm taken."

A look of surprise, following quickly by disappointment crossed her face. "Oh. I didn't realize. I didn't know you were dating anyone."

"It's not common knowledge." She nodded slightly, eyes flitting to the floor in embarrassment before spinning to leave. "Camille," I called. She turned back and her cheeks were tinged a light pink. "For the record, even if I wasn't available this could never happen. You're an amazing HR leader and I'd hate to lose you over a failed relationship."

Smiling, she replied, "Thank you, Mr. Colloway."

After she closes my door, I look at the time. It's already almost five o'clock. I want to get to

Livvy's by no later than seven, so I settle in for another half hour of work or so when my cell rings.

Lena.

I debate on answering it but decide to let it go to voice mail. There's nothing left to be said between us and I don't want to come across as crass and rude, which I most certainly will if I have to listen to her pledge her undying love to me one more fucking time. A couple minutes later, my phone dings with a voice mail, which I promptly delete without listening to and not thirty seconds, it rings again.

My patience snaps, and I click accept, barking into the phone, "For the love of Christ, take a hint and stop calling me."

"Jesus, asshole, take it down a notch," my brother's deep voice replies.

"Shit. Sorry, Conn. I thought you were someone else."

"Well, I'm glad I'm not that someone else. Anyway, I was calling to confirm our dinner tonight with Wellman's at eight o'clock and to ensure you'll be there. Asher thinks your head's so far up your ass you wouldn't remember, but I assured him you would."

Fuck. I didn't. Ash was right. And Conn was calling to make sure he didn't lose.

"How much?" I asked.

"Five hundred," he laughed.

"Wow. Five hundred, huh? That's all I'm worth these days?" My brothers and I regularly make side bets on stupid shit. It started when we were young and would watch Fear Factor. Back then we could only afford to bet our allowance and, of

132

course, it was on who could eat the most worms the fastest, or how long you could let Conn's spider collection crawl on you. One time we bet how high in the air we could each bounce by jumping off the roof onto our trampoline. Ash ended up with a broken arm in three places on his turn when the whole front side gave way and he fell to the hard ground below. Our parents were less than happy, and our trampoline soon found it's way to the local county landfill.

"I had to be conservative because, for once, I agree with Ash."

Chuckling, I say, "Too bad. You could have cleaned Ash out this time, brother. I'll be there. And I'm bringing a date."

A heavy sigh comes through the earpiece. "Do I even need to ask who?"

"No. And I don't need your shit either, Connelly, so leave it alone."

"Right. See you at eight."

"Yes, you will."

Christ, this is not how I wanted to spend my evening with Livvy, but I can't ditch this business dinner either. Wellman's is a local investor group we're tapping to discuss our next potential acquisition. So it won't be an exciting night for Livvy, and maybe not even appropriate to bring her, but I can't bear the thought of waiting until tomorrow to see her again.

In fact, I can hardly stomach the thought of being away from her for one single second, which is why I'm putting plans in place to remedy that. Slowly, but surely, I will entwine my life so tightly with Livvy's, she won't know where she ends and I begin. I will once again become an intricate part of her.

Emotionally.

Spiritually.

Physically.

I intend to make it impossible for her to walk away from me again. No matter the reason.

Chapter 18

Livia

"What's that?" Addy asks, heading my way from the kitchen.

When the doorbell rang, my stomach dropped. Fear had wound its way into my every thought and action. As soon as I'd gotten home earlier, I closed all of the blinds so no one could spy on us from the outside. I'd refused to let Addy open them all day, but wouldn't give her any explanation as to why. I'd even called Alyse to make sure she was okay, trying not to let her know I was worried out of my mind about her. Of course, she was fine. Maybe I'm overreacting. Maybe it wasn't the same guy.

"I don't know." I'm standing at the door, with a very large cream-colored box. A beautiful thick silver ribbon is wrapped around it and the whole package screams mysterious. I asked the courier service three times if they were sure they had the right person and address. They assured me they did. I tried to tip them, but they said it had all been taken care of. Addy grabbed the box, carrying it to the kitchen table.

"Open it," I whisper. I'm terrified of what I might find inside. Oranges? A horse's head?

Jesus, Livia. The Godfather...really?

"You're acting strange today, Livia."

On the other hand, what if there really *was* something from my past in that box? I certainly did not want Addy to open it and prompt more questions. *Shit.*

"Never mind, I'll do it." I scoot her out of the way and tentatively grab the bow, pulling slowly like it's a viper ready to strike if I move too quickly. I gingerly lift the lid of the box as if I expect there to be a decapitated human head on the inside, ready to shove Addy out of the way if I spot even a hint of blood.

But as the lid comes off I see none of those things. No oranges, no heads, no dark, thick red staining the inside. All I see is a beautiful, shimmery silver cocktail dress and a pair of matching, strappy heels along with a cream envelope that has '*Livvy*' scrawled on the outside.

"Holy fuck. Who sent this?" Addy asks. Now she's the one pushing me out of the way to draw the sheath out of its soft tissue bedding. It's short and sleeveless, with a plunging neckline. It's simply stunning. The most beautiful dress I've ever seen. I immediately know who it's from and now my stomach drops for an entirely different reason.

I quickly open the card and read the words that were handwritten by my long-lost love. Addy's breath washes over my neck while she unashamedly reads over my shoulder.

> *My beautiful angel,*
> *I hope you'll forgive me that I*
> *can't honor my promise to give*
> *you space. You see, I've been wandering*

aimlessly in that dark, lonely void
since I last laid eyes on you, and I
don't ever intend on going back. There
will be no space between us ever again.
Be ready by 7:30 p.m. I have a business dinner
at 8:00, and you'll be accompanying me.
I can't wait to see how fucking stunning
you'll look both in *this dress…and* out *of it.*
All my love,
Gray

I gulp and feel a hot breath of desire between my legs at his very blatant claim. Addy screams, "Oh my God!" In. My. Ear.

"Shit, Addy, that hurt." I grab my ringing ear with my free hand, but my other is shaking. My ears really are ringing, but it has nothing to do with Addy yelling and everything to do with Gray's very suggestive message.

He's taking you to dinner. Tonight.
He wants to be inside you again. Tonight.
He's not letting you go. Ever.

Oh God. I'm equally turned on and terrified at the thought of seeing him again after yesterday. I don't know why I'm torturing myself, and him, by even entertaining the thought of going out with him, but God help me, I am. I should pick up my phone and call him to decline. But I don't even know his number.

Shit. Shit. Shit.

Before I can register what's happening, Addy is dragging me into the bathroom and turning on the shower. She mumbles something about hair and makeup and thongs, but none of it's penetrating.

I'm going to dinner tonight. With Gray.

I'm going to have sex again tonight. With Gray.

He still wants you to be his. Forever.

Suddenly my stained Color Run T-shirt is being pulled over my head and my sweatpants pool around my feet. "What the hell, Addy?" I grumble, shaking myself out of my thoughts. I step out of the navy blue fabric trapping me inside. I'm now standing in my utilitarian white bra and underwear while the hot steam from the shower fingers around us.

"Livia, you have less than one hour to get ready. If I have to, I'll strip you bare and wash you myself. Granted, it would be weird, and a line crossed that our friendship may never quite recover from, because I don't really care to either see or wash your coochie or touch your tits, but I'm a good friend, and that's what friends are for. And I'll do it if I have to."

I stare at her with a look of pure horror on my face, I'm sure. *Wash my coochie?*

She grabs me by the shoulders, shaking me. "I will not let you fuck this up. It's obvious this guy is crazy for you and I know you're still in love with him. No normal man sends an expensive dress and fuck-me heels from an exclusive boutique with a message that basically stakes his forever claim on you and tells you he wants to screw your brains out. It's so obvious he's madly in love with you, Livia."

"There are so many things wrong with what you just said. You realize that, don't you?" She laughs and I shake my head, still stuck on the coochie comment.

Stepping behind the shower curtain, I remove my undergarments, grab the sponge and quickly begin to wash. I already shampooed my hair earlier today, so I was out in short order and had barely dried off when Addy appears in the bathroom doorway again.

For the next forty-five minutes, she primped, plucked, curled, lotioned and spritzed me. She was a flurry of hands most of the time. And her mouth kept pace too. By the time she's done, my ears are practically bleeding, but wow...the end result is worth it. My eyes are smoky, my cheeks flush with color and my lashes longer than I could have ever made them myself. She'd thrown my hair up in a messy, but sophisticated bun, leaving a few curled rings to frame my face.

"You look hot," she said standing behind me in the mirror. "If I batted for the same team, I'd do you," she winked.

I couldn't help but laugh. I look up from my seated position, catch her eyes and smile. "Thanks, Addy."

"My pleasure, babe." We sit there looking at each other and I know something sappy is about to come out of her mouth. "I don't know what happened, Livia, but you carry sadness around like a protective coat of armor and I think Gray is your chink. Let him in. You deserve to be happy. You deserve *love*. You know that, right?"

My eyes sting. She was right about the chink, but happiness? Love? *Did I deserve it?* I wanted to believe it. I wanted to grab hold of what was right in front of me, what Gray was offering, never let go and never look back again. But the truth is, I'm scared shitless. And *scarred* beyond repair.

Outside of Alyse, I was never unconditionally loved by another soul until the day I met Gray Colloway. My mother walked out when I was eight, unable to handle my father's gambling and drunkenness. My father essentially sold me. And Peter told me every day how the only thing I was good for was a mediocre fuck and decent punching practice. I think I've convinced myself I don't deserve to be loved. How can a single person go through most of their life without it and feel worthy when it stands right before them?

It took me a long time to accept it, to truly *believe* it the first time around from Gray, but I saw it still burning brightly when I laid eyes on him again, and that little flame I still carried for him all these years turned into a raging inferno. I just don't know if I can take the chance to love with my whole being and lose again. I'd lost Gray once. It would destroy me to lose him again if he found out the truth. And I am terrified he will. How can he possibly understand why I chose to marry someone else? How could he ever forgive that betrayal?

I catch her eyes again and smile sadly. Addy didn't know me. Not really. If she knew all my baggage, would she still think I'm deserving? Doubtful. "Thanks," I manage to choke.

"Whatever it is, Livia, I think you're selling yourself short to believe he won't understand. And if you need someone to talk to, I'm always here."

140

The doorbell rings and all the butterflies sitting in the pit of my stomach take flight at once. I feel their wings fluttering wildly against my insides. I'm nauseous.

"Showtime," she whispers excitedly. I smooth down my short dress, which fits like a glove and shows off every single curve I've managed to gain back over these last two years. I walk to the front door, standing with the knob in my hand so long that the doorbell rings a second time and I jump.

I take a deep breath before turning it, knowing my entire life will change the second I open it.

Chapter 19

Gray

Holy fuck.

That's all I could think when she opened the door and I saw her rocking the dress I'd sent. My cock was instantly, uncomfortably hard. That toddler was going to be difficult to hide in my fitted dress slacks.

I was literally speechless as my eyes traveled slowly down her sexy, curvy body. The silver sheath showed a fair amount of cleavage and hugged her flared hips perfectly, ending at mid-thigh. When I got to the heels, the only thing I could picture was her standing naked in front of me, wearing nothing but those, before I took her against the wall and they ended up digging into my ass as I pumped repeatedly into her. The urge to bail on dinner and gorge on Livvy instead was so great I almost pulled out my phone to call Conn.

"You look mouthwatering, Livvy," I finally manage to utter when our eyes connect. I feather a finger down her cheek, my thumb tugging across her parted bottom lip. I lean into her, my lips a whisper away. Her eyes have darkened and dilated and her chest rapidly expands and contracts with each shallow breath. "My lips ache for yours," I warn right before I claim them, exploring the mouth I didn't get enough of yesterday.

After a brief hesitation, her arms wind around my neck and our bodies mash together, our kiss quickly brimming with passion and longing. I turn her slightly to steady us against the door jam and run my hand up her torso, palming a pert breast, thumbing her hardened nipple through the thin fabric. Her moan has my hand traveling back south, very intent on determining what type of lingerie lay underneath this sexy wrapping.

A throat clearing in the background is the only reason I pull away, but as I do, I tug her bottom lip between my teeth and place one last chaste kiss on her before facing our unwelcome interloper, pulling Livvy close to my side.

A striking tall brunette is bouncing up and down like she needs to pee. She thrusts out her hand toward me with a sly smile. "You must be Gray."

"Addy, stop," Livvy hisses.

I look at Livvy and can't help the broad smile that breaks out as her face reddens. Her roommate knows about me and I'm surprised at how much that warms my blood.

"I am," I reply, turning back toward her, taking her hand briefly in mine.

"I'm Addy, Livia's roommate. Nice touch, by the way. She looks hot." She nods toward Livvy, and I suspect she's referring to the clothes I sent.

"That she does," I reply, but now my heated stare is locked on my woman. She'd look great wearing a potato sack. It's the woman that makes the dress look incredible, not the other way around.

"Have a great time, tonight. Don't rush to bring her home."

"Don't wait up," I reply. Her friend's grin is contagious, and I return it. I have no intention of bringing Livvy back to her apartment. She's spending the night with me, and if I have anything to say about it, every other night for the rest of our lives.

"Umm, hello? I'm right here."

I grab her hand in mine, bringing it to my lips. "Do you need to grab anything before we leave, angel?" *Like all of your belongings?*

"My purse," her soft voice whispers. She's just as affected by me as I am by her and, if possible, that makes my cock even harder. I have absolutely no fucking idea how I'm going to get through the next three hours without being inside of her.

She grabs her purse and a wrap and soon we're on our way to the restaurant. Tonight Henry is driving. He's my part-time chauffeur, but he's so much more than that. He's a long-time friend of the family. He worked for my father for twenty-five years and when I took over my father's company, Henry insisted that I'd also need his services, even though I protested I would never be so pretentious as to need a driver. Turns out, it's not pretension, but necessity, to have Henry handy sometimes; otherwise, I'd be a distracted driving hazard. It's not very smart to host a conference call from the driver's seat as you're navigating Chicago rush hour traffic to O'Hare Airport.

Take tonight, for example. There's no way I could do what I wanted with Livvy on our thirty-minute drive back into the city if I was driving.

144

"Come here," I say. She'd positioned herself as far away from me in the back seat as possible and I meant what I told her in the message I'd delivered earlier. There would be no space between us ever again. Especially of the physical kind.

Her eyes flick to Henry's, catching his in the rear view mirror before landing on mine. Not waiting for her reply, I grab her arm and slide her across the slick seat, pulling her into my lap, against the protests she's voicing. She does that way too much. I want her to beg for my touch, beg for my tongue, beg for my cock. The only time I want to hear her protests are when she's pleading for me to fuck her harder and faster, and then complaining when I'm spent and can't.

"I've been hard for hours envisioning you in those shoes," I whisper, nibbling her perfumed neck. She smells so fucking good, I almost tell Henry to take us to my apartment instead.

"Just the shoes?" she breathes.

"Fuck yes. *Just* the shoes."

"Gray—"

I know that tone and I hastily silence it with my lips, swallowing whatever she was about to say so I don't have to hear it. She quickly melts into me, winding a hand in my hair. I slip the hand not holding her head up the inside of her bare thigh. If I don't find out what she's teasing me with underneath before dinner, I may just blow. Hell, I may blow once I *do* find out.

As I reach the juncture, I feel her radiating heat. As my fingers graze her silk panties, I feel the dampness of her want. And as I slip them

145

underneath the wet fabric, I am scorched by her desire.

She breaks the kiss, trying to squirm out of my arms. "Gray—"

"I need to feel your body quiver in my arms, Livvy, and know that it's me causing each one." If I could get away with taking her in the backseat, I would.

"Not in the car," she breathes, but it's choppy and not at all convincing.

"He can't see anything where you're positioned," I taunt against the shell of her ear. It's true, but I find I wouldn't care if it wasn't. It's only been twenty-four hours, but the burning need I have to bury any body part inside of her is tearing me apart. She's silent for several moments and I know I've tempted her. My intense want for her throbs against her almost bare ass.

"But he can hear," she murmurs against my cheek.

My fingers crawl back up her bare flesh until they slip once again under her soaked panties, caressing her wet, smooth womanly flesh. A low moan escapes her lips. I know she's succumbed when I feel her lashes close against my skin.

"Then be quiet, angel."

Before she has a chance to change her mind, I bury two fingers in her wet pussy and, after dragging through her moisture, feather my thumb over her hardened bundle of nerves. She hides her face in my neck, a gasp escaping her lips before she begins to ride the hand I'm ruthlessly driving in and out.

My Livvy was always so responsive and I'm glad to see nothing has changed. In less than sixty seconds she's quivering in my arms, panting against my neck, just as I'd craved. She bites her lip to stay quiet, but there's no way Henry doesn't know what's going on back here, and I don't give a rat's ass. At least he's discreetly looking ahead, and not back here.

With my fingers still moving slowly inside her sex, as her tremors subside, I rasp, "When I get you home, you're riding my cock. I want to watch you unravel with me buried deep inside you. I need to feel my come coat your insides as you scream my name, Livvy. I need to know you're mine." She clenches my wet digits and it takes everything in me not to rip her clothes off right now.

"Sir, we'll be arriving in just a few minutes."

Once again, she tries to escape, but I refuse. I hold her eyes as I withdraw from her heat and slowly suck my fingers clean. She watches in rapt fascination, her lips parted. "Hmmm, that's all the appetizer I need, baby." She blushes and I love it. I love *her*.

I hold her in my arms, feathering kisses across her temple, her cheeks, her lips until she sighs and relaxes against me. I tighten my arms around her, never wanting to let her go.

Christ, I love this woman so much my chest constricts with the thought of being without her ever again. I honestly feel like my heart may stop beating if I were to lose her a second time.

I simply refuse to think that's an option.

Chapter 20

Livia

The past two hours have been extremely awkward and uncomfortable and I push around the bananas foster that was just set in front me, picking up my wine instead. I think I've had three glasses so far, but it's hard to keep track when Gray keeps refilling it before I've even finished. I know he's trying to ply me with enough alcohol so that it'll be easier to convince me to go home with him, but he needn't worry. I can't get the dirty words out of my head that flowed like smooth melted chocolate from his wicked tongue straight to my core. Since he had his fingers buried deep inside me, he had to feel how every single syllable made me drip more.

God, you're pathetically easy, Livia.

When Gray and I arrived at the restaurant, everyone was already seated. Asher and Connelly are here, along with three men from some investment company Gray briefly mentioned while we were walking in. While neither of Gray's brothers were rude, neither were exactly welcoming either. As much as I wish it was different, I don't blame them. They were left behind to pick up the shattered pieces of their broken brother, and if the shoe were on the other foot, I would echo their sentiments. And I've not given them any reason not to feel otherwise, either.

The other three men have been very cordial all evening and John, a very handsome investment banker sitting next to me, keeps trying to politely engage me in conversation.

"So Livia, what is it you do?" he asks. When we first sat down, Gray introduced me as an associate and I have to admit, it stung a little. I got the distinct impression that I wasn't supposed to be present at this business dinner, and I wondered why Gray brought me in the first place. It made me angry that he felt the need to drag me around like a pet.

"Nothing exciting, I'm afraid. I work at HMT Enterprises as an executive assistant." *For a fucking idiot,* I think, but don't add.

John's eyes flick momentarily to Gray, who is engaged in serious conversation with the others. I wonder why John is paying attention to me, versus the business dinner he's supposed to be participating in.

"Not his," I say softly.

"You look very familiar. Have we met someplace before?" Mental eye-roll. *Really, guy? You can't do better than that?*

I don't know why I feel so out of place being here, but I do. I should be used to polite conversation, I did it all the time when I waitressed, but the way John is scrutinizing me as if he wants to eat me up is making me very edgy. And on the verge of unleashing my inner bitch, which would likely be frowned upon by all present.

"I don't think so. I don't get out much." I take another long sip of the plum flavored alcohol, this time trying to draw it out so he'll take a goddamn

149

hint and get engaged in the discussion he's supposed to be having with the others, versus me.

"No. No, you *do* look familiar. Were you at Firefly last Saturday evening by chance?"

I freeze mid-sip. *Holy shit.* This cannot be happening. I bring the cup to my mouth, almost choking on the very large, very unladylike gulp I take. Is this the guy who I let finger me in the dark, abandoned hallway? Out of the millions of men in this city, could the universe hate me *that* much that she sat him next to me?

"Umm, no. I wasn't." I can't even look at him when I lie. Oh God, I have to get out of here before he says anything else. Before Gray finds out. I'm starting to hyperventilate when he speaks as if he doesn't even notice that I'm two seconds flat from a meltdown.

"Yes. Yes, you were. You were dancing with your girlfriends. My brother and I whisked them away from you, I'm afraid. I danced a few songs with your friend, Kamryn, I think."

The relief I feel at his admission is so great, I close my eyes and choke out a small sob, which hopefully was interpreted as a laugh. He lowered his voice, thinking that only he and I would hear his next statement. "Actually, I was more interested in you, but you looked a little...lost. If you're not seeing anyone, I'd love to take you out sometime."

Oh, how wrong he was. Even before the last word left John's mouth, I felt a strong hand wrap possessively around the nape of my neck and heard Gray's chair slide across the floor, bumping up against mine. Invading my personal space without apology, he leans across until our eyes lock seconds before he takes my mouth in a very public, very bruising and very claiming kiss. He may just as well have whipped out his dick and circled around me because he couldn't have made it clearer that he was marking his territory.

He kisses me until I melt into him, as I always do. Several moments later when he breaks our lip lock, he glares at the man sitting on my opposite side. "She's mine," he growled.

Why did that statement of ownership set my blood on fire? Why wasn't I yelling at him for being a jealous ass? Why didn't I care that we were putting on a show that everyone in the restaurant would be tweeting about later? Because I craved his dominance and possession, that's why. It was always like this with him. He was fierce in everything he did.

Working.

Loving.

Fucking.

Me.

"It's time to go, angel." He finally leans back and stands, his hand still resting on my neck as I follow. It's awkward, but he refuses to let go. Everyone else at the table is staring at us like we've sprouted wings and are about to take to the skies. Asher starts to speak but quickly stops with the daggers Gray is shooting his way.

"Gentleman, we'll be in touch. You're in good hands with my brothers." He grabs the wrap from the back of my chair and places it on my shoulders before picking up my purse and handing it to me. He pulls me into him for a soft kiss before silently guiding us away from the table and through the restaurant exit. I feel eyes follow us the entire way, and I'm pretty sure I even hear the click of a couple of camera phones. *Lovely*.

We wait only momentarily before our car pulls up and the older gentleman that drove us here jumps out to open the door. I don't miss how he won't look me in the eyes. *Great*. My face probably turns twenty shades of red.

When we get settled in the car and pull away, I turn to Gray, who is clearly seething with rage. His jaw and fists are clenched, every toned muscle wound tight.

"What was that about?"

He takes a few breaths before he responds, and even then his voice shakes with anger. "I thought it best to leave before I ripped his fucking eyeballs from their sockets for the way they were eye-fucking you."

I have to bite my lip to keep my smile at bay, but it doesn't work. When his eyes shift my way and he sees my broad grin, he growls and pulls me close.

"Christ, Livvy. Stop." He pulls my lip from between my teeth and I laugh. Until his mouth crashes to mine, that is. And then I moan. And when he lifts me onto his lap so I straddle him, I almost weep with joy. His stiff erection hits in exactly the right spot and I can't help the involuntary movement of my pelvis as he devours me whole. Screw the driver. I want this desperately.

He pulls away and stills my hips. I open my closed lids and our eyes connect. My breath catches at the raw desire and pure love I see floating in his. Those three little words linger on my tongue until I swallow them, but even if I don't say them, I can't hide them either. I wouldn't be able to if I tried.

We sit exactly like this as we drive through the city, silently conveying all the things we can't voice.

I forgive you.

How can you?

Because that's what you do when you love someone.

I've missed you.

I've missed you too.

I wish things could have been different.

So do I.

My body and soul thirst for his. A part of me feels at peace for the first time in years, while the other part is so fucking scared my life is going to crash and burn if I keep recklessly moving forward in this direction. But the side that sighs in peace is slowly overthrowing the fearful one, and every minute I spend in Gray's presence, I convince myself a little more that this may actually work. That we *could* possibly reconcile and live happily ever after.

Why does being with him always make me feel like I'm living blissfully unaware in a fairytale? I know fairytales are bullshit, but for the three idyllic years we were together, I would have adamantly disagreed. I feel myself being lulled into the same false dreamland and I'm so tired of fighting it. I *want* that damn fairytale, even if I don't deserve it and I know it won't last.

He pulls me to him tightly, resting my head on his shoulder and I let him. We sit like this for the next fifteen minutes until we pull up in front of a very tall apartment building close to Navy Pier. We exit the car and Gray tells the driver, Henry, goodbye. Henry tips his head toward me and although I manage a small smile, I flush with embarrassment.

Hand in hand, we enter the building. On our way toward the bank of elevators, Gray politely greets Sam, the security guard on duty. When we enter the steel car, we're alone. Once the door closes, he puts a keycard in a slot, pushes the button to the top floor and tugs me so our fronts are melded together. With my arms around his waist, I look up at him. The predatory look etched on his face makes me shiver in anticipation.

"Do you remember what I told you on the way to dinner?" he rasps, tucking a piece of wayward hair behind my ear.

"Yes," I whisper.

"Good." His smoky eyes drop to my mouth. "That's just round one." His words travel straight to my needy sex and my entire body clenches with impatience. I want him to kiss me, but he doesn't. He devours me with his eyes, instead. My greedy body begs for release again, even though it had one mere hours ago by his hand.

Moments later, the elevator doors open. He drags me into his massive apartment, and suddenly my heart starts to race and my stomach churns with both nerves and excitement.

"Make yourself at home while I get us a drink," he calls over his shoulder as he heads into the spacious living area and around the corner, out of sight. I stand there taking in the scene before me.

The entire space is open, with a large modern kitchen on my left. The countertops are black granite. The greyish cupboards, sans hardware, complement them nicely. All appliances are stainless steel and the island contains a built in flat-top range. This kitchen is a chef's dream and looks very unused.

There's a hallway with a few closed doors to my right, but the sight that really has my attention is the large bay of windows that overlook Lake Michigan and Navy Pier. Looking at nothing else, I walk through the main living space to the cool glass and admire the brightly lit giant Ferris wheel slowly spinning around. Even though it's a tourist trap, I've always wanted to ride it. When you live in Chicago, it's just something you need to do once.

As I wait for Gray to return, I imagine mothers and fathers taking their children up in a gondola for the first time and how they'll tell all of their friends about it at school on Monday. I imagine lovers cuddling together, stealing kisses and touches when they think no one can see, slowly stoking the fire they'll quench later in the privacy of their bedroom.

I imagine happily ever after. And being with Gray tonight, that's exactly what I feel. Happy. I decide I'm not going to overthink it. I'm just going to allow myself to enjoy it and deal with the fallout later.

His body heat warms my back, and a glass filled with dark red wine snakes around my front, which I take.

"What are you daydreaming about?" His husky voice sends chills up my spine and fire down to my core.

"Fairytales," I softly reply.

Our eyes connect in the window's reflection. I not only see, but *feel* love and adoration and absolution flowing from him. For the first time, I truly understand, and *believe in*, unconditional love. I've refused Gray the answers he deserves, yet he can still find it within himself to absolve my unknown sins. I honestly wonder, if our positions were reversed, would I be able to do the same. I'd like to think so, but I truly don't know, and I hate myself for that. I was never deserving of this man and am even less so now.

He turns me to face him and silently takes my drink, which I haven't touched. He sets it on the end table next to us, along with his. I don't need it anyway. My head is already buzzing from the alcohol I had earlier. But mostly it's tumbling from the plethora of emotions currently racing in it. I'm anxious and nervous and horny from our foreplay all evening.

Taking my hand, he leads me through a hallway along the bank of windows and into a large bedroom that I assume is his. We stop at the far side of the king-sized bed covered in a chocolate colored comforter.

A dim light glows from a bedside lamp. Gray surprises me by turning me away from him so my back is against his front. But my surprise disappears once I get a glimpse of us in the floor length mirror and see the fire and lust swim in his eyes as they leisurely rake the length of my body. My breath speeds up and my core dampens. My panties are positively drenched from my earlier orgasm.

"Fairytales, huh?" he breathes. His teeth nip my ear, sending chills down the right side of my body.

"Yes," I reply, equally breathy.

"Am I your Prince Charming, Livvy?" *Yes. You always were.*

I'm floating so high on a cloud of want, I can hardly think as his hands travel slowly down my bare arms, leaving behind a trail of intense need. "No," I manage to mutter. When his eyes flick to mine in the reflective glass, I add, "I think tonight you're the Big Bad Wolf."

The smirk that spreads his lips is indeed wolfish. "You're right, angel. Are you afraid?" he utters softly against my collarbone, his light kisses quietly unraveling me.

I am, but not for the reasons he thinks. And I can't respond anyway. Heady desire has me tongue-tied as he unzips my dress and drops it to the floor, leaving me in a lavender bra and panty set, along with my heels. His hands mold to my lace covered breasts, pulling down the cups to expose my beaded nipples, which he rolls between his deft fingers. Being able to watch what he's doing to me, seeing the pure animal lust that's turned his face into raw need and hard lines is one of the most sensual experiences I've ever had.

My heavy head falls back against his strong chest, an involuntary groan escaping. His lips feather my neck and shoulder and soon my bra joins my dress on the carpet. His fabric-covered steely erection is pressed hard between my cheeks, and I want nothing more than for him to free it and slide it inside me.

"Jesus, Livvy. You're the most beautiful creature ever created. I'm in awe of you." He turns my face toward his, roughly capturing my mouth. The other hand travels down, underneath the band of my panties; into the place I so urgently crave it. "Fuck, you're weeping for me," he groans against my lips. Clever fingers slip through my wet folds and inside me. My walls tighten and another climax calls to me. My body burns to feel the rush of ecstasy that only he can deliver.

His patience finally snaps. He anxiously bends down to remove my panties and I close my eyes and wait for it. I wait for the moment he notices the place I've permanently decorated my body in memorial to him. That's why I didn't want him to remove my skirt yesterday. At the time, I truly thought I wouldn't see him again. It was something I never intended anyone to see, let alone Gray. But now it's inevitable because I simply can't make myself stay away from him and there's no way I can keep it hidden.

I hear a sharp intake of breath and know he's finally spotted it. And I'm terrified of his reaction.

Chapter 21

Gray

My heart stutters. "What is that?" I bend down in front of her and trace my fingers along the grey angel wings folded on top of each other that are inked just to the right of her bare mound. The light is too low to make out the details, so I turn her body toward the lamp, and now my heart stops.

Woven throughout the border of the wings, I can clearly see the scripted black letters: G R A Y. I look up and Livvy's watching my reaction, but I can't decipher the emotions on her face.

Sadness?

Regret?

Torment?

Fear?

All of the above? Unwelcome tears well in my eyes, and I can do nothing but wrap my arms around her waist, burying my face in her warm, soft flesh. Her hands go to my head, holding me tightly to her.

The pain and confusion I've kept buried for the last five years comes rushing back hard and fast and stabs me just as fresh as the first day I truly accepted she was gone and, once again, I find myself asking *why*?

Why did she leave me?

Why won't she tell me?

Why wasn't I good enough?

Am I just kidding myself into believing this time around will end differently? And am I fooling myself into thinking that I can let her back into my life and simply accept her silence when she's put me through ten kinds of hell?

Maybe it makes me weak, but I love her so fucking much, the answer is yes. I will let her back in because I love her. And true love is unconditional and unwavering and sometimes gut-wrenchingly hard. I would give anything and everything I own for her to love me like that in return.

And the bitch of it is, after seeing her tattoo I *know* she does. Who brands themselves permanently with the name of their former lover if they've voluntarily abandoned them? Not one fucking person I know would do that.

Not. One.

"How long?" I choke. I'm literally hanging onto my shit by a thin, fraying string, and the last thing I want to do is break down and bawl like a baby in front of her.

"Six months," she replies so quietly I almost don't hear.

Six fucking months? She just got this tattoo six fucking months ago? She's been pining away for me like I have been for her this entire time and yet she's stayed away from me, leaving both of us to wallow in lonely agonizing misery?

I pull away, wiping the water from my eyes before I stand. "Why?" Now she looks uncomfortable and I don't care. "Why, Livvy?"

"You know why," she barely whispers.

"No. No, I don't fucking know why!"

160

She bends down to grab her bra, but I rip it away and throw it across the room. I'm an ass, making her stand here bare in front of me while I'm fully clothed, but we all do things we regret in moments when we're angry or hurt. For me, this will be one of those moments, but I can't find it within myself to stop. The scab has been picked and it's now bleeding profusely. And a Band-Aid just won't fucking staunch the gush of anguish now seeping out of the open wound.

"Answer the question," I grit, punctuating each syllable. She's quiet for several beats and my fury rises by the second until I'm ready to explode.

"I should leave."

Leave? My derisive smirk causes her to take a step back. "I'm not surprised you would say that. You've been running ever since I've known you, Livvy, and you've clearly perfected it to a fine fucking art form. Except this time, you're not only running from me, you're running from yourself."

She squares her shoulders and stands tall, regardless of the fact that she's completely nude; except for the heels I'd envisioned her wearing. Against my wishes, my dick stirs. Clearly he didn't get the little memo that our plans to worship her have taken a sharp left off the goddamn cliff into the cutting rocks below.

"You have no idea what I've been through," she bites out.

Her indignation digs irritatingly under my skin. "Because you won't fucking tell me!" I yell. She doesn't even flinch, but she can't hide the hurt my words inflict. Livvy could never hide anything from me. I can read her as easily as a Penthouse.

I let my eyes wander down to the place that now bears my name, and fierce possessiveness swells within me, easily crowding out the hurt. Easily overpowering the anger. I think back to the restaurant when that jackass looked like he was ready to eat her for dessert, and I know I'll never let her walk out that door. No matter what. Thinking of her with another man makes me violent. But thinking of her without me just makes me bleed.

I need to convince her to stop running. I need to convince her to let me back into that place that I, and I alone, own. I must get her to trust me with her secrets, so they don't eat us both alive. I have to make her understand that I do, and always will, love her.

I hold her eyes as I unbutton my dress shirt and take off my slacks. She skittishly watches every move I make and the intense lust I'd felt earlier returns with a vengeance.

She's torn. She wants to run, but she wants to stay. My precious angel is in as much agony as I am, but for very different reasons. Reasons that she alone knows and won't share, and it not only infuriates me, it breaks my fucking heart that she won't trust me enough to tell me.

Once all of my clothes join hers, I grab her face and press our naked bodies together. I kiss her mouth, tasting the salty tears that have spilled. "I don't care how fast and how far you run, I'll run faster and farther. I'm not letting you go. Ever," I say, between brushes of my mouth on hers. "Run *to* me, Livvy, not away. I can't live without you again."

I lay down on the bed, pulling her beside me so we're lying side-by-side, flesh-to-flesh. We silently stare into each other's eyes. I want to marry her. I want to have babies with her. I want to grow old with her. I just want to love her all the days of my life. She's my downfall. Now that she's back in my life, I can't fathom a single day without her. I run my finger gently down her face. I know she doesn't want to hear this, but I can't keep it in any longer.

"I love you so goddamn much, Livia Kingsley." Her eyes water again, but I take that as a good sign. "Tell me you love me," I beg. I'm not above begging. I checked my ego at the door a long time ago with this woman. I need to know we're in this together, that I'm not the only one feeling this almost unbearably throbbing intensity between us. Even though I see it in her eyes, I need to hear the words.

"So much I ache with it," she whispers.

Our bodies and mouths meet in a fury of unrestrained desperation. Hands, lips, legs entwined as one. Soon I have her on top of me and am slipping inside her wet, hot heat without preamble. I wanted to take my time worshiping her, but right now I'm too frantic to do anything but make desperate love to the woman I adore. The woman I need to reclaim as mine.

Chapter 22

Livia

Our bodies move in perfect sync, like we've danced this erotic dance a thousand times. We have. Gray's thumb strokes the outline of my wings and that one simple act has me vaulting over the edge into pure bliss. I close my eyes and let my head fall back as waves and waves of euphoria wash over and through me. I hear Gray's low curse seconds before he follows, feeling his hot release bathe my womb.

I want to both laugh and cry. Laugh, because everything he'd described in sensual detail in the car earlier just came true. And cry for all that I've lost, because what I want most with Gray can never be.

"I love you," he rasps, cocooning me in his safety and love.

"I love you, too."

He sighs, holding me closer. It feels good to say it, like a confession. I feel lighter and happier. Light fingers whisper up and down my back and I can't think of anything other than how happy I am. Maybe it's the endorphins coursing through my bloodstream, but, no...it's more than that. It feels incredibly amazing to be held and loved by this man again and the reality is far better than my dreams of it. It's comfort, warmth, home.

"Tell me what you're thinking."

"That I'm happy for the first time in a very long time," I answer softly. I don't mean to confess something that I shouldn't voice for fear of jinxing it, but it's too late to take it back. Other than Alyse and more recently Addy, Gray was the only person that ever made me happy. My mother did, I think, until she left us. Now my faded memories of her are clouded with hurt and betrayal.

A finger hooks under my chin and he tilts my face up. "Me too," he confesses, looking deeply into my eyes. Knowing that he's missed me as much as I've missed him does funny things to my insides. I close the small distance between our lips and kiss him slowly, deeply, deliberately. Our tongues lazily duel. Then he palms my head and quickly takes control. Suddenly I'm on my back and being filled to the brim again.

"Stay," he commands. Gray knows that anytime I'm in his arms I'm as pliable as hot glass.

"Okay." I'd do anything he asked of me as long as he keeps moving...just...like...that.

Our lovemaking is frantic, but tender. Wild, but heartfelt. Desperate and full of passionate longing.

"Christ, Livvy, you feel like heaven," he grates against the column of my neck. Teeth nip at my sensitive skin and another orgasm looms in the background, waiting for just the right pressure in just the right place. Which my talented lover delivers. Repeatedly.

An hour later, sated and exhausted, I snuggle into Gray's side and let my heavy lids fall closed. Just as sleep is pulling me under, I hear, "Stay forever, Livvy."

My last thought, as I succumb to the blackness, is *I hope you want me forever.*

Chapter 23

Livia

I've only been home for two hours when my phone dings, indicating a text message. It's just after nine p.m., but I'm already snuggled deep under the covers. After spending nearly all of Sunday in Gray's bed, making love, I am dead-dog tired. And sore. The man is insatiable. I pick up my phone to read the message, not at all surprised to find it's from Gray.

Gray: u belong in my bed. naked and wet for me. ur body begging for my cock

Tingles race like wildfire to that needy place between my thighs. I guess I'm insatiable too. Gray always had a way of making dirty words sound like the sweetest of music. *Cock* and *fuck* roll off his tongue like a melody that should win an American Music Award.

Me: I was…all day

His response was immediate.

Gray: I want more than a day

My heart flutters and his unspoken words shred me. *So do I,* I want to respond. I want forever. I want the fairytale. But I know that's not in the cards for me and I don't know how to respond, so, like the coward I am, I don't. I know it's a self-preservation mechanism because when the truth comes out, he'll dump me faster than a bad habit and I'll be back at square one in my recovery. Hell...I'll be in a hole a mile deep, and I'll have to figure out how to crawl my way *back* to square one. It won't be pretty. It will be fucking ugly. And I'm not at all sure I'm strong enough to survive a second time.

Gray: I'm sending henry for u in the am

My mind hasn't been far from the unknown man I've seen twice now and while it may be smart for me to take what Gray's offering, I am not about to show up to work in a chauffeured car. Hell no. The train station is only four blocks away from my apartment and there are enough people milling around in the morning that there's no way this man would try anything, if that's even his intent.

Me: absolutely not. pls don't hover. let me do my job or I'll have to find a new one. one that's not at ur company

Gray: over my dead fucking body

Ugh. The man is infuriating. It's one thing to get involved again, but I can't have people at work knowing that I'm sleeping with the owner of the goddamn company. I need this job and I don't need to be fodder for gossip at the water coolers or the break room. It's already bad enough that Wes will be suspicious because he thinks I have a boyfriend and now he'll think it's Gray. No one in that room on Friday could mistake the possessiveness and desire emanating from him. For me. *Shit.*

Me: u wore me out the last 24 hours. I need sleep. stop texting

Gray: goodnight Livvy. dream of the naughty things I could b doing to u if u were here.

I always do.

Me: ur awfully bossy. now you control my dreams?

Gray: I own every single part of you, Livvy. like you do me

I stare at his blatant claim. Yes he does, and I'm having a hard time fighting it. Or him. I knew the second I opened that door last night that I was headed down a path from which I could not turn back. I'm stuck moving forward at warp speed until the mother of all potholes, aka my past, suddenly comes up so fast I cannot veer and I'll sink. *We'll* sink. Will it be this week? This month? Next year? Because it's not a question of if, but when.

Gray: tell me you love me

A smile takes over my face. That was our "thing" back when we were together. He told early on that he loved me, but it took me a long time to say those three words back—over a year of

169

dating. They seem so simple to most people, but to me, they're so powerful and meaningful they almost take on a life of their own. Once I finally confessed, he'd always beg me to tell him again. And I always obliged.

Me: I do...I love u

More than life. More than anything.

Gray: I love u 2, angel. sweet dreams

I throw my phone beside me, lie back on the pillow and wonder what in the hell I think I'm doing. I feel like I've jumped onto a ride that I can't get off of, because the speed is steadily increasing and if I try to get off now, I'll break a leg. But if I wait much longer, I'll not only break a leg, I'll break myself completely beyond repair.

Gray tried his best to convince me to stay the night again, but I couldn't. I need to think. I need to breathe without inhaling his intoxicating scent. I need to keep reality front and center of what my life is like without him, and I can't do that when I am immersed in him. With his arms around me or his cock inside me, it's far too easy to get lost in an alternate reality. One with rings and devotion and white picket fences.

The desire to give myself over entirely to that fantasy is almost too great to resist, so I'll just dip my toe in it instead and that will have to be good enough. I need to keep some distance between us so when my world comes crumbling down around me once again I at least have some hope of surviving. If I start spending every minute of every day with Gray, I know survival won't even be an option. The worst part of being with Peter wasn't the forced sex, never being allowed outside or even the beatings. It was being without Gray.

So I'm going to tuck every moment, every kiss, every touch, every memory into a special place reserved only for Gray. I need new ones to fill that space anyway, because God knows I wore the other ones threadbare during the last five years. And when I'm so far in my pit of despair, I'll pull one out and remember that I was happy once again.

If only for a short while.

Chapter 24

Livia

I walk outside, not at all surprised to find Henry standing beside the black Lincoln Town car that I rode in on Saturday night.

He tipped his head as he opened the back door, "Morning, ma'am."

"Good morning, Henry," I say, walking right on by. I hear the door close and the sound of quick footsteps behind me.

"Ma'am, please. I'm to take you to work today."

I stop and turn, surprised to find that he's right behind me. He's surprisingly quick for a sixty some year old man. "Look, Henry, I'm terribly sorry to have to put you in the middle of this, but I already told Gray I didn't need a ride. I'm perfectly capable of getting to work on my own, believe it or not. And I need to get going if I'm going to catch the train."

I pivot and start walking. I quickly scan the street to make sure I don't see my stranger before picking up my pace. If I did, I'd quickly be changing my mind about that ride, but I don't feel the prickly sense of being watched, so I continue forward.

"Mr. Colloway isn't going to be happy," he calls after me.

"Yeah, yeah," I mumble. I throw my hand in the air, acknowledging him. I don't particularly care if Gray is happy or not. If I thought Gray was possessive before, he's downright controlling now, and while a tiny part of me revels in it, the part that cares about protecting my heart can't give in. I may love Gray with everything in me, but I cannot be dependent upon him for simple things like getting to work.

A few minutes later I'm boarding the Red Line for my twenty-minute ride into the city. As I take a seat on the crowded steel tube, I get lost in my thoughts of Gray and the dreamlike weekend that we spent together. I swear I can still feel him between my thighs. I'm already seeing the small ways he's trying to take control of little parts of my life and I'm torn. Because I want it and need to reject it in equal measure. Somehow, someway, I must keep a small shred of distance between us so I'm not completely lost in him, even though I can think of nothing else I want more.

The announcement for my stop draws me back to reality and I'm quickly exiting the train, along with a horde of others, all diligently making our way for another week of working for "the man".

When I get up to the twenty-sixth floor and to my cube, something doesn't look right and my heart drops into my stomach when I realize what it is. I didn't bring a lot of personal effects to work, but I had a small flowering cactus that Addy had given me on my first day. I had a picture Alyse and me from my high school graduation and one of Kam, Addy and myself at a Cubs game from last summer. We had a great time that hot Saturday afternoon at one of the many rooftop bars that overlook Wrigley

Field. The two pitchers of margaritas we had at this quaint little Mexican restaurant beforehand probably helped too.

But the only three things that I'd brought, indicating that the person who occupied this space actually had some semblance of a life, were gone.

Shit...was I fired and not told? Is this retribution from Wes because of my make-believe boyfriend, or God forbid, he thinks I'm involved with Gray?

"Why are you here?" Wes's voice snapped.

"I...I, uh..." *Because I work here?* Or at least I did.

"You should be up on the thirty-fourth floor. I hear Mr. Colloway doesn't tolerate lateness. But you probably know that already." His caustic tone grates on my nerves, not to mention I have absolutely no idea what this asshole is talking about.

"What do you mean I should be on the thirty-fourth floor?" I'm genuinely confused as to what's going on here.

"What? You don't know?" His laugh is filled with malice. "Apparently over the weekend you were reassigned as Mr. Colloway's new assistant. Better get that pretty ass moving, sugar, you don't want to keep the boss waiting."

"What?" I breathe, not at all believing what I just heard. Disbelief quickly morphs into anger, which is escalating rapidly into pure rage. Why would Gray do this? I told him not to hover. I told him to let me do my job. Just as Wes opens his mouth to make another biting remark, a grey-haired, heavier set woman rounds the corner. And she looks to be on a mission.

"Livia Kingsley?" she asks. Her voice is cheery and she radiates motherly warmth. I nod, unable to speak through the fire building in my belly, which is spreading like hot lava through my veins.

"Good, good. Come with me dear. You were supposed to be upstairs almost ten minutes ago." She starts walking back in the direction from which she came and I have no choice but to follow or be left behind.

"I—I didn't know," I stammer.

"Really? I'm surprised someone didn't at least call you. I mean, it is sudden, but you certainly must have impressed Gray, because he wouldn't pick just anyone to be his assistant. He's very particular. But boy am I glad he did, because I'm down to less than two weeks before I retire and I want to make sure I leave his new assistant behind with everything she'll need to succeed. It's going to be pushing it, but we'll manage, don't you worry, dear."

We enter the elevator and the woman, who has yet to introduce herself by name, still continues to babble, but I've stopped listening. I can't hear anything through the blood rushing in my head and the fury roaring loudly in my ears.

As soon as we exit the elevator, I blindly follow the woman down a series of hallways until we reach a large corner office with frosted windows. The nameplate on the outside says Gray Colloway in large black block letters. His door is closed and I hear voices coming from inside. I don't give a shit if he's hosting the President of the motherfucking

175

United States, I march past the desk that is now supposedly mine and I head straight for that door. I throw it open so hard it bounces off the wall behind it and two sets of eyes turn my way.

One, I'm all too familiar with and is the target of my wrath, but the other belongs to a stunning woman in a clingy white blouse and tight black skirt who is presently standing next to Gray's seated form, leaning over his desk. From where I stand, I can see directly down her cleavage and if Gray turns his head slightly, those girls will practically be smothering him.

"Livia, I'm in the middle of something. Can this wait?" He looks past me, adding, "Bonnie, it's fine." Bonnie must be his current assistant's name and I hear her reply "okay" from behind me.

"Livia?" I mock, stretching out my name into practically three separate words.

"I guess not." He looks at the woman next to him who is now standing so at least I don't have to see her big-ass tits. And Gray no longer has a birds-eye view of her nipples. "Thank you, Camille. I'll call you if I have any questions."

The blond seductress makes her way toward me and surprisingly holds out her hand. "Hi. I'm Camille Hayes, Vice President of Human Resources. You must be Gray's new assistant."

Now not only don't I like the way she dresses, I don't like the way she says Gray's name like she's intimately familiar with him. And as the head of HR, perhaps she should dress a little more conservatively. Like...wear a gunny sack or something so she covers those bad boys up. I look at her hand for a moment like it's a cobra, but decide that I shouldn't take my ire out on her so I extend mine. "Livia Kingsley."

"Camille, please close the door on your way out. Bonnie, everything is fine." Apparently Bonnie didn't take the hint the first time and I'm sure she's wondering what kind of crazy Gray just hired.

Camille walks past me, closing the door much softer than how it was opened. Goodie for her.

"What the hell did you do?" I grit as soon as our audience has left. I want to scream at him, but I'm afraid Bonnie may call security. I can't say I would blame her. I'm feeling pretty homicidal.

He stands and walks over to me with an amused look on his handsome face, which I simultaneously want to kiss and slap off. "What do you mean?"

"You know exactly what I mean. Why am I suddenly working for you, instead of Wes?" At the mention of my current, former—whatever he is— boss, Gray's face looks as stormy as the sky before it opens up, deluging you with its fury. I roll my eyes.

"Wes?" His name drips off Gray's tongue like he'd just eaten a piece of liver, which I know he despises.

"Stop. Fix this," I demand.

"Livvy." He grabs for me and I sidestep him. I know exactly what he's doing. He's using seduction to get what he wants and it's not going to work this time. *Probably* not.

"I mean it, Gray. I'm not working for you. Fix this. Now."

"No."

"No?"

"Correct." As we've been bantering, every step he's taken toward me, I've counter stepped until my back is now against a wall and I have no more moves left to make. His arms have me caged in. My traitorous body thinks this is foreplay and is readying herself for him.

"Why are you doing this?" I breathe.

He leans down, answering directly in my ear. "I'm the boss. I don't have to have a reason."

Bastard. Two can play his stupid chess game. I think he'll find I've improved my skills over the years. "Damn you, Gray. You're going to regret this." I'll make his life a living hell until he relents and ships me off back down to Wes. Who will, in turn, make *my* life a living hell now that he knows I'm involved with Gray.

Shit. I am suddenly in a no-win situation. *Damn him!*

"Doubtful, angel," he says right before his lips descend to mine. I expect another bruising, claiming kiss, but instead it's gentle and reverent and delivers on its intention. To melt my anger away. "You can't hold the fact against me that I want you by my side every second of every day, Livvy. I've been starved without you, and I don't think I'll ever get my fill again."

His words mirror my feelings, but I'm beginning to panic. All the walls I've frantically been trying to build to protect myself from the inevitable hurt keep getting obliterated every time I'm with Gray. How long can I hold out before I just say "fuck it" and throw all caution and common sense to the hurricane force winds that are trying desperately to rip it away from me? I need to talk to my therapist. Get some perspective. Now.

"I'm scared." My voice is so low I don't think he hears me and honestly, I'm not sure I intended him to. But he does, and his reply doesn't provide me any comfort. In fact, it reinforces the reason I need to keep myself guarded, and why I should just get the hell out of Chicago and start over somewhere else, alone.

"Me too." Then my face is in his hands, his intense gaze beseeching mine to believe him. "But I love you so much, Livvy. I'm trying to keep the past where it is and just accept that you're back in my life and that you love me. We'll start over. I want to start over."

God help me, so do I. Can I believe him? Can I trust that he'll leave the last five years buried, so my sordid world doesn't taint the future? I want to, but I just don't know.

His beautiful mouth turns up and I laugh at his next comment. "We'll take it slow."

"I think we're way past slow. We're more like mach ten with our hair on fire." And one, or both, of us is bound to get burned.

Soft lips kiss my forehead. "You may be right, but I won't apologize."

I sigh, reluctantly accepting my fate for the moment. "I should get back to Bonnie. She's probably ready to call in reinforcements any second. She seems awfully protective of you."

He finally steps back, giving me much-needed breathing space. "She is. She's been with me for quite some time. You have big shoes to fill, but I *trust* you, Livvy." The way he emphasized one word in that sentence was not lost on me. He trusts me and wants the same in return. I decide to change the subject instead of responding. Yes, we've already established that I'm a coward of epic proportions.

"And what about Camille?"

"What about her?" he asks, walking back around his desk, taking a seat.

"Have you been with her?" I can't believe that envious question slipped past my gritted teeth, but sometimes that green-eyed bitch is wily and unpredictable. I wanted to kick myself the second it did. I have no right to ask questions like that if I'm keeping my secrets hidden.

A slow smile curves his mouth and his eyes twinkle with amusement. "I like that look on you, Livvy. It makes me hard."

I huff, turn and walk out of his office, closing the door so I can seal out the irritating laughter following me. Bonnie's standing at her desk and our eyes connect, but instead of reprimand, which is what I expect to see, I see delight and a knowing glint only another woman would recognize.

Great. She's onto us, too. I wouldn't be surprised to see an all-company email blast by noon, or even a poster hanging in the break room announcing our little lurid affair. Not knowing what else to do, I simply shrug my shoulders and walk over to her.

It's only then I realize Gray never gave me an answer about Camille, and the seeds of jealousy not only take hold, they start growing roots. Damn him.

Chapter 25

Gray

Between my other responsibilities, I've been pouring over the files Camille pulled. The first one I reviewed was the employment contract on Mr. Nichols and, much to my dismay, we are stuck with him for another eighteen months, or we'll have to pay a hefty severance package that amounts to more than a million dollars. It would almost be worth it to send his sorry ass packing, and I still may do that, but I'd rather find something that would land him behind bars for, oh, say the next fifteen to twenty instead. Unfortunately so far, I've found nothing incriminating.

Imagine his surprise when I moseyed on down to his office on Monday afternoon to discuss his ineptitude at last Friday's board meeting. The fact that Livvy, who was still as green as a newly bloomed plant, knew information on that patent that he didn't not only grated on my last nerve, but it just felt all wrong, so I've also been doing plenty of digging on that this week as well. And when he tried to blame his incompetence on the fact that Livvy was new and he'd had to spend a great deal of time training her so he didn't have time to adequately prepare for the meeting, I wanted to both fire him and cut his tongue out on the spot. I made it perfectly clear his days were numbered and I was watching him like a hawk, just waiting to take him down the second he faltered again, contract or not. I would find some way to make that null and void.

"Sorry I'm late," Conn said before he noticed Asher hadn't arrived either.

"No problem."

Conn takes a seat at the round conference table in the corner of my office, where I'm also sitting, before asking, "So...how are things going?"

I can't help but laugh at the question my brother really wants the answer to. *How are things with Livvy?* I feel lighter and happier than I have in a very long time. It probably shows. "Things couldn't be better," I reply.

Other than Monday night, because Livvy was still a little peeved at her re-assignment and felt like she had to punish me, we've spent the rest of the week together. She's even agreed to go to Detroit with me tomorrow. Since she was supposed to see her sister, I told her to invite Alyse and her new boyfriend to dinner at my mom's house on Saturday night, which she did.

"I'm glad to hear it, Gray." I knew Conn meant it, but I also know him well enough to know he's still worried. Ash, on the other hand, was having a hard time accepting that Livvy was back in my life...for good. "She still coming to Mom's tomorrow?"

"Yes." And I haven't yet warned my mom. I need to make that call this afternoon. As with my brothers, I'm not sure how my mom will react to the fact that I'm seeing Livvy again, but I hope she quickly gets on board because Livvy is here to stay. Forever, if I have anything to say about it.

182

"Hey, sorry I'm late." Ash rushed through the door, breathing heavy as if he'd just run up the stairs. "The meeting with the auditors ran late. They have me by the balls right now. I can hardly get anything else done."

"Sorry about that, brother. Any news yet?" I ask.

"No. Far too early for that. And the lead auditor is a raving bitch. I think she either needs a good spanking or to get laid."

"I'm sure you can help her out with that, Ash," Conn quips.

"Not going there again," he mumbles under his breath.

"Again?" I probe, a smile now on my face.

"Forget I said that." He takes a seat and I start right into business, not wanting to discuss the subject of his bedroom proclivities.

"So, I've met with one of the lead developers still on staff to determine everyone who would have known about that patent. It was only a handful that were close to the details, and most are still employed by HMT. I've already contacted IT and asked them to pull every email, every instant message, every website and any other scrap of information they can get their hands on relative to each of these individuals, plus I've asked them to scour the server for certain words. I'm also pulling the same information on the five people that knew about the patent who are no longer here, including Jeffrey Handy, their former CEO."

"That's going to be a lot of shit to go through," Conn says.

I nod. Yes. Yes, it will and this is something I need to keep on the down low. The fewer people that know about it, the better. But it will take me months to do it by myself, so I plan to assign Livvy her first little project. If it calls for late nights burning the midnight oil, then I guess we'll just have to do that. Together. At my place. Naked. I smile inwardly at the lascivious thoughts I'm creating in my head of every inch of fair, velvety skin glowing in the firelight as she—

"What about Nichols?" Ash asks, scowling. I guess maybe I was smiling outwardly instead. Whoops.

"So far, I haven't found anything that points to him, but I'm suspicious. At minimum, he's an incompetent asshole. At worse, he's fucked us over and will be spending quite a bit of time becoming someone's bitch while pulling laundry duty."

We spend the next hour going over a few other business items before Conn needs to head to another meeting. "Hey Ash," I call, after Conn has already left.

"What's up?"

"Close the door for a minute, will you?" He raises his eyebrows but does as I ask. I'm not even sure Livvy's out there, but I don't want her overhearing this conversation if she is. "You know Livvy's coming tomorrow, right?"

His lips thin. I know I'm right to talk to him before we all show up at Mom's house, and he backs her into a corner, spewing vile and hateful things that she doesn't need to hear. "I won't tolerate you treating Livvy with anything less than respect this weekend."

"Is that so?" Asher crosses his arms, ready for a fight.

I'm not about to throw punches at work, but if he does or says anything that upsets Livvy this weekend, I won't hesitate. Ash crosses his arms over his chest and I know I'm in for a brotherly lecture. Which I don't fucking need, but will have to listen to anyway.

"Gray, I'm not even sure if you remember all the shit that you went through, because you were so blitzed out of your mind during that month and a half you spiraled completely out of control, but I do. I was there every single day, cleaning up your puke, throwing half naked whores out of your house, paying your bills and trying to keep you from slowly, deliberately killing yourself. Hell, I even showered your sorry ass because you'd lost all sense of human hygiene. And some shit you just cannot unsee, brother, but I did it. For you. Because you're my brother and I love you. I've already lost one brother and I almost lost another during what was undoubtedly the darkest time of your life, but it was a dark time in mine as well. And Conn's. And Mom and Dad's. So you'll understand if I don't welcome Livia Kingsley back into our family with open fucking arms because she didn't just destroy you before, she fucking blew you to smithereens. And I don't want her to do it again."

Wow. My head is spinning. Asher and I have never talked about those bleak times, mostly because I tried to shove the memories so deep in my

185

mind, I could almost convince myself they weren't real, but I had no idea that he'd done all of that for me. And I couldn't even touch the topic of Luke, my twin. We never talked about Luke and what happened to him. Ever. But damn if I didn't suddenly feel like a horse's ass because I hadn't really taken my family's feelings into consideration. I'd only thought of myself.

"I'm...I don't know what to say, Asher. I'm sorry."

Asher laid his hand on my shoulder. "Look, I want you to be happy, Gray, and only time will tell if Livia's the one to do that."

"She is," I adamantly reply. "She's the only thing that makes me whole, Ash."

"Fine. But respect has to be earned and she hasn't earned mine, so I will be cordial, but that's it."

I nod. "I can accept that. I guess. But her sister and boyfriend will be there. Can you at least be pleasant to them?"

"Little Alyse? Sure. I always liked her," Asher replies as he walks to the door. I don't miss the brief flare of heat I see at the mention of Alyse's name.

"You and Conn riding together?" I ask.

"Yep. See you there. We'll be there by mid-afternoon, or as soon as I can get Conn's ass out of bed."

"See you tomorrow," I murmur, my mind in a whirl.

As Ash leaves, for the first time I waiver. What if Livvy's right? What if what she's hiding is so damning, it will destroy what we're trying to rebuild? What then? Black spots appear in my vision

186

just thinking about that possibility, so I simply can't. I *won't*.

I suddenly wonder if I've made the right decision by hiring Robert Townley because ignorance truly is bliss. And while it may be naïve and childish to bury your head in the sand, sometimes it's also self-preservation because you know if you don't, something may threaten your very survival. I need Livvy like I need air to breathe. I need her to survive.

No, I decide. Nothing I learn could possibly destroy my love for her.

Nothing.

Chapter 26

Livia

"You didn't eat breakfast or lunch. You sure you aren't hungry, angel?" Gray asks, sliding his hand over mine.

"No. I'm fine." I couldn't even chew a piece of gum right now, I'm so nervous. I have no idea why I agreed to go back to Detroit with Gray, let alone to his house for dinner with his family. It sounded like a good idea when he was buried inside me, promising the next dirty thing he planned to do to my body if I agreed. He kept every one of them, so I had to keep mine.

Ugh. Asher can't look at me without sneering, Conn seems indifferent, and I have absolutely no idea how I'll be received by Barb, Gray's mother. I wouldn't be surprised if she puts a little special seasoning of Kaopectate in my food as a welcome home gift.

"Are you sure your mom doesn't care that I'm coming?" I ask for about the twentieth time.

"Angel, look at me." I pull my eyes from the passing interstate and catch his. "My mom is thrilled that you're coming. Not only is she glad you're alive and well, she's genuinely happy that we're together again. She loves you, just like I do." He brings our joined hands to his lips, brushing a soft kiss on my palm. I'm so distraught I can't even enjoy the tingles it brings to every girlie part.

I'm not sure I believe him. She *did* love me. Until I ruined her son's life. And as a mother, how can you ever forgive the girl who broke your child?

"Want to play this or that?"

I allow myself a small smile. We used to play that all the time on the many road trips we'd take to see friends or our favorite bands or when we just wanted to get away and simply...be.

"Sure." Anything to take my mind off of the uncomfortable setting I will soon find myself in. I wish we could just have dinner and leave, but Gray promised his mom we'd spend the night. I, under sexual duress I might add, agreed to stay at his mom's house, but I've already decided if it's too awkward, I'll be catching a ride with Alyse back to her place, and Gray will just have to deal.

"Okay, I'll start," he says with a slight smirk and a wag of his thick brows. Uh oh...I already know exactly where this game is headed. "Clean or dirty?"

Laughing, I reply with a wink, "Dirty, of course." He joins in my laughter. One question in and I'm already feeling better. I love this man so very much. God, I've missed him. Missed us. "Okay, my turn. Bath or shower?" I smile.

"Hmmm...that's a hard one. Both have their distinct advantages, but I'll have to go with shower. I don't like your pussy hidden underneath all those bubbles."

I gasp slightly, and my heart rate just kicked up several notches.

"My turn," I breathe. "Hair or bare?"

189

He curses before answering and my eyes are drawn to the growing bulge in his tight-fitting dark jeans. "Bare." His voice is pure sex, pure sin, pure seduction. Our heated eyes connect across the tiny interior space of his ridiculously expensive car. Every word he utters makes me wetter and hornier and suddenly I want the drive to go faster so he can fuck my brains out against the closest wall. I want to strip my clothes off and mount him. Right now.

"My turn." His low, raspy timbre is like a magnet directly to my sex, which is now throbbing with its own heartbeat. He could ask me to do absolutely anything right now and I would. Without hesitation. He looks at me before asking, "Front or back?"

"Jesus, Gray." My eyes involuntarily close at his clean words, but filthy connotation. When I open them, his gaze is back out the windshield, but raw lust tightens his face. "Both," I whisper. Because it's true and he knows it.

He closes his eyes with almost a pained look. His chest expands deeply. His knuckles are practically white with how tight he's now gripping the steering wheel. I'm not the only one affected by this little game we're playing, and if he wanted to take my mind off this dinner; I'd say he's hit a fucking grand slam.

I clear my throat, knowing exactly where the next question will lead, but I'm in so deep now, only an orgasm will take the edge off this ache that's now built to explosive proportions in my loins. I think if I rub my thighs together in just the right way, I may detonate. "Sex or masturbation?"

"Fuck, Livvy. *Fuck*." His jaw clenches, and I see his dick twitch. He barks his command without even looking at me. "Lose the skirt and panties. Now."

I quickly pull up my maxi skirt to my waist, shimmying off my silky navy thong. Gray's windows are tinted for privacy, so I'm not particularly worried about anyone seeing me. The thought that someone may only serves to heighten my arousal.

"Spread your legs, baby, so I can see and smell your desire for me."

I turn in my seat, adjusting my seatbelt so it's loose enough I can maneuver, and I prop one foot on the headrest of his seat and the other on the dash. I tilt my pelvis so I'm completely open to him.

When I'm finally positioned, as comfortably as you can in a moving vehicle, he looks over. The burn of his stare lights me on fire and I wonder if that alone can make me explode. Desire rolls off Gray in thick waves, filling the small space with potent pheromones. It's intoxicating.

"Sweet Jesus, Livvy." While I wait for his next command, he takes a hand off the wheel and runs a single finger through my wetness, rimming my puckered flesh. An involuntary moan escapes from deep inside me. "Always so wet for me," he rasps, his voice heavy with lust.

Yes, I know. I feel my want running down between my cheeks, probably staining his leather seats. I can't remember a time when I was as turned on as I am now, doing something so utterly wicked that I'm seriously trying to plan our next road trip.

I just about come when he sucks his finger clean. I desperately need to touch myself, so without waiting to hear what he wants next, my fingers swipe through my arousal, circling my clit. My eyes want to close, but I need to watch what I'm doing to him. I need to watch him come undone with me, even if we are hurtling down the interstate at seventy-five miles per hour.

"Fuck, Livvy. You are the hottest thing I have ever seen. Imagine it's my tongue on you. In you," he growls.

I swirl faster, pant harder and fight to prolong the pure hedonism of this moment, but I was so turned on before I started, my climax is barreling toward me faster than a freight train and after only moments, I'm almost ready to fly. Dirty words roll off Gray's lips like a supplication, his eyes flitting between the road and my active fingers.

Suddenly we're pulling off the side of I94. Gray shoves the car into park while undoing his seatbelt and slams my soaked sex to his greedy mouth. He groans, driving two fingers roughly inside me while sucking hard on my engorged clit. My legs tremble as hot waves of rapture take over my body, making me mindless. I cry out as his talented tongue works me to the edge and over again, devouring every drop of the multiple climaxes he's managed to wring out of me in sixty seconds flat.

When my breath calms, and I can finally peel my eyes open, Gray is staring salaciously into them, a wicked smile on his face. Cars whiz by at fast speeds, our vehicle shaking slightly with each one. "Hi," he says softly.

"Hi." I can barely speak through my post-orgasmic, blissful haze. A place I never want to leave. It's like a wonderland, only better.

"You're fucking delicious. One taste just wasn't enough." He winks and places an open-mouthed kiss over my ink before sitting back in his seat. After redoing his seatbelt and adjusting his hardened dick, he pulls back out into traffic and we're on our way once again. And I'm still lying in this exact same position, legs open wide, unable to move a single muscle, except for the one in my chest. That one is beating wildly with love for this man.

"Baby, you'd best cover up, because if we have to pull back over to the side of the road again, you'll be riding my cock hard and, even with tinted windows, I think it will become pretty apparent to passersby what we're doing. And I'd just as soon stay out of jail today because I have plans for you later."

After I untangle my limbs and pull on my uncomfortably wet panties, I reach over, taking his hand in mine. My head still feels heavy, so I rest it comfortably against the seat, but turn toward him so I can drink in his beautiful profile. "I love you so much, Gray." I'm so happy at this moment, I feel like crying and it's difficult to hold all of the tumultuous emotions I'm feeling inside.

His eyes brim with love when he turns them to meet mine. Raising our entwined hands, soft lips graze mine and a few stray tears slip out when he says, "Not half as much as I love you, Livia."

That's simply not possible, I think. *It's not possible to love anyone as much as I love you.*

193

Chapter 27

Livia

"Mom, we're here," Gray yells as he opens the front door, letting me in first. Well, he more like pushes me in because my feet refuse to move past the threshold. As we stand inside the entryway, with his hand on my lower back, memories assault me from every angle.

The smell of freshly baked bread fills my nostrils, making both my mouth and eyes water. A picture taken at Christmas the year before we were engaged of Gray and his brothers, with their arms wrapped around each other's shoulders, still sits on the thin, long maple table that lines the wall to my left. And Maxwell, the Colloway golden cockerdoodle, whose big chocolate eyes clearly house an old, reincarnated soul, sits patiently at my feet, waiting for my attention.

I kneel and scratch his belly, which he loves. "Hi, buddy. I missed you," I choke, barely able to keep myself in check. I knew coming here would be difficult, but for very different reasons, like rejection and judgment. I just had no idea stepping foot in a house again that always overflowed with so much love would be *this* hard. Because the only time I ever felt such strong family love and unity was when I was in the Colloway home.

Barb rounding the corner with a dishtowel in her hand takes my attention away from Maxwell. I rise and she stops short. We stare at each other, but my vision of her is blurry. You know how you think you're holding things together pretty well until you see that one certain person? And for some reason, seeing that one person not only cracks the dam inside of you, it shatters it into a million, unrepairable pieces?

When I laid eyes on Barb, my dam blew all to hell and suddenly I'm enveloped in her arms, sobbing. "Oh, sweet girl," she keeps chanting, over and over, her motherly arms holding me tight. For all intents and purposes, Barb was like a mother to me, just like the rest of Gray's family was my family too. When I lost Gray, I lost them. This house always felt like home to me, and stepping foot into it again, being unconditionally welcomed by Gray's mother, brings back the same feeling of belonging and acceptance I always had before. And the relief is overwhelming.

"Come on," she says, hooking her arm in mine, leading me to the bathroom. "Why don't you gather yourself, freshen up and meet us in the kitchen. I just pulled some fresh banana bread from the oven."

"Thanks, Barb," I manage to say.

She's at the door of the bathroom when she turns and says, "Livia, I don't know what happened, and I'm not going to ask, but I want you to know that I'm here for you if you want to talk. Anytime. About anything, dear."

I nod, a fresh mixture of grief and happiness spilling. For the first time ever, I want to confess. I *want* to tell another person, besides my shrink, what happened to me all those years ago. Why I disappeared. Why I stayed away. The need to purge without judgment or condemnation or even pity is overwhelming. This burden I carry is so heavy and debilitating, I constantly fight its pull into complete despondency. I want to talk about the baby that I lost. The baby I wanted so desperately, but can barely acknowledge anymore because the pain twists my guts raw. I want absolution from the woman standing in front of me for the pain I caused her and her family.

I don't, though. I simply let her walk out and close the door softly behind her.

But, strangely, I feel relief. Because if I feel like I *might* be able to tell Barb, maybe that means someday I'll be able to tell Gray.

Maybe I'm not giving Gray enough credit.

Maybe I should trust him with my secret.

Maybe he would understand.

Maybe he would forgive me.

Maybe I should tell him about *our baby*.

Maybe.

Chapter 28

Gray

It's been ten minutes and Livvy's still in the bathroom. Two more and I'm going after her. I knew it would be hard for her to see my mom again, because the two of them were very close, and I suddenly realize that I was so self-absorbed during these past few years about Livvy, not letting anyone ask questions or even mention her name, that I didn't understand how much my mom has missed her too. My mom only has boys so Livvy was the closest thing to a daughter she ever had. Then one day she was just gone. I guess we all mourned Livvy, in a way, but I should have paid more attention to my mother's feelings.

"I'm sorry, Mom," I say, gripping the counter I'm leaning against.

"Whatever for, Gray?" she responds. She's like the Energizer Bunny in the kitchen, constantly cutting or mixing or cleaning. She never sits still. She never sits, period.

"For..." I don't even know exactly how to say it. *For being a self-absorbed ass? For never letting you grieve with me? For not comforting you when you also lost someone important?*

But she knows what I'm trying to say and she lets me off the hook, laying a hand on my arm. "It was a difficult time for all of us Gray, and we all handle crisis differently. It's okay." She turns back to chopping onions and I push from the counter to check on my woman.

"I've worried about you, you know."

"I know, Mom."

"Do you?" she asks. She sets down the knife and turns toward me. "I don't ever think I've witnessed a man break like you did when Livia left."

"I know it was bad for a while, but I pulled out of it."

She smiles sadly. "You pulled yourself out of the *worst* of it, you mean. You never pulled yourself out of it completely. You work yourself into the ground. You don't date. I rarely see you smile."

"What are you saying, Mom? That you don't want me with Livia again?"

"No, Gray. That's not at all what I'm saying. I love Livia like she was my own child. What I'm saying is that you look *happy*, son. Happier than I've seen you in a long time." Only what I heard was *"happier than before she left you"* and it brought my mood elevator down a few floors.

"I am, Mom," I say, hoping I sound convincing. Because it's true. I *am* happy, but that little noxious cloud of doubt that I've been trying to shove into a fucking box and bury under two tons of steel, keeps slowly seeping out, poisoning my mind, undermining my confidence in us.

I'm almost to the door when it opens and Livvy walks out, eyes red from crying. And the second I set my sights on her, the cloud dissipates like it was never there. All feels right in my world once again. That's what being in her presence does for me. It centers me. It keeps any uncertainty or misgivings I have about our future at bay. I want to wrap myself up in her and never let go. Hell, I want to climb inside of her and live there for the rest of my days.

Then her back is against the wall, her face in my hands and her lips on mine. Her body softens into me as her hands grip my waist. A quiet moan escapes between our fused mouths and I'm not sure if it came from her or me.

"Get a fucking room, for Christ's sake." My brother Conn's voice penetrates the sexual mist that's heavy around us. "Better yet, go to a hotel, because I certainly don't need to hear the headboard banging or the springs squeaking or any fucking moaning coming from your room tonight, Gray."

Pulling Livvy into my side, I turn to my brother, a shit-eating grin on my face. "Wear earplugs, then."

He walks by us, mumbling something under his breath about not needing that visual.

The rest of the afternoon goes by smoothly. Livvy helps my mom in the kitchen, just like old times, and my brothers and I watch the Wolverines kick some Gopher ass while downing a few Coronas. This feels domesticated...and fucking amazing.

I don't know a lot of men that truly crave, with their entire being, to be tied to a woman for the rest of their lives, but I do. I watch Livvy move around the kitchen in tandem with Mom, like she's done it hundred times before, and I can imagine holidays and barbecues here. I can envision our children running around with their cousins and the house so full of noise and laughter that it will be hard to carry on a conversation. I want that. All of it.

I know we just reunited, and sometimes it feels like this secret she carries is the goddamn Grand Canyon between us, but Jesus, I want to ask her to marry me. Again. I don't want to push her by moving too fast, but I don't know how long I can hold off either. I just don't want her to walk back out of my life.

Being engaged didn't prevent that before. Fuck. That damn toxin is seeping back out and now it has a voice.

The doorbell rings, and now I'm restless, so I rise to answer. When I open the door, I see an absolutely stunning young woman standing in front of me, with long dark hair and big brown eyes. "Alyse, my you've grown up." I grab her in a giant hug, twirling her around like I used to when she was younger. She's laughing, but suddenly stops, and that's when I notice the egghead still standing on the stoop with a scowl on his face and steroids dripping from his pores. I instantly don't like him.

I set her down and extend my hand. "Gray Colloway." He grips it and squeezes like he's trying to crush every bone just to prove his manhood. I squeeze harder. Asshole.

"Finn."

"Finn?" I can't stop the sarcasm that drips thickly from my question. "Just Finn? Like, just Cher?"

He smiles smugly and I want to wipe the fucking floor with it. It's been a long time since I've met someone that irritates the shit out of me before they even speak, but the arrogance oozing off this punk is foul smelling and lethal. He's bad news. And not nearly anywhere in the vicinity of being good enough for Alyse.

"Yes, just Finn." Alyse winces when he pulls her to him and, so help me, I want to haul him out back and have him go three rounds with the Colloway brothers. Then we'll see who's smiling, fucker.

An hour later, Asher grabs another beer from the fridge and leans back against the counter. "What's the deal with Popeye over there?" he asks, clearly talking about Finn. I haven't missed the way Ash's eyes have been running over Livvy's sister... and neither has *Finn*.

The asshole won't let her leave his side and constantly has a possessive arm or hand on her. It's not lost on me that's the way I react around Livvy, but this is different. While mine stems from deep, soul-wrenching love, his is just pure possessiveness. He has a beautiful woman on his arm and it pumps his ego to call her his girlfriend.

Guys like that are a dime a dozen, ladies. Kick their asses to the fucking curb because they are fouler than rotten garbage, and they will suck the very life out of your soul until you're filled with doubt and self-loathing.

And Alyse...I can see she's grown into a hell of a woman who deserves a lot more than what this asshole has to offer. Which is nothing but heartache and possibly a few broken bones if she's not careful.

"He's a tool." I don't know what else to say about the douche. He's currently "between jobs", which means he's a fucking loser who's mooching off of a very successful and beautiful woman. Alyse graduated from college in just two and a half years and started her own auditing firm last year. And come to find out, Alyse's specialty is forensic auditing, which promptly got Asher's attention. I could see the gears clicking a hundred miles per hour in my brother's head. He wants her.

"She's not your type, Asher, so just forget whatever plan you've concocted in that *little* head of yours." I emphasize little, so he knows I know exactly what he's thinking. The last thing I need is for there to be tension between our families because Alyse is the only living blood relative Livvy has and she'll be spending a lot of time with us. And Asher isn't much better than Conn when it comes to running through women at lightening speed. Talk about an awkward family dinner.

I take a swallow of my own beer and turn my gaze on Livvy, who's sitting next to Alyse in deep conversation. She's so damn beautiful it hurts to look at her. I realize that I'm completely whipped, but I don't give a flying fuck. If I could live inside her pussy and never come up for air, I would.

"Did you see that bruise on Alyse's arm?" Ash asks on a low growl.

Yes. Yes, I did. And it's eerily in the shape of a couple of thick male fingers. I bet if we put Finn's up to them, we'd find a perfect match.

"Yeah. Come on, let's get back." I plan on squeezing my way onto the already full couch, even if I have to pull Livvy onto my lap. I just need her as close to me as possible.

It's okay, I own my caveman tendencies.

———————

"What's going on between Asher and Alyse?" Livvy asks while brushing her teeth. I love that we've fallen into our same comfortable routine. It warms my insides.

Just after dinner when bonehead went outside for a smoke that smelled suspiciously like skunk—yet *another* strike against him—Ash cornered Alyse in the kitchen and, while I didn't hear their heated conversation, I saw him pointing to her bruises. And I know a "fuck you" when it's being mouthed, which clearly Alyse was. She's stubborn. A lot like her sister.

"What do you mean?" I knew exactly what she meant, but I was going to nip this thing in the bud with my brother before he got any further down the road with his crazy-assed ideas about Alyse. Asher may like things a little rough in the bedroom, but that's all consensual. He's insanely protective of women and would never, ever harm them. And he detested men that thought they could prey on the physically weaker sex. Finn is a pinhead and it was clear to everyone tonight that he regularly manhandles Alyse. I can already see Ash has appointed himself Alyse's knight in shining armor and intends to slay the dragon that's threatening to harm her. *Has* harmed her already. And Ash is like a dog with a bone. A big, vicious, fucking pit bull. He won't stop until he's shredded the opponent to pieces and they're lying dead in a heap at his feet. The Colloway brothers are a lot alike in that regards.

The look Livvy gives me lets me know she knows I know and I'm not fooling her one bit. "He's just concerned about her, Livvy. He should be," I add.

She rinses her mouth, places her toothbrush on the sink and turns to me. "I know. I'm worried about her too. I don't like that jerk."

Tonight Livvy's wearing short shorts and a tiny white tank that allows me an almost unobstructed view of her luscious, hard nipples. I got hard the instant she walked into the bathroom. Now the only thing I can think about is sucking one of those ripe berries into my mouth through the thin fabric. My head is spinning with a thousand things I want to do to her, each dirtier than the one before.

"I think we're on the same page there," I rumble, my voice dropping an octave. Livvy swallows and I see the pulse in her slender neck flutter. I bring my hand up to thrum one of her hardened nubs. Her eyes close. Her breaths quicken and I can smell her want. I lift her onto the cold granite counter and suck a dusky peak into my mouth, wetting the cloth in the process.

"Gray." My name is a sweet, breathy melody falling from her tongue. One I want to listen to on replay every day. I quickly strip her of the barriers that keep her naked flesh from mine. I find her wet core with my fingers and groan. She's ready for me. She's *always* ready for me.

"I can't be gentle, Livvy," I murmur as I move to the neglected nub and work my fingers in and out of her silky sheath.

Over the last few hours, I've had to have quite a few heart to hearts with my dick, who begged me to lock ourselves away the second we stepped foot in this house and fuck his woman long into the night. I've refused him, but now I'm letting him out to take over fully.

"Ready to fly, baby?" Her eyes flare in sweet submission, making my cock weep so much my boxers are now coated.

With a flick of my wrists, my underwear lands at my feet. I pull Livvy to the edge, plunging unceremoniously into her warmth. We both moan in sublime pleasure. Holding her head where I want it, I ravage her mouth the way I've been dying to since she had her legs spread for me in the car earlier.

"You're it for me, Livvy," I rasp against her lips between thrusts. Deep, shallow, shallow. Then so deep, I feel her cervix on the tip of my cock. My eyes roll back in sheer rapture. Her walls are hugging me so tight I'm not going to last. Her legs are wrapped around me so snuggly, it's almost painful, but fuels my raging desire for her all the more. "I love you so fucking much it hurts." I don't know what it is about being inside her, but my deepest thoughts come flowing out without a filter.

"I love you, Gray," she mumbles against my neck. Every time she utters those words, my heart skips a beat.

I fuck her just as promised.

Hard.

Rough.

Raw.

"Get there, angel. I want to come together." I reach between us and feather her clit, which hurtles her immediately into space. Fusing my mouth to hers, I swallow her cries of ecstasy just seconds before I follow, coating her with my seed. Hot jets of semen bath her insides, and my breath catches at the thought of creating a life with her. We've not once even discussed birth control, so I have to imagine she's on something to prevent pregnancy, but I wish she wasn't. I want to see her belly swell with our child.

Holding her eyes, I confess, "You're my everything, Livvy." And before I can hear her response, I once again capture her mouth with mine.

Minutes later, snuggled in bed, with my future at my side, I feel more content than I ever have. I hold Livvy close until I hear her breaths even out and know she's sleeping. As I let my consciousness fade, I begin to plot my next move. Very soon, I will have a ring on her finger and share her bed every single night.

And I will have her for the rest of my life.

Chapter 29

Livia

It's been over a week since I've seen Peter, and that means it's been over a week since I've seen Grant. Where Peter goes, Grant goes, so while a part of me gets excited to see my only friend here, at the same time I don't because I know Peter won't be far behind and then I'll most likely be spending the next few days recovering from my fresh physical and emotional injuries. But that's okay. I relish the time between visits from Peter, even if they are spent in bed, healing.

After two and a half years here, while I'm not allowed outside without either Peter or Grant, I at least have the run of the house, even though I'm watched at all times.

I look down; testing the sprained ring finger I got during our last "visit." The swelling is almost gone, the bruising faded to a deep yellow. My previously black eye has faded to a nice greenish-yellow as well.

I'm sitting at the kitchen table, eating a turkey sandwich for dinner, admiring the beautiful sunshiny summer day from inside my opulent prison when I see Grant walk in.

"Hi," he greets tentatively, a sad smile on his lips. He, too, knows what being back here means for me.

"Hi," I choke. Suddenly no longer hungry, I barely swallow what's in my mouth and push the rest

of my sandwich away. "Where is he?" I don't really want to know the answer, but not knowing is even worse.

"He's a bit behind me. Got held up."

I relax marginally as he holds out a hand. "Let's go for a walk outside."

My gaze nervously flicks back to the entrance. He knows as well as I do that there are cameras all over inside and outside this house, tracking every person's movement at all times.

"It's fine, Livia."

"Okay," I answer shakily. I take his hand, the electricity running up my arm as it always does when he touches me, and let him lead me outside after punching in a series of super secret security codes. Ones that change daily. Trust me, I learned that very early on. That day didn't end well for me.

Once I hit the balcony, I look to the clear blue sky and take a deep breath, drinking in the smell of heat and flowers and freedom and wish, like every other time I'm outside that I could just take off and run and never look back, but this place is a fortress in the middle of nowhere. I wouldn't get far. Also been there, done that. I wasn't allowed back outside for almost six months.

We walk down the stairs, side-by-side and onto the path that leads through the lush gardens Peter favors. Even though we're outdoors, neither of us is foolish enough to think that we can speak freely, so our voices are quiet.

"Livia...you know I'd do anything for you, right?"

"Yes."

"I'm working on something, but it may take some time."

My gaze snaps to his and for the first time since I landed in this god-forsaken place, I have a small sliver of hope that I may actually get out of here because while he didn't say those exact words, I know what he means. Grant would never get my hopes up artificially. "Can't you just...you know?"

He doesn't look at me, but even from the side I can see pain and anger swirling his eyes. His jaw ticks furiously. He knows exactly what I'm asking because I've asked many times before but the answer is always the same. "It's more complicated than that, Livia."

I'm quiet for several minutes, angry that a man that carries a gun on his person at all times won't just pull the damn trigger against the one who holds both of our lives in his hands. "How much time, then?"

"I don't know, but I need you to be strong. No matter what."

I swallow hard and nod. Could it be a day, a month, another fucking year? I don't know, but I know Grant is my only way out of this hell alive. I just hope it's not too late. "No matter what."

He doesn't dare hold my hand, but in a show of unity, he briefly brushes his arm against mine. Tears want to well, but I don't let them. I can't or I'll never stop.

We stay outside for another half hour until Grant says he needs to get some things done for Peter. And hours later, as expected, my worst nightmare returns.

"I own you, you little cunt!" He slaps me across the face and pain explodes in my cheek. "When I tell *you to be in my bedroom, waiting for me at eleven sharp, I mean you are to be waiting, with your legs spread, like the whore you are, at exactly eleven sharp."*

It was ten fifty-nine, but who was counting? The rules changed every day. Sometimes he'd summon me and then I'd wait all night. He'd never show. It was another Peter mind-fuck special. He constantly tried to invent ways to torture me. To break me. And after I lost my baby, he succeeded. For a while, anyway. Grant put me back together. He made me strong. Gave me hope this wouldn't be my life forever, and after today, that hope has been renewed.

I mumble my apology and after a few more blows, I sink into my safe place, forgetting about the torture I'm about to endure. I'd rather take a beating every single day than take anything of his inside of me. Luckily for me, Peter's impotency once again comes out to play, taunting the master of persecution himself. It always makes him more violent but saves me another tear in my already shredded soul. I smile inwardly. I think Peter's "condition" is fitting, and makes me a firm believer in what goes around comes back around.

In the background, I hear an insistent, loud knock on the door, which pulls Peter from his rage and his fists from my battered body. Distantly I register Grant's voice and then Peter is gone and Grant is at my side once again.

"I'm sorry I couldn't get to you in time." He picks my prone form from the carpet and carries me from a monster's room to my own.

"It's not too bad this time," I reply through a swollen lip and nearly closed right eye.

"Fuck, I wish I could get you out of here," he growls under his breath. Barely controlled rage shakes every muscle in his body.

"Soon," I reply quietly, sinking into the safety of his arms. It's the only place I am safe.

"Not soon enough."

I bolt up in bed, confused and trembling. Gray mumbles and shifts beside me, still in a deep sleep. I choke back the sob that wants to break free.

I'm free. I'm free. I'm free.

I keep repeating that to myself until my heart rate calms and my breathing slows. Until I believe it.

Needing a moment to myself, I head quietly to the bathroom and sink down to the cold tile floor, crying softly into my hands. I am so broken inside; can I ever truly be free? Can I ever truly be happy? Can I really put that nightmare completely behind me and move forward?

Jesus, I *want* to with everything in me, and never more so since I laid eyes on Gray at that fundraiser. In those moments when I'm with him, I feel like it's possible. In fact, I think I might even be able to, but with each day that passes, this secret between us grows heavier and weighs more than I think I can carry on my own.

How long until he starts questioning me again, especially with my frequent nightmares? I'm lucky that he's a deep sleeper, because this is the third one I've had this week. The nightmares that I'd managed to keep mostly at bay have been coming more often since I've reconnected with Gray. The guilt I feel deep inside by keeping this secret is eating me alive, tearing me up and I'm being punished by having to relive every horrible, torturous moment.

Pulling myself together, I splash cold water on my face and quietly pad back to bed, slipping in silently. I turn away from him, not wanting to disturb his slumber when I feel his fingernails lightly run up and down my back, and my tears quietly start anew, rolling into my pillow.

Gray always used to scratch my back to help me sleep, and the simple gesture brings me peace, the likes of which I haven't felt in years. I've lost count of how many times I've felt his phantom fingers comfort me during those interminable days. It's the simple things, like this, that I used to miss the most.

After a few minutes, he slides next to me and pulls me close and into his warmth, wrapping a possessive arm around my waist.

"Bad dream?"

I nod, unable to choke out a single syllable through the knot in my throat. I feel so loved, yet so tortured at the same time. It's exhausting keeping up this façade, keeping this cancerous story hidden from the man I love.

"You know you can tell me anything, right? You can trust me," he whispers quietly, but it sounds like a shout in the darkness of night that covers us in evasion and avoidance.

What is it about the protective cover of nightfall that makes us believe we can shed our skin and purge our sins without repercussions? Why do we feel this false sense of security that anything we confess is forgivable when someone can't see our face?

"Maybe someday," I eventually reply, and this time I mean it. Could I be doing both of us a disservice by staying mute? The more I'm with him, the more I think maybe so.

"I love you, angel. You're safe now." I'm safe. *Then why don't I feel like it?* Why do I have this bad feeling that everything I want is right within my grasp, but if I reach for it with both hands, they'll slip through the hologram, a sick taunt of all I will never have.

He pulls me tighter and after several restless moments, I finally talk my brain into shutting down and let the dark take me again. As I drift off, this time I pray for clarity and direction and faith.

Faith in me.

Faith in Gray.

Faith in *us*.

Faith that whatever it is we're building here is strong enough to endure the truth when it finally comes out because with every passing day I feel the noose tightening more around my fragile neck.

Chapter 30

Gray

This is the third time this week. She thinks I don't know, but I do. I just don't say anything. I don't want to push her. Make her defensive. Give her an excuse to pull away from me, when I'm trying to pull her into me.

By the way she cries out and mumbles incoherently in her sleep, her dreams are bad. The only thing I can ever make out is "no" or "stop" and every time I hear those pained words, my gut clenches in agony. I want to take away her sorrow. I want to banish her demons. I want her to trust me with whatever she's hiding because it's clearly killing her slowly but surely.

I feel like we're building a glass house on a shifting mound of sand, and each small settling of the treacherous grains causes microscopic fissures in our fragile structure, endangering the foundation. And the thing about cracks is...they spread. They weaken. They destroy. Until pretty soon the whole thing you've spent every ounce of energy building will implode on itself, and we'll be left with nothing but shattered rubble and cuts so deep, the scars will never heal.

But now I'm starting to wonder...is it the secrets that will break us, or the truth?

Chapter 31

Livia

"I wish you could be here. I miss you," I whine.

"Me too, baby. I'll be home tomorrow night, after my meeting." This is the first night that Gray and I have spent apart in weeks. He's out of town meeting the CEO of a company GRASCO Holdings is looking to buy, and I'm surprised at how much I miss him already. And with how much he's become ingrained in my daily life, even when I tried to avoid it. But I'm on the ride now, so I've decided I'm just going to enjoy it until it stops.

"Call me when you get home. No matter the time."

"Yes, sir," I reply saucily.

"Oh angel." His voice drips with seduction. "I can't wait to hear you say that when I have you underneath me. When I'm buried balls deep and have given you so many orgasms you can't remember your name and I can get you to agree to anything I want."

Oh my. As usual, his words jump on the express line directly to my sex and my pussy dampens for him.

"Oh really? You're pretty confident." I hold up my finger to Addy, who's bouncing impatiently in my bedroom door. The bedroom that I've not spent one night in for the past three weeks.

"I have reason to be." His smoky voice is full of sex and sin and promise. Promises he can, and will, deliver on. And I look forward to enjoying each and every moment of the wickedness he'll lavish on my body tomorrow night when he gets home from his meeting. I have a surprise planned that will blow his mind.

"And what are you going to sex me into agreeing to this time?" I cajole.

"Come on," Addy whispers. "I can't be late to my own party." I nod my head that I've heard, but I can't seem to make myself end this conversation. I want to celebrate Addy's twenty-eighth birthday with her, but I also want to be in Gray's arms, doing normal couple things, like watching TV or reading a book. I crave normal, and these past few weeks we've easily fallen back into our same routine, only this time it's more intense. And definitely more passionate.

I'm so caught up in Addy talking in my other ear that I almost don't hear Gray's response. But the minute his words register, I freeze. My lungs stop working and I don't know how long I go without taking a full breath.

"What did you say?" Because as I replay his words, I'm not at all certain I heard them correctly. I *couldn't* have.

"You heard me, angel."

"Gray—"

"Stop. We're not going to have this conversation a thousand miles apart, but I mean it,

216

Livvy. Now, go have fun with your friends. I can practically hear Addy bouncing on the floor. I love you, angel."

"I love you, too," I manage to say. I drop the phone into my lap and stare straight ahead, Gray's words tumbling around and around in my head. Words I can't believe he really meant, but I also know Gray. He doesn't say things he doesn't mean.

"What kind of sexual haze did he put you in this time?" She shakes my shoulders. "Wow, it must have been really good."

"It was," I mumble.

"Come on, let's go. Kam's in the car downstairs waiting."

"Yeah, let me just grab my purse." And give me a couple of minutes to pull my shit together. I look down at my hands. They're trembling.

"Okay, but I'm going down. She's got a bottle of champagne already open and I can hear the bubbles seducing me all the way up here!"

She bounded out, none the wiser of the turmoil my addled brain was now in. I spend a couple of minutes in the bathroom, getting myself together before heading down to meet my friends. I decided to put Gray's words away for the evening and revisit them tomorrow with a clearer head.

Unfortunately, that's easier said than done.

Chapter 32

Livia

Kam had reserved a small private room at the back of this upscale club and it's filled to the brim with family and friends of Addy's. The doors are open and people are milling about between the room and the club, which is already hopping for a Thursday night. And I had the unfortunate luck to run into John, who Kam invited for some reason. Apparently the asshole decided that since he couldn't have me, he'd settle for Kam. And believe me when I say that when I get a moment alone with her, I'll make sure she knows what a d-bag he is. I have yet to see Kam fall for a guy, but I certainly don't want her first time to be with this vag-sniffer, no matter how good-looking he is.

"How have you been, Livvy?" a deep voice asks as I'm helping myself to a second piece of cake. It's stuffed with some sweet decadent filling that I can't seem to get enough of and I don't care if it just ends up on my thighs. It's too good to pass up.

"It's Livia, and I'm good. Thanks." I don't even turn to look at the intruder because I know exactly whose brown eyes I'll be staring into.

"My bad. I heard Gray call you Livvy at dinner." *Gray?* Like he knows Gray well enough to be on a first name basis. This guy is such a loser.

I spin on my heels and John's standing so close, my plate hits his chest and my cake goes flying. "Oh my God, I'm so sorry." He grabs a napkin from the table, and pulls at my blouse, smearing the frosting that's splattered on me.

"Stop," I spit. "You're making it worse." And this feels too intimate. Having another man's hands anywhere near me just feels wrong.

"Sorry," he mumbles. I push my way past him and through the club to the bathroom. A few minutes later, with the blue stain mostly gone, and now sporting a giant wet spot on my pink shirt, I'm making my way back to the party when I spot him.

The stalker.

Only he's not looking at me. He's looking at John, and by the thin line his lips are drawn into he seems mighty pissed. I'm conflicted. I feel panicked, but a strange sense of relief at the same time. I haven't seen him since that day at the café, but I've still felt his presence occasionally. And by the way he's staring John down like he wants to cut off his dick, I get the feeling he's protecting me, which is the relief part. But I don't know why, which has my heart racing and my blood running cold. Has Gray hired this man to keep an eye on me? If so, why? Is he suspicious?

I return to the party, making it a point not to acknowledge the man watching me. Watching *out* for me...whatever. I try to stay out of his line of sight, hiding in the back corner of the room. I also make it a point to stay as far away from John as I can, which doesn't seem too hard since he'll talk to anything with cleavage.

"Ah! I love this song!" Addy screams as the new funky Bruno Mars tune blares through the speakers. "Alright ladies, time to shake some ass," Addy announces, her words slurring together a bit.

"Oh, not tonight, Addy." The last thing I want to do is put myself on display with my unknown protector watching every move I make. Besides, I can't seem to concentrate on much of anything besides Gray's emphatic response to my question earlier.

"And what are you going to sex me into agreeing to this time?"

"Making you my wife."

"Making you my wife."

My wife.

Wife.

Wife.

"Sorry, chica. Not taking no for an answer. It's my birthday, which means you have to do what I want." Addy grabs one hand and Kam the other and between the two of them, they drag me practically kicking and screaming to the dance floor.

But once there, the infectious smile that Addy has on her drunken face spreads to mine, and I end up spending the next hour dancing with two of my favorite people in the whole world. My friends love me, flaws and all. Secrets and everything. And I feel blessed.

"Hey, looks like you have a couple of admirers, babe. And one of them looks like he wants to eat you up." Kam whisper-yells in my ear so she can be heard over the blaring music.

220

I shouldn't turn, but I can't help myself. I see my unconventional stalker, as I suspected I would, but then my eyes lock onto the familiar hazel ones of the man leaning against the bar next to him—eyes I haven't seen for two years—and it makes my knees almost buckle. I feel a rush of heat so potent, I nearly melt on the spot.

Those eyes.

That earlier sense of relief I had disappears quicker than my father's paycheck used to. Because now I know it wasn't Gray that sent this man.

It was Grant.

The last words he had said to me before he left me alone in this city came rushing back, as if he'd spoken them only yesterday.

"Will I see you again?" Grant is the only steady thing I've been able to rely on for years and he's leaving me. Alone. I want to cry, but I don't dare let myself because I know I won't be able to stop.

"No, baby. You need to get away from everything and everyone, including me. If you see me again, it means you're in danger."

Before I can speak, he grabs my face, and he doesn't just kiss me, he devours me like he's trying to memorize how my lips feel underneath his, just as I'm doing. He moans into my mouth, pulling me closer. I feel his stiff erection prodding my stomach and God help me, I want him. I've wanted this for months, but neither of us would give in to our desires. If Peter ever found out, he would have killed us both. As quickly as his mouth was on mine, it wasn't, and then I'm watching him walk away without so much as a backward glance or a way to contact him.

221

So if Grant is here, it means only one thing. That I haven't escaped my past, as I'd thought. No. My past was now staring me directly in the face and I don't mistake the worry and concern I see. And the only way Grant would be here, watching me, was if something was terribly wrong.

Chapter 33

Livia

"I have to go," I mumble, making a beeline for Grant, who has now pushed himself off the counter and is heading in my direction. Our eyes haven't left the other's. It makes my heart flutter and I'm instantly disgusted with myself for feeling even a twinge of anything for another man.

Addy grabs my arm, stopping me. "Livia, what's going on?" she asks, in a worried voice, alternating between Grant and me.

"Nothing." I try to move forward, but the grip she now has on me is almost painful. "Addy, it's okay." I look at her, pleading to let me go and not ask any more questions. She knows this look well.

"Okay, fine, but if you don't come home tonight, I'm calling the cops." She finally releases her kung-fu grip.

"For god's sake, I'm fine. Grant won't hurt me." And that's true. It's not Grant that will hurt me, but some other unknown enemy. Apparently Grant has gone to very great lengths to protect me since he's had someone following me for a while.

"Grant?" Her brows draw together in confusion, eyes flitting back and forth between us. Grant turns his attention to Addy and you'd have to be blind not to notice that he's looking at her like she's prey.

223

I smile at my overprotective friend. "I need to go." I give her and Kam a quick hug. "I'll be leaving with Grant, and don't worry, Addy, I'll be home tonight. He's just a friend, that's all." *A friend that you were once attracted to*, my traitorous lady parts remind me.

When I reach the edge of the dance floor, Grant is waiting for me. Now that I'm finally in front of him, I don't know what to do. It feels like a betrayal to Gray to hug him, but it feels equally wrong not to embrace the person who means so much to me and to whom I owe my life. But in the end I don't have to decide because suddenly I'm wrapped in his strong arms and can do nothing but hang on while he drinks me in. His scent wraps around me and it's so comforting, it's unnerving.

I pull away and he places a lingering kiss on my forehead.

"Your friends?" He nods to the dance floor where Addy and Kamryn are watching us with keen interest.

"Yes. Addy and Kamryn."

"Addy the brunette?" he asks, his gaze finding her again.

"Yes."

He acts like he doesn't know her, which confuses me because he found her in the first place. To this day I'm not sure how he knew about her or that she was looking for a roommate, but in the end, it worked out and we are the best of friends. She wasn't there when he helped me move in, but still. I never asked, because quite frankly I didn't want to know, but all that's quickly forgotten when he says those four dreaded words that never lead to anything good.

"We need to talk." Entwining our hands together, he pulls me through the throng until we reach the bar and the man that's been following me. "Thanks, man. I'll be in touch," he addresses my stalker, pulling me toward the exit without so much as an introduction.

"Grant, what's going on?" I ask as he drags me quickly down the sidewalk and around the corner. Even though my mind is racing and I'm having a mini meltdown as to why he's here, I can't help but appreciate how very good he looks in his tight, well-worn blue jeans, fitted tee and black combat boots. Except that his hair is a little shorter, he looks exactly as I remember him.

"Not here, Livia." He walks at a clipped pace until we reach a nondescript, dark blue Kia Rio another block and a half away. It's clearly a rental, as the Grant I knew would never drive such a car. He'd be on his bike. That, and the Hertz receipt I see sitting on the console are dead giveaways.

Ever the gentleman, he opens the passenger door and waves me in. I huff and comply, my short black dress riding up my bare thighs as I make my way into the small interior. Grant notices and even in the low light, I see his eyes darken. When I hear him curse under his breath, I quickly pull it down as far as it will go—which isn't far—not wanting to give him the wrong idea.

Quickly he's settled and we're on our way. Grant clearly remembers the way to my apartment;

because I'm not giving directions and he's not asking.

"Are you going to tell me what the hell you're doing here and why you've had someone following me?" Now that the shock of seeing Grant has worn off, I'm suddenly starting to panic. I feel my throat swell and my lungs constrict. One, two, three, four, five. In, out. In, out. Breathe, Livia. Breathe. I take in slow, raspy gulps of air, trying to calm myself.

"Baby, are you okay?" Grant places his hand over mine and squeezes. I calm slightly, but his endearment feels wrong. I can't let him think there is something more here than friendship. I love Gray with every fiber of my being and nothing will ever change that.

"Grant—" I start, but he interrupts.

"It's okay." He releases my hand and I feel oddly bereft. I hate myself. Grant is a friend and I do love him. One of the closest that I have. *Had*. I reach over and take his hand back in mine. He looks over and smiles, and suddenly an intense calmness come over me.

"I missed you," I say. It's true. I've missed Grant something fierce and I didn't realize exactly how much until just now.

"Me too," he replies softly, with a soft squeeze of his fingers.

"Are you going to tell me what's happening?"

"When we get to your place. Will we be alone?"

"Why?" I ask, tentatively. I trust Grant with my life, but I don't want to put either of us into an awkward position by having to turn down his advances, because I can clearly see his want for me flashing like a neon sign.

He turns his head and smirks. I may be in love with Gray, but even I am not immune to Grant's charms. "Just to talk, baby. Nothing else."

I sigh in relief. "Yes, it's still just Addy and me, and that was her party we just left." And suddenly I remembered that I didn't bring my purse, which means I don't have my phone or my keys. I groan and throw my head back against the headrest. Gray will be freaking out if I don't call him soon because it's already close to eleven. And we won't be able to get into our apartment until Addy gets back. *Shit.*

"What is it?"

"I forgot my purse. Which has my keys. And my phone."

"Don't worry." He doesn't elaborate and I don't ask. I know Grant has a sordid background since he was mixed up with Peter, but we've never talked about it.

"I need my phone."

"Here, use mine." He pulls it out and hands it to me. I can't call Gray from another man's phone. There will be too many questions. Questions that I simply cannot answer. So instead, I dial Addy's number and luckily she answers. It's noisy and I can barely hear her.

"Addy, it's Livia," I yell.

"Are you okay?" She sounds panicked and I hear her yelling for Kam.

"For god's sake, I'm fine. I just forgot my purse. Can you grab it when you come home? I need to call Gray. He'll be worried." Grant stiffens beside me and releases my hand at the mention of Gray's name. I look over at his handsome profile and notice his jaw ticking. The tension in the car suddenly feels so thick, it's cloying. "Thanks, babe. See you in a bit," I tell Addy as I hang up. I'm confused at Grant's reaction, but by the way he's working his jaw, I think it's best not to ask.

"We only have about a half hour. She insists on coming home to save me from the Big Bad Wolf," I laugh, only half kidding.

"She's naïve," he mumbles.

The rest of the ride is tense and quiet and I don't push for answers like I want. The twenty-minute drive is one of the longest I've taken and by the time we reach my apartment, I've conjured up every single horrific scenario I can possibly think of, each one worse than the one I'd made up before. When we finally get out of the car, I think I've convinced myself Peter has risen from the dead and wants me back.

When we get to my apartment door, Grant pulls out a couple of screwdriver-looking things, sticks them in the lock and begins twisting them. Within seconds, I hear the lock turn. He does the same thing with the deadbolt and in less than thirty seconds, we're in. I look at him and he silently dares to me ask, which I don't.

Once inside, I head for the kitchen, pulling out a bottle of white wine from the fridge. For a woman who rarely drinks, I feel like that's all I've been doing these past few weeks. "Want a glass?" I ask Grant.

"No." He's leaning against the kitchen counter, arms crossed, watching every move I make and it's starting to make me uncomfortable. I feel like he's waiting to drop a Hiroshima bomb on me that will scatter my molecules to the wind and I'll be forever lost. After I pour a healthy glass for me, I turn to him.

"Stop stalling. Tell me why you're here." I'm losing the battle against the water works and my eyes tear up involuntarily.

"I think you need to sit down." There is concern and something else I can't place in his voice.

"No. I don't want to sit. Just tell me why the hell you're here." *And then fix it so I can go back to my fairytale life with Gray.*

Reaching out, he takes my free hand in his and leads me to the couch. He sits me down, taking a seat on the coffee table facing me. Our knees touch and he hasn't let go of my hand. I know this ritual well. He's grounding me. He's making sure I don't break apart into a million pieces right before his eyes. He's done this a hundred times before. *God, this is going to be bad.* I just couldn't possibly have predicted how cruel the universe would be to me. Again.

"A video surfaced a few weeks ago."

Chapter 34

Gray

It's nearly midnight and I haven't heard from Livvy yet. I've tried her twice, but my calls just go to voice mail. We texted a few times earlier in the evening, but I haven't heard from her for nearly two hours and I'm trying not to worry. I'm sure she's just on the dance floor having fun with her friends and I don't want to seem like a controlling, possessive boyfriend who can't let his woman out for a night of fun.

Never mind the fact that's exactly what you are, asshole.

I take another swig of my single-malt bourbon to chase away my anxiety. I trust Livvy. It's the rest of the entire male population I don't trust. Livvy's an extremely beautiful and desirable woman, even if she doesn't think so, and I know every heterosexual man at that bar will be salivating over her. When she described, in detail, what she was wearing, I begged her to put on a sack, or sweatpants, but she scoffed, saying no one would pay her a lick of attention when she was with Addy and Kamryn. They were both beautiful in their own right, but they didn't hold a candle to my Livvy.

To take my mind off the fact that my beautiful woman is a half a country away, and probably being eye-fucked by every male within a twenty-yard radius, I turn my attention back to the latest report that Livvy put together in her research of the HMT personnel. She's done a great job these past few weeks at organizing and combing through the inordinate amount of documentation and data that Camille pulled together for me, but so far we've come up with nothing that points to a leak inside that organization. But I know it's there, and I will find it...eventually.

I'm about half way through the report when my phone rings and I pick it up without looking at the caller ID, fully expecting it to be Livvy. Only the female voice that grates through the speaker is not Livvy.

"Gray, it's Lena."

Christ.

I sigh loudly, hoping she'll hear and take a fucking hint. "What do you want, Lena?"

"I wanted to talk. You've not answered any of my calls or texts." *Then get a clue, you stupid psycho stalker.*

"It's over, Lena. I'm not sure what there is to talk about." I stand and walk to the mini bar to pour myself another two fingers of the caramel liquor. I'm going to need it for this conversation because as much as I want to, hanging up on her just isn't the right thing to do. Maybe this will give her the closure she needs and she will leave me the fuck alone.

"It's not over for me," she says softly. Her sniffles make my eyes roll. *For the love of all that's holy.* Yes, it's challenging to find a mentally stable, somewhat intelligent, attractive woman who wants

231

a no-strings relationship. And clearly Lena falls into the mentally *unstable* category.

Fuck me.

"I'm not sure what you want me to say, Lena. I was up front with you from the very beginning. I told you it was just physical and that I was emotionally unavailable." Because Livvy has my heart now and always.

"I love you, Gray." I sigh heavily, throwing back the entire glass of bourbon in one swallow. The burn feels good.

"Lena, listen to me and listen good. You don't love me. We fucked. That's it. Don't make this into something it's not. And please don't call me again. You need to move on."

I hang up without waiting for a response and flop down onto the bed, my head turning to look at the digital clock. *12:06 a.m.* Asher and I have a 6:30 breakfast meeting with the CEO of Hammond Consulting, a small financial consulting group we're interested in buying. I should be sleeping, but I can't. Not without making sure Livvy is okay. I'm just picking up the phone to call her again when it rings.

Livvy.

"Angel, it's late. Everything okay?"

"Y-yes. Why wouldn't it be?" She's lying. I can tell by the wobble in her voice. She is not okay in the least.

"Livvy, what's wrong."

"Nothing." I sit in silence, waiting for her to tell me. To trust me. "I just got into a fight with Addy, that's all." I don't know much about Addy, but I don't think that's what's wrong. Disappointment rushes through me hard.

"I'm sorry, baby. I'm sure you'll kiss and make up."

"I'm tired, Gray. Do you mind if we just talk about this tomorrow?"

"Are you sure that's all that's wrong, angel?" *Please tell me the truth.*

She sighs, responding quietly. "I miss you, Gray. I wish you were here." Her voice sounds teary, like she's been crying. I ache with the need to hold her. To comfort her. To fuck her into confiding in me.

"I wish you were in my bed."

"So do I," she whispered.

We were silent for what seemed like several minutes before she spoke again. "Gray?"

"Yes, angel," I reply softly.

"Will you stay on the phone with me until I fall asleep?"

"I'd do anything for you, Livvy. Anything. I love you."

"I love you, too."

About thirty minutes later I hear soft, even breathing and I know she's finally asleep, but I'm loath to hang up, so I don't. I put my phone on speaker, lay it down on the pillow next to me, and fall asleep to the quiet sounds of the woman who has me firmly by the balls. And I've made my peace with that.

Chapter 35

Livia

I made Grant leave before I called Gray last night. I just couldn't have another man here while I talked to him. I needed Gray. I needed him with a desperation I hadn't felt in a very long time. I wanted his arms around me, protecting me from everything and everyone.

I almost spilled the entire sordid story over the phone last night. My walls were crumbling in around me and he was my only reinforcement. He was the only thing that could possibly save me. Even from myself. It was a little alarming at how much I'd come to depend on him because the thought of not having him in my life again did things to my mind and body I can't even describe. Sheer panic didn't even come close to defining how I felt if I had to live without him again.

Grant would tell me very little about the video, but I knew what was on it. I shouldn't be shocked at anything Peter did, but once again I find myself being surprised. I had no idea he'd ever videotaped the depraved things he did to me. While Grant told me he's pulled all copies from the world wide web or the cloud or whatever mystical, magical playground the Internet has become, and programmed an alert to pop if it resurfaces, he hasn't yet validated the source of the leak. But that's not why I was panicking. It's one thing to *tell* someone your deepest, darkest, most shameful secrets. It's another thing entirely to have them personally *witness* it. If Gray ever saw that video...

"A video surfaced about a month ago."

My blood froze and I could only shake my head in denial. I didn't understand this. Any of this.

"I've shut it down, but I'm working to track the source. I'll fix this. I promise."

"Why? I don't understand," I whisper. Confusion swirls like a black cloud of smoke in my head. Why would someone do this and why now? Two fucking years later? Why can't they just let me be? I feel like Peter is reaching beyond the grave, haunting me, taunting me, intent on ruining my life forever.

"I don't either, baby."

"Am I in danger? Is that why you have someone watching me?"

"I don't think so, but one can never be too sure when dealing with psychotic bastards." He's now taken the wine and placed it on the table, holding both of my hands. "Look at me."

I do.

"I'll take care of this." I believe him.

"Why are you helping me, Grant? Why have you always helped me?"

He breaks our gazes, looking down. When he looks back up, my breath catches. "Why do you think, Livia?"

Now it's my turn to look away. I knew Grant cared for me, but... His finger hooks under my chin, lifting it.

"He's the one, isn't he?" He doesn't say Gray's name. He doesn't need to.

"Yes."

His lips thin and he nods. "Does he know?"

I shake my head.

Then he surprises me by leaning forward to place a soft kiss on my lips and it feels like goodbye. "I'll fix this for you, Livia. I'll make sure he doesn't see it."

"Thank you," I choke through the lump in my throat. Tears stream unbidden down my face and my nose is starting to run, but he doesn't care. He moves to the couch and holds me tight, and I shouldn't, but I let him.

"Tell me about him," he says softly when my tears dry up.

So I do. It feels good to finally tell another person about my history with the love of my life, even if it feels wrong that that person happens to be the only other man that I've ever cared about.

My phone rings, bringing me back from the conversation I had last night with Grant. He told me he'd be in touch, but also gave me his number in case I needed to reach him, and for that, I was grateful. It felt comforting to call him if I needed to.

Before I answer the phone, now on its third ring, I do what I've always done to deal with my overload of shit. I compartmentalize. So I shove this new problem in a fresh box and I shut the lid. My boxes are stacked high and my compartments are getting cramped. I pray Grant can fix this before it does any damage because I'm worried if he doesn't, I won't have any space left when I really need it.

I finally answer, surprised to see the caller is Gray. "Hi."

"Hi, angel. Feel better this morning?" I cringe at his reminder of my lie last night but warm at the endearment. I missed his arms around me, and the comfort of his presence when I tossed and turned in my sleep.

"Yes. It's all good. Why are you calling? I thought you were supposed to be in a meeting?"

"I was, but we ended early. I'm catching an earlier flight, so I'll be home by late afternoon now." His voice dropped low at the end of his sentence.

"That sounds promising," I tease. I glance around the office to be sure no one is eavesdropping, but I'm all alone.

"I want you waiting for me at my apartment by four." Those words send fire between my legs and make my nipples tingle. Boy, oh boy, does he have a surprise in store when he walks through his door today.

"Well, I don't know. That would mean leaving work early and my boss is kind of a hard ass."

"Really? He has a hard ass, do you say?"

Laughing, I answer, "Yes, the hardest, tightest set of buns I've ever had the pleasure of feeling underneath my lips. Or tongue."

"Jesus Christ, Livvy," he groans. "Do you know how uncomfortable a two-hour flight with a raging hard-on is going to be? Not to mention how many flight attendants I'm going to scare."

I stifle my laugh. "Hurry home," I say breathlessly, ending the call.

The rest of the day drags and finally it's three o'clock. I'm packing up my stuff to leave when Gray's line rings. I debate on whether to answer or let it roll to voice mail, but decide to do my job. "Gray Colloway's office."

"Is Gray available?" a sultry feminine voice purrs. Whoever she is, I don't like her. The familiar way Gray's name rolls off her tongue makes me burn with jealousy.

"I'm afraid he's not in today. May I take a message?" I'll be damned if I'm going to offer voice mail. I want to see what this the woman with the sex kitten voice wants.

"Tell him Lena called and that I need to speak with him urgently."

"Of course," I respond so sweetly my teeth ache. "Can I get your number, please?"

"Oh, he has my number, darling." Then she hangs up, leaving me to stare blankly at the phone in my hand, the dial tone mocking me from the other side.

Guess what, darling? That's one message that won't get delivered.

Chapter 36

Gray

My flight was delayed half an hour and traffic was backed up for miles due to a six-car pileup on I90. It's after five and I should have been home an hour ago. I texted Livvy that I'd be late, but never received a reply. My cock aches with the desire to release deep inside of her. I have this raging, primal need to taste and touch every inch of her milky skin and stake my claim on her. Make sure she knows she belongs to me, and no other. It's archaic and not at all necessary, but I can't shake the violent urge I feel to do it anyway.

I open my apartment door expecting Livvy to greet me, but the only thing that does is the scent of vanilla, sultry music and candlelight. I shut the door, leaving my suitcase by it and take a few steps inside, but freeze at the vision that greets me from the informal dining room.

Fuck. Me. My cock jumps.

A completely nude and blindfolded Livvy is spread out on my table. Her hands are crossed at the wrists and placed gracefully above her head; one slender ankle positioned delicately over the other. Her back is slightly arched, her glossy red lips parted like she's already in the throes of ecstasy, and the shadows from the candles surrounding her dance like entwined lovers over her flushed skin.

Two flutes of bubbling champagne sit at the head of the table, waiting to be enjoyed.

I stand there for what seems like an eternity drinking her in. She's so goddamned beautiful, I'm struggling to breathe. Every man's fantasy come to life, but she's all mine. She's my everything.

My life.

My breath.

My very fucking sustenance.

My cock has never been so hard.

"Christ, Livvy. You're a goddess," I finally manage to murmur as I walk the length of the table and slowly, deliberately drag a finger lightly from her toes all the way to her fingertips. Her breath hitches and I watch as goose bumps break out along the path I've taken. I walk around the other side, repeating the same process; this time edging closer to the parts of her I want my hands and mouth on most.

On my way back down, I trace her angel wings, which still makes my gut twist each time I see them. I'd be lying if I denied the fact that having a part of me etched on her skin forever isn't ego boosting.

"Gray—" Her voice is thick with desire and she's on the verge of begging already, but I plan to stretch this out as long as I can before I sink between her thighs. I just don't know how long I'll be able to hold out. Her body is like a siren's song. I feel the sensual spell she's weaving over me, and I want to succumb.

"Shhh, angel. Don't move. Don't speak," I command softly. This is my show now. I'll be directing every movement, every shudder, every moan. Unable to resist, I lean down and suck a beaded nipple between my lips. She exhales on a rush, but other than arching her back further, she doesn't move and she doesn't talk. "Very good, baby."

I remove the candles from the table because while they create nice ambiance, I don't need one dropping to the floor and starting the carpet on fire when I'm fucking her raw like an animal. I leave the champagne because I plan to use that very shortly.

The next sentence comes out gritty and rough, my longing for her unable to be contained. "I want to do very naughty things to you, Livvy." Even in the low light, I watch her skin flush and her chest expand with shallow breaths at my promise. I know how much she craves for me make good on those wicked things.

"Open your legs." She immediately complies, knees falling to the sides and my eyes are glued to her slickness. Her body weeps for me already. My heavy cock pounds, insistent on being freed from its confines so it can be one with her, but I make him wait. The rest of me wants to enjoy her first. Jesus, I want to bury my face in her pussy and spend days enjoying the taste of her on my tongue as I repeatedly make her come. I run two thick fingers between her dripping folds, gathering her juices.

"Taste your need for me." I run a wet finger over her parted lips and inside her eager mouth, where she does exactly as I demand and if possible, I swell even more. Our lovemaking to this point has run the gamut...frenzied, rough, sweet, sensual and

241

everywhere in between. But this…this complete submission from Livvy is what I've craved the most. I've needed it more than I even realized. And now I'm trying to convince myself to take it slow when all I really want to do is ram my cock home and fuck her hard until she agrees to marry me.

I walk around to the front of the table and grab the glass of sparkling wine. "I'm going to play your body until it sings for me," I whisper against the shell of her ear before taking a drink, savoring its sweetness on my tongue. Two of my favorite flavors are right here in front of me. Mine for the taking. "Do you want to know how the rest of this night will go?" I continue softly.

"Yes," she breathes.

I quickly divest my clothes and take her mouth in a bruising, claiming kiss. I savor her taste, her texture. *Her.* I nip her earlobe, laving the hurt when she gasps. As I work my lips slowly down her body, I whisper each wicked act against her pebbled flesh. Minutes later when I reach her toes, I suck one into my mouth, mesmerized by the look of rapture on her face. "I will have you in every way possible tonight, Livvy."

She groans and her hips involuntarily shift. And while I want her at my mercy, suddenly I don't want her eyes hidden beneath the black fabric. I need to see them cloud with lust and roll back in utter euphoria with everything I'm about to do to her. "Oh God. Gray, do something. Please," she pleads. It makes me rock hard when she aches so badly she can do nothing but beg for me and for the pleasures she knows only I can lavish.

I remove the blindfold, softly kissing each one of her eyelids before she opens them. I'm entranced by her and it takes all of my willpower to continue down the path I have laid out in my mind, because all I want to do is pull her up and slam her against the closest wall while I impale her on my shaft.

Instead, I rise and take another sip of the champagne, but rather than swallowing, I wind my arms underneath her thighs, pull her to my mouth and latch onto her already hard clit. I let the bubbles fizz around her sensitive flesh before I swallow. She cries out, pushing her pelvis further into my face. I suck her with fervor until she explodes in my arms, my name rolling off her tongue like a prayer. I don't stop until the shudders subside and she releases the vice grip her legs have on my head.

Scooping her up in my arms, I ravage her mouth for several minutes like a starved man before I can't stand not being inside her a second longer. I turn her around and gently push her torso down on the table.

"Arms above your head, hands flat on the table, Livvy."

"Gray, please. I ache."

I want to inhale her. Own her. Crawl inside her and never come up for air. My body is a live wire, every nerve ending a tiny spark that fires with each brush of her flesh on mine.

"Let me enjoy this gorgeous view first," I reply roughly, caressing her flawless porcelain skin, starting at the top of her spine. Bending down, I run my tongue between the crack of her ass, circling her rosette, and the long moan she lets out breaks the

243

thin thread of restraint I've been hanging onto since the second I walked into my apartment. I stand, find her entrance and slam home in one hard thrust. She feels so fucking good I almost come instantly. I have to bite the inside of my lip to redirect my mind from anything else besides coating her with my seed prematurely.

"You're a fucking vision," I rasp, withdrawing almost all the way before pressing into her again, slowly this time. I watch my cock, slick with her juices, sink into heaven and close my eyes in pure ecstasy. Nothing in my life will ever feel as good as this. I slowly push into her again and again until she begs for more.

"Harder. Harder, Gray."

I lean down and gently bite her shoulder, whispering, "No, angel. I'm going to make you come undone. Mindless with desire."

"I am," she pants. "I already am." She reaches around to grab my ass, trying to make me move faster. I move them back.

"Don't move," I growl. Ecstasy calls us, but I deny it. *Not yet.*

Holding her in place, I savor our joined flesh as I thrust slowly, intent on setting my own pace. But all too soon pure euphoria engulfs every cell in my body and I can't hold back any longer. As her walls pulse, I stand, tighten my grip on her hips and drive harder and rougher, wringing every morsel and shred of rapture from Livvy's lips before we both fly apart. My apartment fills with our cries of passion and professions of love.

Minutes later, I'm still inside her heat, our breathing finally evening out. My legs feel like Jell-O and my body is spent, but I've never felt more content in my life. I'm going to marry this woman. And if I have my way, it will be soon.

Chapter 37

Livia

Strong, comforting arms hold me and I lay quietly, relishing every single body part that's still sore and tingling. I slowly replay each sinful moment on the table, on the couch, in the shower, against the wall. The way I sucked him off in front of his full-length mirror was one of the most erotic things I have ever done. The ecstasy that pinched his face and every corded muscle while he held my hair to guide himself in and out of my mouth was a sight that will be forever branded into my memory.

Gray gave me so many orgasms I lost count. I remember the exact whispered words when I told him I couldn't take any more. *"I've had years to learn your body like only I can. I know your every moan, your every tremble, every hitch of your breath, and what each means. I know when you've had enough and you aren't even close, angel."* The words still send shivers down my spine.

His soft snore indicates he's still in a deep sleep and while I have to use the bathroom, I don't dare move. I can't. I'm soaking in the feeling of his body underneath mine, and the scent of sex that still permeates the air all around us. It's only eight a.m. and I should still be tired, but I'm not. My body hums like low volt electricity runs just beneath the skin.

I drink in his beautiful face while he's so tranquil. He looks younger in sleep. His thick, inky lashes lay gently on the top of his cheeks. I always wondered why some men get blessed with lashes that women pay to duplicate. Of course, I could say that about every feature on Gray's face. His full, pink lips are perfect and I love to run my tongue along the dip at the top. Sharp, angular cheekbones are high and sculpted. And his eyes. His eyes are simply enthralling. Whenever they latch onto mine, they trap me in their depths and I never want to leave. I clearly hear every word he silently speaks with them. It's like we have our own secret, wordless language.

The urge to spill my past was on the tip of my tongue all night, but it kept getting pushed back inside with each round of new pleasure he'd give me. I was greedy. I didn't want it end. And I knew with my confession it would. By the time neither of us could take any more, shortly after three, I fell asleep in his arms within seconds. I woke up in exactly the same position.

My mind is still in a sexual haze, remembering how many times and ways we made love. Gray was true to his whispered promises earlier. He always is. It was almost as if we were trying to soak in as much of each other as possible because it would be our last night together.

How prophetic.

Chapter 38

Gray

"Angel, let me come take care of you," I urge.

"No. I look like death warmed over, and I don't want you to get sick." She sounds weak and tired.

"I'm afraid it's too late for that. We had our tongues in almost every body part possible last night, so if you're sick, I'm already infected. Let me come over and rub your back."

Livvy had spent most of the day throwing up, convinced she had gotten the flu from Addy, who was sick with it last week. She insisted she go home to recuperate. I'd vehemently disagreed, but lost the battle. As her future husband, it's my job to take care of her in sickness and health and I told her as much. Then she promptly ran into the bathroom and dry heaved because there was nothing left in her stomach.

"I'll be fine. I think maybe you wore me out last night and my defenses are weakened."

I smile. "Exactly how weakened are they?" I ask in a low voice. *Weak enough to agree to marry me if I ask? Weak enough to tell me why you left?*

She chuckles lightly but takes a few moments to respond. When she does, I suck in a breath. "Pretty weak."

"Livvy..." It's one word, but it says so much. Pleads for everything she's been denying me. Answers.

The silence is deafening. Will she tell me anything? Will she finally trust me with the truth? Do I really want to know?

"I'm sorry I hurt you, Gray," she says quietly.

Yeah, I'm sorry too. "Will you ever tell me why?" Now that she's opened this can of worms I can't stop myself from asking. It's been close to a month since I hired Robert Townley. The only time I've heard from him was four days ago, and it was short and sweet. *"Have a lead I'm following."*

"I...I want to. I just don't know if I can."

I sigh and lean back against the headboard of my bed. "This secret, whatever it is, is going to eat away at us until there's nothing left." I don't want to put a voice to it because it makes it too real, but I have no other choice. No matter how bad this is, she needs to tell me if we have any chance of making it.

"I know," she whispers.

"Dammit, Livia. I want to marry you, have kids with you and grow old with you. I want to just simply accept that you're back in my life, but the truth is, I don't know when you're going to pick up and walk back out of it again without a goddamn word, and I'm telling you right now, that will annihilate me."

"I won't. I swear it. I'm not going anywhere, Gray. I love you."

The words were out of my mouth before I could stop them. "You loved me before."

She sucked in a sharp breath. "I never stopped loving you. I just...had to go away for a while."

"Why? Tell me why."

"Gray, please. Give me some time," she pleads. And it just makes me angry, this lack of trust she has in me. In *us*. We've been back together for a month and not one word. It's always the elephant in the room, except either the room is shrinking or that big, fat, grey animal is getting bigger because it's getting to the point where it can no longer be ignored. My resentment is burning hot again and it's clear that poisonous cloud has completely escaped its confines and I don't know if I can shove it back in.

"Time? You've had five years, Livvy. Five years to contact me and put this to rest, but you didn't. And we wouldn't even be together if I wasn't the one to pursue you. *Again*." And if I'm honest, that's probably what hurts the most.

"I—"

"You know what, you should get some rest. We'll talk about this another time."

"Gray—"

"I love you, Livvy." And I hang up before she has a chance to respond or I say something I'll truly regret. Words are powerful weapons, once spoken you can't take them back and it's impossible to sidestep the venom they spew. I want my forever with Livvy and if I start spouting off words that come from a place of hurt, I know I'll just make things worse.

For the next few hours, I pour myself into work and I try to forget it all. The hurt. The pain. The betrayal. I try to forget the days that I drank myself into a stupor to numb the bone-deep agony. I try to convince myself it's probably a good thing she went back home tonight, but I never was a very good liar. Even as angry and hurt as I am, I still want her by my side. And what kind of fool or sucker does that make me? I'm an addict and Livvy is my drug of choice, no matter how harmful she may be for me.

Finally at midnight, I'm exhausted. I've fallen asleep sitting up twice already. I'm just turning off my reading lamp when I get a text and as I read it, I realize all the euphemisms and idioms created about skeletons in the closet are true. That door is better left closed. With a fucking industrial sized padlock so thick there's no way to ever pry it open.

Seconds, minutes, hours tick by as I stare at the three words that send my entire world spinning and crashing to the ground once again, destroying every shred of trust I had foolishly and carelessly rebuilt with Livvy.

These would be the words to end us and now it's crystal clear to me why she kept her silence. She betrayed me in the worst possible way.

"She was married."

Chapter 39

Livia

It's Monday morning and I haven't heard from Gray since we got into an argument and he hung up on me Saturday night. I tried calling him several times yesterday, but my calls went to voice mail and my texts went unanswered. I considered taking the train into the city, showing up unannounced at his apartment but decided against it. And frankly, I was being a chicken because I knew if I showed up at his place, I wouldn't be able to avoid it any longer. But I also know I *can't* wait any longer before telling him every despicable detail. My stomach is twisted into a million knots that I have no hope of unwinding at the thought of him knowing my deepest shame.

My fairytale is at its end, only in this final chapter, I'm no longer the princess that the prince will woo, and we won't ride off into the sunset and live happily ever after. No. I'm the witch, the sorceress, the bad guy. And I'll single-handedly deliver the poison straight to the prince's heart. The poison which will effectively kill his love for me. In this sad and imperfect ending, no one survives unscathed.

Knowing what fate has in store for me, in between bouts of throwing up yesterday, I cried. I sobbed. I ached. Addy comforted me, not knowing what was wrong. She never once asked, never cajoled. She was just there for me. And when I asked her why, she simply said because she's my friend and that's what friends do.

I'm still not feeling much better this morning, but managed to drag my ass into work. It's now eight-thirty and I haven't heard from Gray. He's already missed two meetings and I've called him twice. I'm starting to get a very bad feeling that I may have waited too long or pushed him too far. No matter how upset he is with me, Gray not showing up to work is not like him. He's dedicated and devoted to his company. I'm getting very worried, so I do the only thing I can.

He answers on the second ring. "Asher, it's Livia."

"Yes?" It sounds like I'm the last person he wants to talk to. Well, guess what? Right now, the feeling's mutual because I know in about two seconds, I'll feel his hatred for me like a switchblade to the gut.

I take a deep breath. "I can't reach Gray and he's already missed two meetings this morning. I'm worried."

A string of low curses flows fluently under his breath. "What did you do?"

It hurts, but I deserve that. "We got into an argument on Saturday night and I haven't heard from him since."

"Fuck! Jesus, Livia. I knew things between you two would end this way," he hissed.

Me too. "Please, just make sure he's okay and let me know what I should do with his calendar."

"I'll call you back as soon as I know something."

Not knowing what else to do, I go ahead and cancel his meetings for the morning, but all the while I'm thinking the same thing I thought to myself weeks ago when he moved me into this position. This was a bad idea. We are too intertwined with each other's lives and when that cord severs, which I knew was inevitable, it will be that much harder to deal with the shit pile we'll both be left with. And not only will I have lost Gray for a second time, I'll also be out of a job. But I let him do it without barely a protest. I needed to feel that connection with him again and, I too, wanted to spend every single second of every single day with him.

To keep my mind busy, I go through Gray's emails and find the invoices that need his signature. I print off two that came in over the weekend. I enter them into the system but am missing the tax ID number on a new vendor, so I call them.

"Townley Consulting," a young voice cheerfully answers. I wish I could answer the phones this morning with half as much enthusiasm. As it is, I can barely muster a mumbled hello.

"Yes, I have an invoice for thirty thousand dollars sent to Mr. Gray Colloway over the weekend, and I need a couple pieces of information before I can process it."

"Certainly. What do you need?"

I look over my form to make sure that I get everything I need because I don't want to have to call her back again. The first time I did this, I had to

254

call the vendor back three times. "Umm, tax ID and...type of services rendered. I need a description."

She puts me on hold for a couple of minutes and returns with the information. "Okay, the tax ID is..." she rattles off a series of numbers quickly. "And the type of service is a background check."

Background check? *Oh my God.* Pieces are clicking together so fast I can actually hear them. My hands shake and my lungs feel like I can't get enough air. "Can you be more specific," I ask, trying for nonchalant, but failing miserably.

"I'm sorry, but it's confidential. I can't give you any more information than that."

"Yes, of course. Thanks," I mutter before hanging up. Just as I disconnect, the phone rings again.

Asher.

"He's fine. He's working out of his New York condo for the week. He said he'd take his meetings by phone."

The final piece falls into place. Suddenly this bad feeling I've had in the pit of my stomach since yesterday solidifies into a solid, hard mass. Thick, heavy and suffocating. It's threatening to choke the life out of me.

Gray knows. That's why he's been avoiding me.

"Did..." I had to clear my throat before I continued. "Did he say why?"

"He just said he had some shit to sort through."

"Okay. Thanks, Asher," I manage to strangle out. I hang up and sit there staring into space for the longest time, dumbfounded.

The betrayal I feel at his actions is white hot. He told me I could trust him. He had me believing I could tell him *anything* and he would understand. I was finally beginning to think it was true. That it may actually be possible to break open this deep wound that was nearly healed, bare my stained soul to him and that he may possibly understand. Accept me. And still love me, regardless.

But it was all lies. This entire time he had someone checking into my past. A past that was supposed to be buried so deep no one would be able to find it. That's what Grant had said. Yet, somehow he had. And he didn't even have the balls to confront me to hear my side of the story.

It makes me angry, even if it is unfounded. Even though I know that I'm the one that dug this fucking crater that we've both fallen helplessly into, but it doesn't stop the sharp sting of his duplicity.

I wonder what he knows. I *have* to know what he knows. I have to get him to talk to me.

Me: why did you run away?

Several minutes go by and, once again, I don't think he's going to answer, but when he does, his caustic words shatter my fragile heart.

Gray: that's rich, coming from a woman who probably holds the world record in that sport

Me: gray, what's going on? please come home. I'm ready to talk

Gray: it's a little too late for that Livia. I know

My blood freezes and my heart sinks. So it's true. He does know. He went behind my back, digging into my private life. And he paid a lot of fucking money to do it. Oh my God, I can hardly breathe. My fingers tremble. The keypad is blurry through my watery eyes as I type my response. Even though I was dreading it, I was going to tell him on *my* terms, in *my* own way. Eventually.

Me: u know what exactly?

Gray: everything

Nonononononononono.

Me: meaning?

Gray: u did what u swore u wouldn't. u annihilated me

My hands fly to my mouth and my cell drops to the carpeted floor. It lands face up, and even feet away, his words mock me. He knows the truth. He knows I left him for another man, even though I didn't want to. Does he know why? Does he know I was raped, tortured, beaten? Does he know about the baby? I lean over the garbage can and dry heave. I couldn't keep anything down before and now my stomach churns like a wild carnival ride. A ride that I want off of, but I can't find the exit.

257

The next few days pass by in a blur. I barely function. I come to work, answer the phone, but I couldn't tell you what I do from eight to five. I'm like a robot, set on autopilot. I don't remember walking to and from the train station. I can't sleep, but when I do manage a couple of hours, they aren't filled with hauntings from my past anymore. They are filled with glimpses of a future that I will never have.

The one that troubled me most and sent me into a near tailspin was a vivid dream of Gray and I having a baby. We had a boy and he was tiny and pink and perfect. We named him Jax. After I had awoke in hysterics, Addy had to sleep with me that night, holding me like a child. She begged me to call Dr. Howard and make an appointment, but I don't think I can possibly transform my pain into words that will make any sense.

None of what happened makes sense. I'm in the worst kind of depression and I don't know how to pull myself back out. The only reason I keep going to work is that I hope Gray will come to his senses and come back to the office so I can see him. Convince him to listen. Hear my side of the story.

The world is now colorless and drab, a spiteful, mocking mixture of nothing but swirling and muted greys. Without him, I'm launched back into that dark, lonely place that I was before, only now it seems so much gloomier, lonelier. More despairing. I feel dead inside and I know my life will never be the same.

I can't keep anything down. I've lost several pounds and my new clothes now hang on me. I stopped wearing makeup because it won't stay on longer than fifteen minutes. Crying jags tend to do that. And like a crazy stalker, I have texted and called Gray repeatedly, but he doesn't answer.

I tell him I'm sorry, I tell him how much I love him, I beg him to let me explain. He never responds. I don't know when he's coming home. I get so desperate I even call Asher and Conn and beg them to convince Gray to talk to me. Asher said he wasn't getting involved and Conn told me he'd see what he could do. I don't hold out much hope.

This feeling of debilitating agony right here? This is exactly why I ran away from Gray at the fundraiser. This is the reason I didn't tell him whenever he demanded answers. This is why I stayed away from him when I escaped my prison. I knew he would never understand the decision I made. He could never accept that I'd been with someone else, even if it wasn't of my own free will. He would see me as the damaged goods that I am

I'm gutted. Destroyed.

My worst fears have come true and the pain this time is far, far worse than I could have possibly imagined.

Chapter 40

Gray

I swirl the dark liquor in my glass until it forms a little funnel in the middle. I watch it go around and around, threatening to suck anything down to the bottom that has the unfortunate luck of getting stuck in its vortex. How apt, given that's exactly how I feel. I'm stuck in a dizzying maelstrom of despair and depression that is threatening to suck me to a bottomless, black pit, destroying me once again.

I take another swig of the pungent alcohol and stare into the nothingness. My apartment is dark, except for the moonlight that shines through the open blinds, and even the moonlight makes me ache. The beams remind me of the brightness of Livvy's eyes when I make her come. The shadows that play on the walls from the cumulous clouds passing high overhead remind me of the candlelight dancing over her naked flesh when she was laid out on my dining room table like a sacrifice.

Fuck.

Another swallow. I can't feel the warmth of the alcohol coursing through my bloodstream anymore because my body is numb. But my mind isn't. Why can't I forget about her? Why have I had to fight the nearly overwhelming urge this entire week to hop the next plane home and bury myself inside her, forgetting everything I've learned. I'm disgusted that my thoughts keep drifting back to the way her expression transforms in the throes of pleasure when my face is buried in her pussy, or the sheer tranquility I feel at the simple act of just holding her in my arms.

Almost a week later I can still smell her, taste her, feel her body against mine. I let my heavy head fall back against the couch and stare at the ceiling, barely blinking. Blinking is overrated. Apparently I haven't had near enough alcohol to make me forget yet, but I know that's not true. I've already finished almost three-fourths of a bottle of one-hundred-thirty-proof bourbon. I'm three sheets to the wind or just plain lost in the wind, but I can't get my fucking mind to shut off. I can't stop thinking about *her,* and mourning a future that has once again been violently ripped away from me.

A lone tear of humiliation streaks down my cheek, rolling into my ear. I am in utter agony. The pain in my heart radiates throughout my entire body and I can't seem to get it to stop, no matter what I do. I rub my chest, feeling the hurt physically constrict it. This is a million times worse than losing her before. I thought she had run away. I thought she had abandoned me. And it turns out she just played me and left me for another man. How did I not see that one coming? Is that what they mean when they say love is blind? *No.* Love isn't blind. It just makes you plain fucking stupid. Love and hate are on the opposite sides of a sharp blade, and if you tip too far to either side, you'll get sliced apart. It will be bloody and it will be painful. I should know...I've been on both sides now. Twice.

Townley sent me a brief one-page summary of his findings. Actually it was one paragraph. I paid thirty thousand dollars for about fifty earth-shattering, ego-bruising, gut-wrenching words. She married a man named Peter Wilder two days after she left me. She must have been seeing the asshole during at the same time she was me and I guess he was the better man. Had more to offer. Maybe he was richer than I am. Maybe he had a cock the size of an anaconda. It pains me to wonder what he could offer her that I couldn't. And the only reason she wasn't with him any longer was because he was six feet under.

I'm overwhelmed with emotions that I simply can't deal with. I have to turn off my brain. I need a reprieve, if only for a brief fucking moment. I close my eyes and try to let the drunken haze take me into blessed oblivion when I hear my locks turn and my door open. Never mind that I don't know that many people in New York, let alone anyone that has a key to my apartment, but I don't move. I don't think I can. I tell my limbs to defend me, but they won't respond. I hear voices in the background and I vaguely wonder if I'm going to be robbed. Maybe they'll kill me and put me out of my sad misery. At this moment, it would be a blessing.

I'm mentally trying to place where I left my cell and if I can reach it in time when the lights turn on and I'm temporarily blinded.

"What the fuck," I yell, throwing a protective arm over my pupils before they're scorched.

"Well, at least he's alive. Shitfaced, but alive."

"What the fuck are you doing here, Ash?" I slur.

"Check the condo for any naked women that may be passed out," he directs someone. Like I would be able to get hard for another woman. I never will be able to again. I'll be one-handing it for the rest of my life to my memories of the only woman I'll ever love. How pathetic is that? As much as I want to, I can't hate her. I still love her deep down to my core, even after what she did to me. What seems like an hour later, I hear my other brother respond, "Clear."

"Why are you here?" I moan. I want to wallow in my despair and misery alone. I don't want help. I don't want to be saved. I don't want anyone to try to console me and tell me everything is going to be alright. It will never be all fucking right. Ever. Again.

And remembering what Ash said in my office I sure as fuck don't want my brothers to bathe me. "And if you so much as look at my junk, I'm cutting yours off. Just as soon as I don't see two of you."

"Come on, Gray, let's get you to bed." Then, with a brother on either side, they drag me from the couch into the bedroom, throw me unceremoniously onto the mattress and strip me down to my underwear. The last thing I remember before I pass out is the sad looks on my siblings faces at my condition.

Or my predicament. It doesn't matter...it's one and the same. A big pile of stinking shit.

Moaning, I roll over, holding my head. I feel like a tractor-trailer hit me when I wasn't looking. The last time I felt like this was...*fuck*. Everything comes rushing back like a dam that just burst. The entire week that I've tried to erase through self-medication flashes back like a bad movie stuck on instant replay.

She was married.

I groan when I sit up, grabbing my throbbing skull. I sit there for several agonizing minutes before I notice three aspirin and a glass of water sitting on my nightstand. Then I remember that my brothers are here and for once, I'm grateful. I need to be surrounded by my family. Learn from my past mistakes and lean on them, not push them away.

I down the medication, stumble into the bathroom, and half an hour later, I feel marginally better. My skin is still pink from the scorching water I let pummel my aching flesh. It felt good to redirect the pain for a while away from my soul to another body part.

I throw on a pair of faded jeans and blue polo shirt and pad barefoot into the kitchen. Conn and Ash are sitting at the island, heads together in a low, heated conversation that I can't hear. As soon as Conn spots me, they stop, both heads swiveling toward me, gauging my mood. I ignore them and walk to the coffee pot, pouring myself a cup of the strong brew. I wish it were bourbon instead. I could use the hair of the dog about now.

"What happened?" Conn finally asked, breaking the silence. I take a deep breath and try to find the right words deep inside me and force them out.

I was a fool.

I was duped.

I was played.

I was deceived in the worst possible way.

But I can't. I can't say any of them, because every time I try, they get stuck in the top of my constricted throat, so I walk to the living room, grab the brief report and throw it on the counter in front of them. A couple minutes later, two sets of eyes look up at me questioningly.

"I fucking knew it," Asher hissed. "I knew she was hiding something. I knew she would do this to you, Gray."

"Wait a minute, both of you." Conn...always the most level-headed one of the group. "Is this from a reliable source?"

I nod. Robert Townley is one of the most sought out private detectives in the United States. For a reason. He wouldn't be as successful as he is if he gave out bogus information.

Conn shakes his head in disbelief. "I don't know, Gray. Something doesn't feel right about this. I don't think Livia would do this to you. I see the way she *looks* at you. Like you're her entire world. Have you talked to her?"

"No," I reply flatly. I can't stomach hearing any more lies. Even if they have been lies of omission.

My younger brother stares me down. "You should. You owe it to both yourself, and to her, to get some straight answers. Even if they're answers you don't want to hear, Gray. You deserve to know the whole truth, if for nothing else, so that you can get some closure and put this shit behind you once and for all. You won't have any peace until you do."

Conn's right. I need to stop being a pussy and confront her, but I don't know if I'm ready.

"She's not doing much better than you, by the way," he continues. "She's pale and has a blank look in her eyes and she's lost a visible amount of weight this week already."

My gut clenches, his words like a knife tearing into my already shredded soul. I don't want to care, but I do. I don't know if I'll ever be able to stop. "I don't know if I'm ready to see her yet."

Asher speaks up. "I'll take care of things, but you need to come back home. You need to get back to Chicago, Gray. You've got a fucking company to run and you can't do it by conference call much longer."

I nod. That's one of the reasons I've stayed away because I just cannot see her sitting outside my office door every day, but I don't have the heart to do something about it. At least Asher can reassign her somewhere else so I don't have to run into her, until I sort out what I'm going to do. God, I'm a fucking pussy.

"Yes, fine," I finally agree.

I take my coffee cup and walk to the bay of windows, looking out at the crisp morning sky. I talk to the window, to my brothers, to no one at all. I just talk, because I need to get the words out of me.

"I remember when I brought Livvy here for her birthday the first year we were dating. We'd only been together just a couple of months. She'd never been to New York, never seen a Broadway play, so while I'm not much of a theatergoer myself, I took her. We saw *Cats*. I'll never forget that night. I knew I was falling in love with her already, but that sent me plummeting over the edge and I knew I didn't want to live a day without her.

"My God, she was mesmerized by the play and I was mesmerized by *her*. I'm not even sure I saw any of it because the only thing I could do was watch her and her reactions. She looked like a kid who'd seen Santa Claus in the mall for the first time. She was captivated and childlike and in such awe and I thought to myself, *I* can give her this. I *want* to give her this. I would do anything in my power to make this woman happy for the rest of her life."

No one speaks for the longest time.

"You'll move past this, Gray. You got over her once. You can do it again."

I shake my head. "I never got over her, Ash. I don't think I'm capable of *ever* getting over her. She's strength and sunshine and dreams all rolled up into this magical little being. You remember what I was like when I met her. I was a bumbling idiot."

"I remember," Ash replies quietly.

"She's still all of those things and so much more now. She's not perfect, but she's *my* perfection. I've never met another woman that even comes close to what she gives me and I know I never will. She's tattooed on my soul and there's not a thing or a person that can ever erase her mark and I don't know what to fucking do about it."

Conn lays a comforting hand on my shoulder, squeezing. "I watched you go through hell when you lost her the first time. I watched you slowly bounce back over the years never quite being who you had been before. But over these past few weeks, Gray, I've watched you become the man you used to be. You're happy, you smile, you've got that gleam back in your eye that was dull and lifeless before. Give it some time, but then talk to her. You both deserve that even if things don't end up the way you want them to. At least this time you'll have some closure."

I nod, knowing he's right, but also wondering where I'll find the strength inside to possibly let the woman I know I can't live without go a second time. Only this time it will be *me* running away and I'm just not sure I can get my feet to move in any direction but where she is.

But I also don't know if I can ever forgive her betrayal either.

Chapter 41

Livia

It's mid-afternoon on Saturday when the final nail in my coffin is hammered in, and for some reason, this one hurts the worst. It's been a week since I've touched or seen or talked to Gray and every passing day is worse than the one before. I had an emergency appointment with Dr. Howard this morning and I could hardly talk. Most of the hour I spent crying. I feel like after a week of constant weeping, that well should be dry, but my treacherous body keeps making more moisture to replenish what I've lost.

The doorbell rings and my stomach goes into a free-fall. Maybe it's finally Gray, but as I look through the peephole, disappointment floods me and I take a resigned step back at who I see on the other side. This is not good.

"Camille, what are you doing here?" I ask as I open the door. It's a rhetorical question because I know exactly why she's here. Somehow I manage to keep the waterworks at bay as she produces a severance agreement, effective immediately. It's grossly over-substantial, two years worth of pay and benefits for a month of work. Now I just feel like a whore he's trying to buy off. I want to rip up the papers in front of me into a thousand pieces, burn them and send the ashes back in a box with a big *Fuck You* scrawled in magic marker across the top.

But I don't.

While it crushes my heart just as if he'd reached into my chest and bled that aching muscle dry with his own two hands, it's clear he doesn't want to see me again. This is his goodbye.

So if he wants to buy me off, I'll let him. I'll use the money to move and start a new life somewhere else. I can no longer live in the city that I've come to love if he's in it. At some point in the future, if I happen to run into him, especially with another woman on his arm or pushing a baby stroller, I'll lose it. I'll never be able to accept that he's not mine. Over the past five years, I've always thought of him that way, even when he wasn't. Maybe I'll move to a small town in Wyoming where no one knows me and I can live a simple life, alone. The country sounds like a good place to start fresh.

I don't ask questions as she goes through the terms of the agreement. Quite frankly, I don't give a shit what it says. I blindly sign, and turn over my security badge and the key to Gray's office. As Camille hands me the meager personal effects from my desk, she says, "I'm very sorry, Livia. Truly."

Me too. I nod. I believe her because you just can't fake that kind of sincerity. She's just a pawn. Sent to do Gray's dirty work. Not only does he not have the decency to hear me out, he doesn't have the balls to fire me himself. It pains me deeply to learn he's not the man I thought he was. He's a coward, but then again, so am I.

After she leaves, I sit in silence at the kitchen counter. My thumb absently circles my angel tattoo, a habit I've fallen into since I got it, and even after all of this, I still don't regret it. No matter how badly it ends, how can you really regret your one true love? Regretting it is like wishing it never existed. Even with as much agony as I'm in right now, I would never do that. I'll love Gray with my entire being for the rest of my life, regardless of how he feels about me. That kind of bone-deep love can either be transcendent or the worst kind of agony. I guess mine now falls into the latter category.

My stomach lurches. It's still not right and I've felt weak and tired for a solid seven days. *Probably because you've hardly eaten a stitch of food.* Severe depression will do that to a person, I guess. An hour later when Addy gets home from the store, I'm in the same spot, staring into space. She doesn't ask me if I'm okay anymore because she knows I'm not. And now, I'm even less so, knowing that I have nothing to look forward to come Monday morning.

"How's the stomach today?"

"Ehhh."

"How many times have you thrown up?" She eyes me, daring me to lie.

"Twice." Four if you count the dry heaves.

She turns from putting away the groceries and leans against the refrigerator. "Have you taken a pregnancy test?"

"What?" I breathe. I think of the many times Gray and I had unprotected sex, but I can't get pregnant. Addy doesn't know that and I just can't tell her. Peter robbed me of that at the tender age of twenty-three, so my baby making days are quite over.

"No, Addy. I'm not pregnant. I'm just depressed." And I wasn't sick like this the first time I was pregnant, I want to add but don't, because she doesn't know about that either. God, I'm a cesspool of secrets. I'm so sick of it all.

"Whatever you say, but my flu lasted twenty-four hours. Yours has lasted a week. I think you should take one anyway, just to be sure. You could have morning sickness."

I shake my head, not responding. There's no way I'm taking a fucking pregnancy test, just the thought alone rips my heart out anew.

As she rounds the island, she spots the severance agreement sitting on the counter. "What the hell is this, Livia?" she asks, picking it up and scanning it.

I shrug. "My walking papers."

She throws them down in disgust. "God damn him! I can't believe that asshole! He doesn't deserve you, Livia."

I smile, but it's weak and sad. I love that she's indignant on my behalf, but it's misguided. If only she knew the truth. All of it. The only thing she knows is that we broke up and Gray won't return my calls. My eyes tear again.

"No. I think it's the other way around." I slide off the counter and head to my room. I shut the door, lie down on my bed, and sob.

Chapter 42

Livia

A very warm, clearly male body spoons me. Sturdy, thick arms are wrapped tightly around my waist and for a moment I'm confused. For just one teeny tiny millisecond in time, I think they're Gray's, and everything is right again, but then, in a flash, I remember they're not.

They're Grant's.

And the all-consuming grief hits me again hard and deep. "What time is it?" I croak. My mouth is parched and I'm nauseous again, but not as much as earlier. I need to pee, but I can't make myself get up. I'm so utterly...drained.

"It's just past seven," he replies softly in my ear. He smoothes down my hair, pulling it away from my face. "You need to eat, Livia. You've lost too much weight just in the week since I've last seen you."

I barely remember Grant coming into my room, laying behind me and pulling me into his calming body, willing his stoic strength into me. He whispered words meant to comfort, but they only made me cry harder until exhaustion finally took me under its magical spell. That was apparently only two hours ago. I was hoping two months, or maybe another two years had gone by. Maybe then this all-consuming grief would abate somewhat.

"I can't." I peel his arm away and sit on the edge of the bed, looking down at the floor, gripping the comforter like a lifeline. He never said how he found out or why he was here, but it was clear he knew something had happened with Gray. I have a sneaking suspicion my roommate had something to do with it. Whatever the reason was, I wasn't going to question it. I'm glad he's here.

I *need* him. I need someone who loves me to guide me through the treacherous, rocky paths of this hell I've found myself in once again so I can come out of the other side. I'll be battered and bruised and bloody, but at least I'll *be*. Grant is my raft. The vessel that will save me from the violent, murky ocean waters I now find myself callously tossed around in. I can't be without him. I'm unable to do it alone this time.

"How long are you staying?" I don't even try to keep the pleading out of my voice.

I feel the bed dip and then he's beside me, drawing me close, laying my head on his shoulder. "For as long as you need."

I choke on a sob. "I'm so glad you're here."

"Stay here, baby, I'll run you a bath."

That sounds heavenly. "You don't have to do that."

He tilts my head upward so our eyes meet. His compassion ruins me. "I want to."

I just nod. Five minutes later he leads me into my adjoining bathroom where a steamy, lavender bubble bath awaits. "When you're done, come into the kitchen. I'm making you something to eat and you're going to eat it. No more excuses."

274

"Okay." My stomach revolts at the thought of food, but it's pointless arguing with Grant.

He places a soft, reverent kiss on my forehead before leaving and I stare at the vacant space long after he's gone. As happy as I am that he's here, I also wish he wasn't. I wish it were Gray drawing me a bath and forcing me to eat. I wish it were Gray holding me in his arms and his lips touching my skin.

I wish.

But it's not. And it won't ever be again. I look at the counter, where the Zoloft Dr. Howard prescribed me this morning stares me down, daring me to swallow a pill...or the whole bottle. I open the childproof cap and gaze at the contents inside that can bring me either fog or peace. For the first time, I can understand my sister and her despondency so much better. I don't know how long I regard the tiny, powerful pills before I decide that I want neither and flush them down the toilet.

I brush my teeth, throw my hair up in a messy bun and quickly strip, sliding into the perfectly warm, scented bath. Taking a deep breath, I truly relax my body for the first time in a week. The warmth surrounding me even makes my nausea calm. My mind is a different story, but, hey...baby steps.

I must drift off to sleep because suddenly I feel a hand on my shoulder and I startle, my body jackknifing up in the water. Bubbles run down my naked breasts, baring too much, and now I'm staring into the lustful eyes of my savior. Grant has seen me naked a number of times, just never when I wasn't covered in blood and bruises. He clears his throat and looks away. "I was worried about you. You've been in here almost an hour."

I quickly slink back under the protective bubble layer, and then I remember the game of *this or that* Gray and I played in the car and his preference for showers. Lack of bubbles. My face falls. Suddenly I'm regretting flushing my reserve of medication. I could use some nice, thick fog clouding out my suffering about now.

"I'm sorry. I must have fallen asleep. I'll be out in a minute."

Grant is now staring intently at me and neither of us says a word for what seems like minutes. The air is thick with something I don't want to name.

"Sorry." He stands and retreats quickly, leaving me confused in a pool of cooling water. Five minutes later, dressed in a pair of baggy sweats and a Detroit Lions tee, I stroll into the living room, where I find Addy and Grant talking quietly on the couch.

"Hi," I say, breaking up their little party.

Grant jumps up and comes to stand in front of me. "You okay?"

"Better."

Taking my hand, he drags me to the island that separates our living room and kitchen and sits me on a bar stool where he presents, with a flourish of his hand, the supper he's whipped up.

Chicken noodle soup.

I laugh until I cry. He steps between my legs, wrapping his arms around me. "Still your favorite, right?"

"Yes," I nod.

"You're weird. Eat up." He kisses the top of my head and walks to the other side, where he leans on his elbows and watches me. I take a few, tentative bites. While it's pretty tasteless, it seems to sit okay, so I eat a few more until I have half the bowl gone. I push it away and he silently pushes it back.

My eyes challenge his. "You're not my father."

"You've eaten about fifty calories, if even."

Huffing, I take a few more spoonful's and look back up. His brows arch and my eyes roll. "Grant, really. I'm full." He holds my gaze, silently telling me to finish. "God, you're so stubborn."

"Don't even go there, Livia," he laughs.

A couple minutes later my entire bowl is gone. Half an hour later, it's being flushed into the Chicago sewer system.

"God, I'm so sorry," he says as I open the bathroom door.

"I told you I was full," I tease, but I'm so weak, I have to hang onto the wall for support until he puts his arm around my waist and walks me to the couch.

"I think you were just trying to prove a point."

"Trust me, I'm not." I'm starting to get a bit worried about the fact that I can't keep anything down and I can see the worry on Grant's face as well.

"Addy tells me you've been throwing up for a week."

I look down the hallway at Addy's closed door. She's made herself scarce since I came out from my bath. "Addy has a big mouth."

"Addy is a good friend," he counters. I sigh. He's right.

"What else did she tell you," I ask, desperately wanting to change the subject. He sits down on the other end of the sofa and pats his lap. I lay my head on it, facing away from his body and curl my body into a fetal position. He runs his fingers through my hair, gently massaging my scalp. The air of melancholy that follows me everywhere is once again suffocating. I suddenly want to fill our small apartment with music that's as sad as I am and cry into a glass of wine. Unfortunately it neither sounds good nor can I keep it down.

"If you're not better tomorrow, I'm taking you to the emergency room."

"Stop, Grant. I'm fine. I had the flu and now I'm just... Unless they can fix a broken heart, there's nothing they can do for me." They'll just want to prescribe more pills, and I'm not sure I want to take them. I'm not even sure I can keep them down.

"They can run tests and make sure nothing else is wrong and give you something for dehydration. Jesus, Livia, you can barely walk you're so fucking weak."

"What happened with the video?" I ask quietly, changing subjects again. I'm not going to the stupid emergency room over a damn broken heart. That's like calling 911 because your cat crossed the road and it's stuck on the other side. It's just plain stupid.

"It's all handled. As of today." His voice is terse and angry.

I turn so I'm looking up at him. "Who was it?"

He lightly traces my eyebrow with his finger, his hazel eyes following the curved line it draws. The gentleness of it belies the anger I see swirling around him. He's so beautiful with his unruly hair and devilish eyes. I wish I could fall in love with him, making Gray just a memory. If there was anyone else I could fall in love with, it would be Grant, but I know it will never happen. And even if it did, I'd always be holding something back. Something reserved for another man.

"Just someone who was trying to hurt me."

"You? Why?" That makes absolutely no sense. Why would a video of me hurt Grant?

His fiery eyes search mine. The intensity in them takes me back a bit. "Because they know my weakness."

It takes me a minute to understand what he means. *Me.* "Oh," I manage to say. It's amazing how much Grant can say without really saying anything at all. I don't ask any more questions about it because I really don't want to know.

"What do you do now, Grant?"

A smile turns one corner of his mouth. "I'm a PI and I do some bounty hunting on the side. All legit."

I can't help but smile. "I'm glad." And I am. I was hoping Peter's death meant a different life for both of us. He never belonged there.

I turn back over, not able to hold his smoldering gaze any longer. Grant resumes playing with my long locks, but suddenly it feels different. Intimate. "Gray fired me," I say quietly, changing subjects yet again, trying to get away from *us* and whatever seems to be happening here.

His thighs tense and his hand stills. "Yeah, well Gray is a fucking asshole and he doesn't deserve you."

"That's the same thing Addy said, almost word for word," I laugh. I sit up, regretting the loss of his warmth. "But it's not true. I'm the one that's undeserving." I stand and walk to the window on shaky legs, holding onto the sill for support. "I knew it would end like this when he found out. I've ruined us both. I should have never gone back to HMT after that day. It would still be hard, but I wouldn't be shattered beyond repair like I am now. I'm so broken." My voice cracks on those last three words.

Then my face is in his hands and his eyes are blazing with a fire I've rarely seen. "Baby, you're not broken, just bent. Remolded into a new, unique you. A stronger version. Christ." He pauses, gathering his composure. "You listen to me and you believe every word I'm about to say. You are an incredibly strong and brave woman who has endured horrors that most people could never even imagine, let alone survive. And to be able to put that behind you, and actually thrive like you have? Jesus, I don't know anyone else that could have done that. And if Gray Colloway can't see that, then *he's* the one that's undeserving, baby, not you. If he can't accept you, all of you, as much as you want him to be, he's *not* the man for you."

He couldn't be more wrong. Gray *is* the man for me. His chest heaves with the exertion of his impassioned speech. I stare into his stormy eyes, swirling with passion and conviction and swallow hard, tears running down my face. I reach up, placing my hands on biceps. "Are you that man, Grant?" I don't know why I ask the question, other than to reassure myself that I could be desired by another man.

A throaty rumble leaves his lips and he tilts his head back, eyes closed. That pained look I saw in the car last week is back. Then he pulls my forehead to his, looking deeply into my eyes. "I will always be here for you, Livia. I will never leave you alone again. I promise."

Not really an answer, but that's okay. My question was self-serving and came from a place of pain and despair that I'm trying desperately to soothe any way I can. I love Grant, but I am *in* love with Gray, and it was an unfair question for me to ask when I know how Grant feels about me. Hell, maybe he's in the same place as I am, just over me. I frown at that aching thought. I don't want to hurt Grant.

Then he's holding onto me as tightly as I am him. Even though I don't want him to leave, I also don't want us to do anything that will damage our friendship because God knows, I won't make it through this without him and right now I'm feeling a little too vulnerable and, in my grief, I can already see myself making a very stupid mistake here. One that will lead us down an unrighteous path. Then I'll lose both of the men I love. "You can leave. I'll be okay."

He chuckles. "You trying to get rid of me, babe?"

"Yes."

"Tough shit. I'm staying."

I sigh into him, grateful that he's not letting me push him away. He scoops me up in his arms and carries me back to the couch. Once he has us settled lying down so my back is against his chest, he turns on the TV. He grabs the throw from the back of the couch, placing it over me. This position feels too intimate, but I can't move because his body heat warms me in all the places that I feel cold and numb. Which is everywhere.

"What are we doing?" I ask quietly.

"We're going to veg and watch a little Property Brothers."

"Oh, I love those guys. They're pretty easy on the eyes."

His body shakes with laughter. "Yep, that's what I was going for."

I feel his lips in my hair. He pulls me closer with an arm around my waist, and I can't help the little shred of peace I feel, albeit ever so small. At this point, I'll take it and be grateful for it, even if I know I'll wake in the morning and it'll be gone. It gives me hope that at some point in the distant future I'll be able to at least get back to where I was before I saw Gray again for the first time two months ago now. It wasn't really living, more like existing, but at least I didn't mope around and cry all day, every day. And right now, I'd settle for just existing, instead of sitting on the edge of despair, looking down the sharp, deadly rocks below, praying for the strength to turn and walk away from the calm they'll ultimately bring me.

"Grant?"

"Yes, sweetheart?" he replies softly.

"Thank you for being here."

His lips on my temple comfort me. "There's nowhere else I'd be."

I can't keep my eyes open and even though it's not even nine, it doesn't take long before I'm drifting off into the most peaceful sleep I've had in seven days.

Chapter 43

Gray

It's almost midnight and I'm standing outside Livvy's door, debating whether to knock. I've been pacing for almost ten minutes. I've gone up and down the staircase three times. I expect the cops to show up any minute. The old lady across the hall has stuck her nose out twice, and by the scowl she's given me, she probably thinks I'm some sort of stalker. It's midnight, for Christ's sake. Aren't old people in bed at like...four?

I arrived back in Chicago several hours ago, and in my lonely apartment, all I could hear were Conn's words echoing off the walls. *"You owe it to yourself, and her, to get some straight answers."* I also can't seem to forget his other comment about there being something wrong.

Before I left New York, I went into my bedroom and called Townley. I asked him if he had any more information than what he'd already provided me and he gave me an abrupt no. He told me the same thing I'd thought when he delivered this earth-shattering report. *"Sometimes the past is dangerous. Leave it where it belongs."* And after those cryptic words, in no uncertain terms he told me never to call him again.

As much as I try to talk myself out of it, I still love Livvy. I can't see myself ever getting over her.

Even when I thought she'd left me, I still loved her. All these years I've pined for her, like a lovesick fool. There will never be a time when I don't love Livvy. So I do owe it to both of us to have a sit-down, and while I could have chosen a better time than the middle of the night, I simply couldn't wait a minute longer. My soul aches for her. My eyes thirst to drink her in again. I've listened to every one of her voicemails and read every single text a dozen times in the last twelve hours.

But I also have to know why she betrayed me and I need to do some deep soul-searching to find forgiveness. Right now I'm too hurt to even think about that. Answers first, forgiveness later. Before I can change my mind, my hand raises and pounds loudly on their door. I knock several times before it swings open and a very irate Addy stands in front me, pulling the sash tight on her short robe.

"What in the fuck are you doing here, asshole? And you do realize it's the middle of the fucking night, right?"

"It's Saturday night. Not like you have to get up and go to work tomorrow."

"Oh. My. God." She starts to slam the door in my face and luckily my foot makes it in the crack just in time to stop it from breaking my nose.

"Fuck," I curse, shoving it back open.

She stands there with her arms across her chest and her legs spread like a warrior princess preparing to protect all that she cares about in the world. And maybe she is...her friend. "You need to leave. You've already done enough to Livia. She's a barely functioning, vomiting, zombie wreck."

285

"She's the wreck?" I ask indignantly, even though all I remember now is the throwing up part and Conn's comment about her losing weight. My stomach twinges. "Did she tell you what *she* did to *me*? I think you have the wrong version of the story here, sweetheart. You know what, this is none of your business." I push past her and head down the hallway to Livvy's bedroom, all the while Addy's pulling my arm, trying to stop me.

And the second I throw open her door, I know why. I feel like someone has reached inside my body and violently ripped out every single organ I have. My lungs won't work. My stomach is in my shoes. My bleeding, beating heart is lying on the floor at my feet and my soul is...my soul is crumbling right before my very eyes.

My girlfriend, former fiancée, and woman that I love to the depths of my very being is laying in the arms of not only another man, but a man who I never thought I'd see again. Never wanted to see again. A man who is dead to me.

My twin brother.

Chapter 44

Livia

I awake from a deep sleep to sounds of yelling and screaming and furniture being broken. Blinking several times to clear the haze in my brain, I take in my surroundings. I'm in my bedroom and Grant isn't here. My door is wide open, the hall light spilling into the darkness. A quick glance at the digital clock shows it's after midnight. I hear Addy screaming *stop* and wonder what in the hell is going on. I'm decent, still dressed in my sweats and t-shirt, so I quickly head out into the living room, but I'm so dizzy, I have to stop half way down and hang onto the wall for support. When I finally make it to the edge of the hall, what I see stops me short.

Gray is here. And on the ground trading punches with Grant. Gray's mouth is bleeding and his blue polo shirt is ripped down the front. Blood pours from Grant's nose and the black t-shirt he's wearing is pulled almost over his head.

Addy's running around hitting them both with a yardstick, trying to break up the fight. If they both didn't look like they wanted to kill each other, I'd almost laugh at how utterly ridiculous she looks wielding a three feet long piece of wood that's doing about as much good as a plastic baseball bat.

"Hey!" I yell, weakly. Not one of the three acknowledges me. My vision starts to blur and my ears buzz. My head feels heavy and their voices sound further away every second. I've fainted once in my life before and this feels an awful lot like that. "Hey," I yell again, but it comes out on a whispered croak.

The last thing I remember before I crumble into a heap to the floor is three sets of eyes latching onto mine. I try to fight it, but can't stop the darkness from coming for me.

The inside of my mouth feels like I've swallowed paste. An annoying beep chimes in the background. I reach over to turn off my alarm, but my hand hits air. I lay still, struggling to open my eyes, but low, angry voices in the background cause one to crack.

Gray and Grant are in the corner arguing, and their voices continue to get louder and louder. Even from here, I can see both their faces look worse for the wear. Gray has a swollen lip and the beginnings of a black eye. Grant still has dried blood on his face and his cheek looks swollen. Their clothes look disheveled and there's a trail of dried blood dotted down the front of their shirts.

I look around and see Addy curled up in a chair, sleeping. I'm in a room that looks sterile with dingy yellow walls and that hard tile looking floor that seems that it would be indestructible, even as the earth burns at the end of days. A window with dirty looking plastic blinds sits in the middle of the far wall and a small TV hangs in the corner of the ceiling.

I'm in the hospital. *Shit.*

"Stop," I croak, but my weak attempt at speaking can't be heard above their escalating voices. I try to sit up, but still feel too tired. I take a deep breath and say it again, this time getting their attention. They both rush to either side of my bed, but neither touches me. It makes me sad and a fresh set of tears well up again. I'm so sick and tired of crying, I could scream. The fact that I'm unable to control my emotions this past week, when I've had them locked tighter than Fort Knox for years is just plain pissing me off. I swipe at the moisture and strengthen my resolve.

Grant pushes a button on the side of my hospital bed, which slowly sits me up. I look down and notice I'm in a hospital gown, instead of my sweats and t-shirt.

"How are you?" he asks softly.

I shake my head. I don't really know how I am. "How long have I been here?"

Gray answers, "Twelve hours."

Twelve hours? I do remember coming to a couple of times, but it didn't register where I was. "Did they admit me?"

He nods. "You're severely dehydrated." He points to the IV that I only now notice is attached to a tube coming out of the top of my hand. "They ran some tests, but won't give us any information, because we're not family." I wince at his last word. Gray and Grant feel more like family to me than anyone else, except Alyse.

289

"I'll call for the nurse," Grant says, pushing another button on the side of my fancy bed that apparently has everything I need for a comfortable stay. I want to go home.

"You need to leave," Gray spits, each word dipped in venom, directed at the man on the other side of me.

"I'm not leaving her unless she tells me to." The smugness on Grant's face is going to earn him another punch. I shake my head. Testosterone duels wildly in the air. It was so obvious they were each trying to stake a claim on me, but there is only one man I belong to, and I don't think he wants me any longer.

"I'm thirsty," I say, trying to defuse the situation. I'm simply too exhausted for this bullshit and this is not the place. Gray happens to be on the side with the water pitcher and quickly pours me a glass, holding it out to me. His coolness toward me cuts deep. I take it and he avoids any brush of our fingers. Once again, I have to hold back the tears.

"How do you know him?" Gray asks, nodding to Grant as I'm taking a drink. His tone is clearly accusatory and now I'm finally piecing it all together. He came to my apartment last night and found me in bed with Grant.

Oh shit. I cannot get into this here, in a hospital room. Grant is a huge part of my story, and someone I care deeply about, but I was going to leave his name anonymous in my rendition of my horror story to Gray. And I certainly never intended for Gray and Grant to meet. "He's a friend."

"A *friend*? Jesus, Livvy, how many other *friends* do you let into your bed?"

Grant starts to round the bed. "You are out of line, brother. I've told you repeatedly that there is nothing sexual between Livia and I. This entire situation is on you, and you alone." Grant waves in my direction. "Her face has been hanging over a toilet for an entire week because you do what you've always done. You avoid conflict. You shut out anyone who you think doesn't live up to your precious high-horse standards. Why don't you just be honest with yourself for once in your fucking life?"

Wait a minute. *Brother*? Why are they talking like they know each other? *Brother*? "What's going on here? Grant, do you know each other?"

They continue their conversation like I haven't even spoken. "This situation lays squarely at Livvy's feet, not mine. You have no idea what she did to me, or to us. Looks like it didn't take her long to move on, though. Just like five years ago."

I suck in a sharp breath at his wounding words and now I know. I know this is the end of us. Any hope I had been harboring deep inside me that he'd listen to me, understand and accept me for who I am just went flying out of the three-story hospital window.

As if he just heard what I said, Gray turns his head toward me. "Grant? Is that the name he's going by these days?"

My eyes volley between the two, confused. Grant's jaw is clamped shut and if looks could kill, Gray would be ten kinds of dead by now. I've only ever seen Grant that mad when I woke up from losing my baby, two days later. "I – I don't understand what's going on here," I whisper.

Gray's snicker is bitter and full of disdain. He holds Grant's eyes and punctuates every word like he's wielding a blowtorch, each one creating a fresh third-degree burn. "Classic. Well, *Livia*, *Luke* here, is my twin."

"Your twin?" I breathe. "No. No. No. No." I shake my head in utter disbelief. "You told me your twin was dead." When we first started dating and I asked Gray about his family, he told me that his twin brother, Luke, had died and they never talked about him. It was too painful for the family. I brought it up to Gray once after that and he got upset, so I never did again. And neither did anyone else. He wouldn't even show me a picture. It was as if Luke had never existed and I always found it more than odd. And sad.

"He's dead to *me*."

I felt so many things at that moment I couldn't separate them all. Confusion, betrayal, pity. Why didn't Gray tell me the truth about his brother? Did Grant—Luke, whatever—know about Gray this whole time? I look back on the first time I mentioned Gray's name and the furious look that came over Grant's face. *He knew.* And how could Gray have such hatred for his own flesh and blood that he'd simply disown him and tell people he's dead? How could his entire family do that?

I look into Grant's eyes because I don't know if I'll ever get used to calling him anything else, and I search for the truth. I see sorrow, regret and an apology, and I know that Gray isn't lying. I turn my eyes to Gray and I see anger and loathing. For me or Grant, I'm not sure.

Before anyone else could speak, the door opens and a pretty, young-looking woman in a long, white coat and blue scrubs walks in. She carries a clip chart and has a blue stethoscope wrapped around her neck. The glasses she's wearing make her look smart and trustworthy. "You're awake. Good. How are you feeling, Livia?"

"Better." I'll say anything I need to in order to get released. But surprisingly, once I attune to my body, I realize that I mean it. I do feel better, at least physically. Emotionally, though, I'm worse than before.

Both Gray and Grant have moved to the foot of the bed, and Addy has joined them, smartly—or maybe not so smartly—standing between. I cringe at everything she's overheard in the last five minutes.

The doctor walks to the right side of the bed, checks my vitals and then my heart and lungs with her cold little piece of equipment. "Everything sounds good."

She turns to the two men I love most, but whom I don't seem to know at all. "Gentlemen, miss, can we have a minute alone, please."

Addy smiles and squeezes my foot, leaving silently. Gray and Grant both grumble, but walk to the door. Gray walks right out, but Grant looks back, his eyes begging for forgiveness. I look away. I need time to digest and think about what the hell just happened. I have so much hurt inside me, I don't know what to do with it all.

"So your *friends*…" she pauses at the word, and I smile weakly. "…tell me that you've been unable to keep anything down for a week. Is that true?"

"Yes."

"Nothing? No water, no food?"

"Not much."

"How many times a day have you been vomiting?"

"Several," I answer. No reason to hide the truth.

"And how much weight have you lost?"

I sigh. "Five pounds, probably. Maybe more."

In an unusual move, she sits on the edge my bed, facing me. I guess I don't know what's unusual for a doctor, but sitting one's bed seems to fit that bill. She sets the chart down beside her and holds my gaze.

"Are you under any stress?"

I look down and will my moisture away. "Yes," I reply quietly. So much, I don't know what to do with it all.

"And I take it those two have something to do with that."

My laughter is weak. "It's complicated." That's the understatement of the century.

She nods and smiles sympathetically. "It usually is."

"So what's wrong with me? Some sort of flu bug?"

"Well, you have what's called hyperemesis gravidarum, which causes severe, frequent vomiting

294

and can last for a specified period of time, although it varies with each individual."

Hypergrav, what? That sounds very bad. "How long does it last? Can you give me something to make it go away? Like medicine? I can hardly even function, doctor."

Smiling, like she has a secret, I'm afraid to hear what's going to come out of her mouth next. "I'm afraid it can last up to nine months, although most of the time it starts to dissipate significantly after the first trimester. And there are some reasons you could be experiencing such a severe case. Heredity, multiples, a history of motion sickness..." She keeps talking, but I can't hear any more words. I stopped listening after she said *first trimester. First trimester?* No...

"Livia? Are you listening to me?" The pretty doctor is now shaking my shoulder.

"Umm, I think you need to back up. Are you trying to tell me I'm *pregnant*?" I'm about to hyperventilate. There is absolutely no way I can be pregnant.

"There's no doubt. Your blood tests confirm you're pregnant. And I'm afraid you have severe morning sickness, Livia. It's not uncommon, unfortunately. It's inconvenient, and in your case, severe enough we needed to get you rehydrated with fluids. I've given you some vitamin B6, which generally helps with the worst of the nausea. There are also some herbal remedies you can try, like ginger, which can sometimes help. Maybe even some acupressure cuffs on your wrists. You should take vitamin B6 every day, and I'll leave you with a list of other things to avoid that can cause the nausea to flare, but mostly, I'm afraid, you'll just have to give it time."

I'm shaking my head furiously. "I need you to stop. I *cannot* be pregnant. I can't *get* pregnant." Each word I speak sounds shriller.

She sighs, like she's frustrated she has to go over this again, but I can't help it. She has to be wrong. "And why do you think you can't get pregnant? You're a young, healthy woman."

Yes, who had her family's future ripped away from her when she was a mere twenty-three years old. I begin to cry, sobbing uncontrollably into my hands. I feel the bed dip and her small arms come around me, trying to comfort. "Livia, there are other options."

I shake my head because that's not the problem. Something I never thought was possible has happened.

I'm going to be a mother.

I couldn't be happier and more distraught at the same time. I have a life growing inside of me that Gray and I created together, and now he can't even stand the sight of me and thinks I'm sleeping with his *brother*.

Oh God.

I have absolutely no idea how he'll feel about this baby. What I don't want is pity. I don't want for him to stay with me simply out of loyalty to this child. The man I *thought* I knew would do that. I guess with my new discovery about his undead brother, I'm not even sure of that anymore. I'm unsure of a lot of things. What I'm not unsure of, however, is how much I love Gray Colloway, and how much I already love this little life growing inside of me.

Twenty minutes later, my mind spinning with our conversation and my news, Dr. Culross walks out the door, leaving me alone in the deafening silence. She said I could be discharged after this next batch of fluids is gone, which will be in about three hours. Three hours that I need to think. I asked her to tell Gray and Grant that I was tired and needed some undisturbed rest.

I need time to figure out what I'm going to do next.

Chapter 45

Gray

Luke and I have hardly spoken a word that hasn't been hateful and hurtful since he opened his eyes and saw me standing in the doorway of Livvy's bedroom. A flash of guilt left as quickly as it came, and it took everything in me not to rip him apart that very second. The only thing that stopped me was how tranquil Livvy looked.

Even in sleep and the low light, I could tell she wasn't well. She had bags under her eyes and her skin looked pale and sickly and a pang of guilt hit me so hard, it nearly buckled my knees.

I had done this to her. I had left her all alone, without explanation, without discussion, over fifty words from some asshole who was probably trying to get back at me for blackmailing him. And it was like a sucker punch to the gut when Luke called me out on it in front of Livvy, because he was right. This laid squarely at my feet, not hers.

I said some cruel things to her, things I couldn't take back. Things I wasn't even sure I meant. I don't know if they're sleeping together, but I know love when I see it. And Luke is clearly in love with Livvy. I could see it in the gentle way he held her in her bed, and the way he's watched her lying helpless in that hospital bed. And it makes me seethe with rage and jealousy and murderous thoughts.

I don't trust him as far as I can spit and my trust in Livvy sits precariously on a high cliff, where a brief gust of wind could easily knock it over. I want to give her the benefit of the doubt, but the cards are stacking up against her awfully quickly. Married two days after leaving me and then I find out she knows, and is "friends" with my gangster brother. I feel positively sick, wondering what she's really been up to these past five years.

I stare at my brother across the waiting room. Luke and I were inseparable growing up and then one day everything changed and I never knew why. Luke became a completely different person. Withdrawn, angry, defiant. He started smoking. He got tattoos. He fell into a rough crowd, initiated into a gang at eighteen and started selling drugs. By the time I realized what was going on, it was too late to pull him back. I tried. I begged, I pleaded, I guilted. Nothing worked.

After graduation, we went our separate ways. Me to college. Him to live a life of crime. When I heard he got mixed up in the mob, I was done with him. Our family was done with him. Our father was sick with shame and worry and guilt. I think our mom has kept in touch with Luke all these years, although she'll never say one way or another. She would never betray his trust like that. She wouldn't do it to any of her other kids, either. My mom is a fucking saint.

I've asked Luke repeatedly how he met Livvy and he refuses to say. He only repeats his answer, "that's her story to tell." I'm growing very tired of being kept in the fucking dark. By everyone. I clearly see they share a secret between them, a secret that *I'm* not privy to, a secret I know is about these past few years. I want to tie him to that fucking chair he's sitting in and torture him until he spills everything. Had I not come by Livvy's apartment last night, or at all, would she have just moved on with my brother? Would she fall in love with him, if she wasn't already, and marry him and live the life that *I* want with her...with him instead?

God, it makes me so sick, I can't even think about it.

"I have to go," I say, rising from the blue, pilled chair that I've been sitting on for the past two hours. Yes, it's a cowardly move and one I know I'll regret making, but right now I just need time to think. And I can see that Livvy clearly trusts Luke, although if she knew everything about him, she wouldn't. Hell, maybe she already does and that's the kind of man she wants. My head is so jumbled and confused right now, I don't know which way is up and if I stay, I'll just end up spewing more hateful words that I'll never be able to take back.

Luke just shakes his head in disappointment. I ignore him. The last person I need condemnation from is my mobster brother. His statement stalls me for only a moment. "You're making a mistake. She loves you, Gray."

"You are unworthy of her," I snarl, willing my feet forward. I heard his soft words, but they don't register until long after I'm gone.

"At least you and I agree on something, brother."

300

Chapter 46

Livia

Grant peeks his head in as I'm pulling on my jacket. Addy brought me fresh clothes a little while ago when she heard they were cutting me loose. When he told me Gray had somewhere to be and had left without saying goodbye, I broke down and cried again. He held me and let me weep. That was an hour ago.

"Hi," he said, trying his hardest to be cheerful.

"Hi," I replied, trying my hardest to reciprocate. He smiles at my pathetic attempt, making me laugh.

Taking a seat beside me on the small loveseat, he pulls me close. "How are you feeling?"

I turn to him. "That's a loaded question." His smile is sad and I look away. "Physically, I'm doing much better. Whatever concoction they gave me seemed to work." I'd not said a word to Grant about the baby, he just thinks I have some sort of super flu bug.

But Addy knows. It was hard to keep that secret when I handed her the scripts I was given to fill, one being prenatal vitamins. She just hugged me, not saying a word. I could see the dozen questions she was thinking, but wouldn't ask.

Does he know?

Are you getting back together?

What will you do?

They were questions mirrored by me. None of which I had the answers to. We had a whole silent conversation in the span of thirty seconds and then, like a good friend, she left without speaking one judgmental word, even if she was thinking them.

"Did you know? About Gray?" I turn to look at him when he's silent for too long.

"Not until I had you followed. I didn't know all those years ago. I swear."

I nod, silent for a few moments as I mull his answer. "You should have told me."

"I know," he replies softly. "I'm sorry. I just didn't know how."

I sigh deeply. "Well, those who live in glass houses and all, right?" I'd been thinking about this for the last three hours. Who am *I* to judge *him* for keeping secrets when I've done the same exact thing to Gray. And apparently he's been doing the exact same thing with me. Oh, what a tangled web.

"Should I call you Grant or Luke?"

"I go by Luke now, but you can call me whatever you want, babe."

"You look like a Luke," I say after a few beats.

He twines our hands together and we sit in silence for several minutes, waiting for Addy to return so we can leave. "Tell me what happened with Gray. How he even found out? I thought I'd done a pretty damn good job of burying that so no one could ever find it."

I lean my shoulder into him, throwing him off balance. "Me too." I stand, not able to sit any longer. "He hired a private investigator. Townley

302

Consulting. If you can believe it, I found out when I had to pay an invoice that came in last week. He told me he trusted me, that he'd wait for me to be ready to tell him, but we got into a fight about it last Saturday night on the phone and he hung up angry. Then, starting on Sunday, he wouldn't return my calls or texts and I didn't see or hear from him again until I woke to a WWE wrestling match in my living room yesterday."

This is one of the things I loved most about Grant...Luke. He owned everything he did. He didn't look sheepish or apologetic about my dig. Instead, his face lit up with a brilliant smile. "I was defending your honor. He was saying some pretty nasty shit."

"I'm sure he was," I mumble.

Addy walks in, cutting our conversation short, which is probably a good thing. I don't want to know everything that Gray said. It would only hurt worse.

Chapter 47

Livia

Three days later I still haven't heard from Gray, and with each day that passes, my anger grows and my sadness deepens. Luke, I'd finally gotten used to calling him that, is with me almost constantly, even though I'd told him repeatedly I would be fine alone. And because he is around constantly, he is starting to get suspicious that I no longer had the flu.

While the B6 that I took daily and ginger powder that I put on everything helped, they didn't eliminate the morning sickness. I only vomited once or twice a day now. But my stomach is still pretty queasy and I didn't have much of an appetite.

"You should go see him. Gray is a stubborn asshole," Luke said. We are watching a movie on Lifetime. Luke's been complaining about it the whole time. He'd do anything to get out of it.

"I know." We've had this discussion several times already, but I think Gray's absence is pretty telling. He's trying to move on, get over me. *But he came here the other night to talk, Livia, so that must mean something. And you're carrying his baby. He deserves to know.*

He grabs the remote, shutting off the TV. "Hey, they were just getting to the good part," I whine.

"Let me tell you how it ends, babe. Man wrongs woman. Woman retaliates. Woman victorious. It's how all these fucking movies end."

"Wow, cynical much? And how would you know how Lifetime movies end?" I tease.

"It's television for women. How else do you think they end?" I laugh as he stands in front of me, holding out his hand. "Now, no time like the present."

My smile falls. "But it's after nine."

His brows arch and his hand wiggles, urging me to take it, not buying my bullshit excuses. "He needs to know, Livia." His voice is soft and coaxing, but firm. Yep, he knows and he's not going to let me put this off any longer. "I'll take you."

I put my hand in his and less than thirty minutes later, we're idling in front of Gray's building. I've had to practice my deep breathing most of the way here because now the nausea is all due to my nerves, instead of the baby.

"You okay?" He reaches over squeezing my hand.

"Yes. No. I'm nervous." My right leg is bouncing so fast, the entire car is shaking.

"I know, baby."

"Will you wait for me?" I don't even know if Gray is home, let alone if he'll see me.

"Until you tell me to go."

I let go of his hand and open the car door. With each shaky step I take toward the building, and Gray's apartment, my stomach churns faster. I feel sicker. My legs are like liquid, almost unable to hold my slight weight. When I reach the lobby, I wave to

Sam and head to the elevator. I finger the card key Gray gave me with trembling hands, barely able to insert it into the thin slot.

The elevator ride goes all too fast, and then I'm standing in front of his door. It takes several minutes to get the courage to knock, but I finally do. After only seconds the door opens, and I realize that I should have called first.

Because it's not Gray that answers the door, but a tall, beautiful blonde. The same woman I saw hanging from his arm like an ornament at the fundraiser. That day seems so long ago now. And not only is it bad enough that she's answering his door, what makes it worse is what she's wearing. Or what she's *not*.

"Can I help you?" she asks sweetly, acting like she belongs there.

I stand mute, blinking rapidly like a fool. I can't take my eyes away from the fair expanse of her legs peeking out from underneath the bottom of the mint green button down of Gray's that she's wearing. And when my eyes travel up, it's clear she's not wearing a bra, her cleavage peeking out from just the three buttons she's managed to thread.

Finally, saying nothing, I turn and call for the elevator. Luckily for me, it hasn't been called down yet and the doors open immediately. I step in and don't turn around, unwilling to see if Gray's joined her in witnessing my shame.

When the doors close, I fall to my knees and vomit. Then I curl into a ball and commence nuclear meltdown. I don't know how long I lay there. I don't remember anything, except that suddenly I was being lifted by a pair of strong arms and cradled to a male chest.

Luke has always been there for me whenever I've needed him. Every single time without fail. Looks like maybe he's the only man I can count on now, because Gray has clearly left me standing alone in his rear view mirror.

Chapter 48

Livia

I lay quietly in the dark, listening to the sound of my bathroom faucet dripping. The steady rhythm is soothing and should lull me to sleep. It doesn't. I'm mentally exhausted, but can't seem to fall into that black nothingness that I crave so much. Every time I close my eyes, I see *her*. Images of Gray kissing her slender neck or slowly unbuttoning his shirt and removing it from her perfect body or the sounds he'll make when she goes down on him. They haunt me. They'd obviously been very busy tonight. She looked like a woman who'd been well attended to when she answered the door, and I have first-hand knowledge of the sort of attentive lover Gray is.

Luke's warm body spoons mine and for once, I don't want him here, but he refused to leave. I think he knew if he did that I'd truly be lost. He may be right. I'm having a very difficult time not letting myself be pulled down by this massive undertow that's sucked me firmly in its grasp. It's one thing to know that I've lost Gray, it's quite another to know he's with someone else less than two weeks after we're apparently through. How is it possible for your heart to still beat when it feels like it's broken and bleeding out? I never understood that cruel trick the universe played.

As much as I want to succumb to this despair, I have to stay strong. For the baby. Even if Gray doesn't want me, this baby needs me, so I can't let myself fall into that dark place that's whispering so seductively for me to join. It's enticing, but I need to resist. I know sooner or later I'll have to face Gray and tell him about the pregnancy, because I have to believe that he'll want to be a part of his baby's life, even if he doesn't want to be part of mine. And I would never keep Gray from his child.

Gently lifting Luke's arm, I slide slowly out of bed. I pull on my robe and open the door, careful to avoid the loose floorboard that squeaks when I step out into the darkened hallway.

Making my way to the kitchen, I pull a few saltines from the cupboard. Opening the fridge, I stare longingly at the milk. One of many things I've been told to avoid to help the morning sickness. I grab a bottle of water instead. Sitting in the dark at the island, I think back to Dr. Culross's explanation of how I ended up pregnant.

"I had a procedure done with coils or something placed in my tubes. I was told they'd prevent pregnancy."

"Well, not every procedure is foolproof, Livia. Did you have the follow-up visit where x-rays are taken to ensure sufficient scar tissue had formed? That's what blocks the sperm, but it takes several months for the tissue to form, so that last step is critical to ensure the procedure worked."

I shake my head.

"Well, then I guess you're lucky you haven't gotten pregnant before now. If you truly don't wish to

have children in the future, you'll either have to have it re-performed or choose an alternative method of birth control."

Dr. Culross had no idea of my history. She had no idea that I hadn't even had sex in the past almost three years, until recently, and she certainly didn't know the man who used me as his plaything before couldn't have children. She never asked me why, but I could see the question in her eyes about why someone so young would have such a life altering procedure.

As I sit here in the dark and think about the circumstances that led me here, that led *us* here, for the first time I have a deep-seated need to tell Gray what happened. Not for sympathy, not to win him back, but for closure. For both of us. Maybe if he knows why I left, why I really stayed away all this time, he'll truly believe it wasn't him. I need him to believe that. I've been exceedingly selfish keeping this to myself and I need to make things right. He needs to understand that I *didn't* abandon him, at least not in the way he thinks.

Maybe then we can both put this part of our lives behind us. It makes me incredibly sad to think that's a real possibility, even though I saw evidence of that with my own two eyes tonight. To know that I may have to see him in the future with another woman, or other children, when we swap weekends with our child almost brings me to my knees with sheer, raw pain.

Resolute in my decision, minutes later, pen and paper in hand, and a soft glow from the lamp adding just enough light, I begin my confession. It takes four tries, but an hour later, with my deepest shame now in writing, I strangely feel a little bit lighter. I feel a tiny bit of peace lingering around the dark edges. I hope it does the same thing for Gray.

When I glide back into bed, Luke puts an arm around my waist, pulling me close. "Feel better, baby?"

I nod and close my eyes, finally able to drift off into a light, fitful sleep.

Chapter 49

Gray

This week isn't much better than the last. I go through the motions, not even sure what decisions I'm making anymore. I attend meetings. I sit on conference calls. I blindly sign documents without even so much as a cursory review. I could have sold our company ten times over by now and not even known it. I can't get Livvy out of my mind. And I can't get the image of her in Luke's arms out of it, either. It's forever scorched there, the outline of it still smoking.

I've sat outside of her apartment every night for the past three days, but I can't force myself to go up and knock on her door. I can't see her in his arms again. Last night I saw them walk out together and get into his car. He held open the door and they were laughing. They looked like a couple. I don't know how many times I have to be destroyed by this woman before I give her up or give up on her. I never would have pegged myself to be such a glutton for punishment.

As I watched her, I noticed she looked better, not nearly as peaked as she did when I up and abandoned her in the hospital without so much as a goodbye. I don't even know why I care anymore, but I do. I can't make myself stop.

I sat there long after they left, doing nothing but staring into the night. I was in so much pain seeing them together I couldn't even move. An hour later when I returned to my apartment, I had another problem to deal with.

Lena. In my fucking shirt and nothing else.

That conniving bitch had sweet-talked Sam into letting her into my apartment, making him believe we were back together and that she'd just misplaced her key. Because she'd been to my place several times, he believed her. Sam felt terrible. I told Lena if I ever saw her, or if she so much as thought about contacting me again, I would take out a restraining order. Psycho bitch.

A sudden loud commotion outside my office gets my attention and I'm almost to the door when it flies open, knocking me back a few steps. Seconds later I'm on the floor, my cheek feels like it exploded. I look up and Luke hovers over me, fists clenched, ready to strike another blow.

"A simple hi would have worked," I grumble, licking the blood off my lip as I stand. My temp is in the doorway, eyes as wide as saucers. "It's fine, Allison. Shut the door on your way out, please."

"Are you—"

"Yes. Shut the door." The last thing I need is for the entire office to hear what I'm afraid is about to go down, although I'm pretty sure they'll hear plenty of muffled shouting here very shortly.

I walk back to my desk and calmly take a seat. What I really want to do is lay my brother out flat on the ground. "Do you mind telling me what I did to deserve that? I think I'm the one that should be throwing the punches. You are fucking my girl, after all."

He shakes his head, taking a seat. "I've told you repeatedly I'm not fucking Livia. We are friends. That's it." I watch his eyes closely as he speaks. I remember when we were kids and Luke lied, his left eye would always tick slightly. It didn't take long for my parents to catch on and Luke was always the go-to kid when they wanted to get the truth.

No tick.

"But you want to." *That* much, I know. And I want to strangle him for thinking that way about her.

"You're one to talk, Gray, given the fact that just last night you were fucking some whore in your apartment." Luke's jaw clenches.

My brows draw together in confusion. *Lena?* How the fuck does he know about Lena? "Then you have been misinformed."

"Really?" he smirked. "So you're telling me the blonde in your apartment, wearing nothing but your shirt, was what? A maid? A co-worker dropping off some work papers? A neighbor stopping by for an egg or a cup of sugar, perhaps?"

"How do you know about that?" Now I'm getting fucking pissed. I have no idea what Luke is into these days, but if I find out he's following me we will have some serious problems.

"Why don't you ask Livia?"

"Livia?" I whisper. "Why would I ask Livia?" That sick feeling that's been my constant companion for the past couple of weeks is knocking violently deep within the walls of my gut. I know exactly what he's about to tell me and I feel positively ill.

"Because your whore answered the door last night at about nine thirty when she came to talk to you, since you've been too much of a pussy to nut it up and chase after the woman you claim to love."

I think back to when I saw them leave Livvy's last night. Had I not sat there, drowning in my own pathetic pool of sorrow, none of this would have happened. Maybe Livvy would be back in my arms this very moment. A string of expletives rolls low and rough off my tongue. My brother watches me closely, gauging my reaction to his little bomb. "It's not what it looked like." My excuse sounds lame and unbelievable, even to my own ears.

A ghost of a smile crosses Luke's lips. "Riiiight."

I don't deem his comment worthy of a response. The only person's opinion I care about is Livvy's, and I need to make sure she knows what she saw wasn't at all what it looked like. *And maybe neither was what you saw between Livvy and Luke.* I let my head fall back against my chair and gaze up at the ceiling. This whole situation is one big clusterfuck. Luke is right and I hate it. I do need to man up.

"Why are you here," I ask tiredly. All of a sudden I'm exhausted. Constantly carrying anger and hurt takes a huge emotional and physical toll on the human psyche. I've been carrying them both for over five years and I'm tired. I want Livvy in my life, but I realize I don't know if that's really possible anymore. All that water under the bridge seems to have risen to flood level stages and threatens to spill over its banks, washing the entire bridge away with its enormous power.

Luke stands and paces, running his hands through his shaggy hair. "I really don't know why, Gray. I may not be worthy of Livia, but you sure as fuck don't deserve her either with the way you've treated her these past few days."

"I—"

He continues, talking over me. "But for some fucking reason, she is blindly in love with you and has been since the day I met her. The Gray I used to know wouldn't take a paltry paragraph of loosely thrown together facts at face value without digging and picking and pulling apart each word until he had the whole fucking story."

"She married another man after she'd agreed to marry me!" I roar. "What other story do I need?"

Luke stops, staring me down, his blazing eyes mirroring mine. "The real one."

Then I realize that he was referencing the report that Townley had given me. "And how do you know about the report?"

"Probably bad form to have your PI bills sent to your work email when your girlfriend has access to them. Livia's pretty good at putting two and two together."

"Fuck." Then I realize that Townley only sent the bill to my work email, not the report. "That still doesn't explain how you know about the report. Or what's in it," I accuse.

His smirk grates on me. "I have my sources."

We're silent for several tense minutes. "What happened to her, Luke?" My quiet voice drifts over the desk and hangs in the air like poisonous mist, ready to sear my skin with its deadly toxin.

"I've told you. That's Livia's story to tell and only hers. But I can assure you, whatever you're thinking, you are dead wrong." His words ring with such conviction, it scares me.

Standing, I walk to the window and look out into a city teeming with life. I inanely wonder what types of problems the people walking the sidewalks of Chicago below me are dealing with in their own lives and if they're half as fucked up or complex as mine. "I don't know if it matters anymore. I don't know if we can get past this."

Snorting, he bites, "If you really think that, then you're even more of a self-absorbed, self-righteous prick than I thought you were." I hear something whisper across my desk and turn to see an envelope that Luke's thrown down, my name scrawled across the front. I raise my eyes to lock with his. "And if you really think that, then you don't deserve answers. You deserve to be kept in the dark for the rest of your sad, lonely life. You don't deserve *her*."

I face him, my arms crossed protectively, like I'm trying to shield my heart from the cuts each truthful word inflicts. "You never told me why you're here."

His mouth turns up in a sad smile. "I'm doing it for Livia. *I* would do anything for her." Then he turns and leaves much differently than the way he arrived, closing the door softly behind him. His last sentence lingers in the air, the unspoken challenge heard loud and clear.

My twin may be in love with Livvy, of that I have no doubt, but he's trying to push us back together, instead of tear us apart. And right now, tearing us apart would be so very easy to do. We both believed hurtful lies that aren't true. As insanely jealous as I am of Luke, I also have to respect him for his selflessness. I rub my split lip absently, another injury to add to my marred face, just starting to heal from Saturday's altercation.

Just then, an odd thought pops into my head and I remember the story our mom used to tell us when we were younger about how they named us. Luke was always to be named Luke, but my parents had a different name picked out for me. When I was born, they said the name didn't fit, so I became Gray instead.

I look at the closed door my twin just walked through. The original name they'd picked out for me was Grant.

Chapter 50

Livia

"Did you see him?" I ask anxiously when he walks through the door.

"Yes." He walks to the refrigerator and takes out a beer.

"And?"

Luke leans against the island and tips the brew to his lips, taking a long gulp. "And I did as you asked." His eyes wouldn't meet mine.

"Thank you," I reply quietly. "I'm sorry. I know this is hard for you." I've unfairly put Luke into the middle of this shit storm with Gray and me, even though I knew what it would do to him. He wants me for himself, but he loves me enough to take my confession to the man *I'm* in love with. His twin brother. A brother who tells people he's dead. God, I hate myself more with each passing day. I seem to have one thing down to a science. Hurting the people I love.

He downs his bottle in one more giant gulp before setting it down hard on the counter. He pulls me to him, burying his head in my hair, holding me close like he's trying to crawl inside. The gesture is tender and filled with love and heartbreak. We stand silently there for long minutes, arms wrapped around each other.

I have this near overwhelming urge to kiss him because I know a goodbye when I feel one. I'm breaking inside. I *need* him, even though I know it's wrong to lean on him so much when he's hurting just like me. *Because* of me. Then he kisses my temple, warm lips lingering, before he leaves me and walks back to the front door.

"Yeah, it was hard," he says almost inaudibly right before he walks out, leaving me standing there alone.

A single tear streaks down my face. I've lost so much. I don't know how much more loss I can take. I place a protective hand over my belly, where the baby that Gray and I created grows and I pray that, for once, God will be on my side and let me have something good in my life.

Chapter 51

Gray

I stare at the thin envelope my brother left on my desk like it's full of razor sharp thorns that will bleed me dry if I prick myself. My hands tremble as I slit open the sealed flap and take out the three pages inside. I'm nauseous, the sandwich I ate for lunch churning madly in my stomach.

These are my answers. I knew I was about to learn something that I no longer really wanted to know but had no other choice. There are times when burying your head in the sand simply isn't a viable option any longer. I guess that's where I am.

I look at down at Livvy's handwritten letter. For minutes I just stare at the salutation, afraid to go any further. Then I start to read. Several times throughout the letter, I have to set it aside because it's simply too agonizing to continue and my tears blur the words. It takes me nearly half an hour to get through it.

My Dearest Gray ~

I know I'm taking the coward's way out by writing you a letter instead of telling you this in person, but I can't stand to see the shame and hurt, and even possibly disgust you'll have for me after I tell you everything. I only hope that someday you'll be able to understand,

and possibly even forgive me for my actions and the suffering they've clearly caused you.

Please believe me when I tell you, if I could have done things differently, if there were any other path than the one I chose, I would have taken it. I would have done *almost* anything to be with you and share the life I'd already envisioned us having together. And you'll see, once my story is finished, therein lies the problem. That one little word, *almost*, is what changed everything for me. For us.

Mine starts out as a true love story. A fairytale. The one that romance writers will try to emulate. But it's not possible, for there is no greater love story.

The fairytale starts when a young, naïve, working girl meets a cocky, confident, persistent, beautiful boy. The second she laid eyes on him, he took her breath away and she knew he was The One. He was fierce and loyal, intense and loving. He would sweep her off her feet and become the love of her life. He was her future husband and father of her children. He stole her heart and imprisoned it deep within him, so it would become forever his. In her entire lifetime, there would never be another that could have it because it was no longer hers to give. He was her soul mate. Her life. Her very breath. Her reason for living.

Her everything.
He was you. He *is* you.

But every story has a villain, and this one is no different. My fairytale quickly morphed into a horror story. I know this will be difficult for you to read, Gray, and for that, I apologize. I can assure you, however, not more difficult than it is for me to know you'll be reading it.

The morning after your proposal, I got an urgent phone call from my father. He was crying and sounded scared. I thought Alyse was in trouble again, so I left you a note and rushed home. It turns out Alyse was in trouble, just not in the way I'd thought. You know my father was a gambling addict and apparently he owed some very bad men a lot of money. Money he didn't have, so their payment came in the form of a young, innocent eighteen-year-old girl who had already suffered so much. A girl who wouldn't have survived a day, let alone three years, with a monster.

You understand why I couldn't let that happen.

Fifteen minutes after I arrived home I was taken away and the next day, I was forced to marry a fifty-five-year-old monster and mobster named Peter Wilder. They didn't know about you, Gray. And I couldn't let them. I would not endanger your life, or Alyse's. If I'd tried to warn either of you in any way, you'd have stopped at nothing to find me and I have no doubt Peter would have taken great pleasure killing you just to spite me. So I followed every instruction to the letter and prayed I'd find a way out. That I'd find my way back to you before it was too late. It turns out my way

323

out wasn't until three years later, but it was far too late by then.

It wasn't a marriage of love or convenience or even hate. It was a sacrifice that needed to be made in order to change my sister's fate. And I was the only one that could make it. Alyse has no idea, and it must stay that way.

Please don't ask me to detail all of the horrible things I endured during that time. It was traumatic, it was horrific and whatever you're imagining, it was probably worse. Peter Wilder was not a nice or decent man. He didn't buy me jewels or take me on extravagant vacations. He didn't love me. He barely tolerated me. But I'm here. I survived, and that's all that matters. Peter is dead and I'm free. I've had extensive counseling and, although I still have my days, for the most part, I'm better. Only my love and memories of you got me through those dark days and I'm so grateful that I have new ones we've created these past few blissful weeks. You will never understand how much that means to me.

You need to know that Luke saved my life. Luke worked for Peter, that's how we met. And although I don't know his story, I knew he didn't want to be there. He didn't belong with them. He was kind-hearted and soft and he had what none of the rest of them did. A conscience. If it wasn't for Luke, I'd be dead. He cared for me the many times I was beaten and when Peter died of a stroke a little more than two years ago, he single-handedly got me out of hell and into a new life. He set me up in Chicago, gave me money and found me a place to live. I haven't seen or heard from him since then until just a couple of weeks ago. I think perhaps the man you thought you knew isn't the same man anymore. You should give him a chance. Get to know him again. I actually think you'd like him and would be able to see the good in him that I do.

I'm not going to lie to you. I love Luke. We have a bond and a friendship that's unique and he was there for me when I had no one else. I won't give that up. I won't give him up. Not even for you. But I'm not in love with Luke. I'm in love with _you_, and I have been every day for the past eight years. I think it's true what they say that we don't get to choose who we fall in love with. We just fall and hope for the best, no matter how the story ends. I will never regret us. I will never regret our love because regretting it means I wish it never happened and, for so many reasons, I could never do that.

You can probably now understand why I didn't tell you all of this before, even though you had every right to know. I warred with myself every day for the past two years on whether I should find you, but...I was scared. I wasn't the same woman you fell in love with and I didn't know if you could love this new version of me. The tainted version. I thought too much time had passed. I thought you'd hate me. I thought you'd be with someone else and I couldn't bear to see that. I thought a lot of things. None of them good.

And when fate placed us in each other's paths once again, even though you deserved it, I just couldn't make myself say the words. I was selfish. Truth be told, I didn't want you to look at me differently. I didn't want to lose you again. I couldn't understand how you could still want me, how you could possibly forgive me after everything that I had done to you and I didn't want anything to shatter the fragile relationship we were trying to rebuild. But a relationship can't thrive on lies or half-truths or secrets. I wasn't the only victim in this story. I know you were left confused and angry and hurt and you deserve closure, even if it's hard to hear and hard for me to say. I was wrong to keep this from you for so long and I'm so very sorry.

I understand if this is too much for you to handle. Truly I do. It's a lot for anyone to wrap their head around. I think maybe these answers have come too late for us and I'll never forgive myself for ruining what we had yet a second time. Even though I stayed away, please believe that I've ached to be with you every single day. These past few weeks I've felt more alive than I have since the last day I saw your beautiful face.

I want you to know that, while it will hurt, I'll be okay without you. I understand if we can't be together and if this secret I've kept has damaged us beyond repair. I have nothing but love in my heart for you, and I always will. You're it for me. You'll always have my heart under lock and key, unavailable for any other man.

I pray this gives you the answers you've been seeking and provides you the closure you need. I hope someday you can find it within yourself to forgive me, move on with your life and be truly happy. You deserve that and so much more, Gray.

Forever yours,

Livvy

When I've finished reading the last sentence, I let myself finally break down.

I cry for Livvy.

I cry for me.

I cry for all that we've lost because of a sick, addicted old man. A man I would kill if he weren't already dead.

I cry for the unknown pain and suffering that she went through while I was simply stuck spinning my wheels in bitterness and anger.

I cry for the sacrifice she made for her sister. For me.

I cry for the many ways I've failed her, both then and now.

I get the message. She's letting me go. She's telling me it's okay for *me* to let *her* go. But I'm *not* letting go. I'm not letting *her* go.

327

Then I do what I should have done a week and a half ago. I step up to the fucking plate and I make plans for my future. A future which includes Livvy. Because despite everything, despite what she thinks, it's not too late for us. I will never love another woman. I'm never giving her up. *I can't.* She's my everything. She always has been. The only way I can truly be happy is with her.

She's not the only one who's had her heart stolen, forever unavailable to another.

Chapter 52

Livia

"I told him. Well, I wrote him a letter." I pick imaginary lint from my jeans, not wanting to see her reaction.

"And?"

"And what?"

"How does that make you feel?"

I look up into the compassionate, aging face of my psychiatrist whom I've seen for the past two plus years. I've come to have a great deal of respect for the woman who brought me back from the brink of despair with her quirky techniques and soul-searching questions. For the first year, I happily took anti-anxiety medications, like the good little patient I was, but I got tired of the fuzzy, mind-numbing effects and found that I could cope just fine off of them. Of course, the year of intensive therapy probably had something to do with that.

"How does that make me feel?" A question she asks a dozen times a session. "Honestly? Sick to my stomach."

"That's not an emotion, Livia. That's a physical symptom of the emotions you're feeling."

Snorting, I add, "Okay, fine. I feel anxious and embarrassed and helpless."

"Why?"

"Because I'm afraid he won't want me anymore," I whisper softly. I think back to the nearly naked woman who answered his door last night and it cramps my stomach. He's made it pretty clear he already doesn't want me anymore already. I guess maybe my mind really just hasn't accepted it yet. I don't know why *hope* enthralls us in her wicked, twisted spell, making us believe things that aren't really true, but she does. And she does it well.

Writing that letter was the right thing to do, but it doesn't mean it was easy and handing to Luke was probably the hardest thing I've ever done in my life.

I've been checking my phone obsessively since Luke left me this morning. It's now almost five and I haven't heard a peep from Gray. I guess I didn't really expect to, but I'd be lying if I said I wasn't gutted all the same. I also haven't heard from Luke. I've texted him twice with no response. I'm equally worried I won't see him again for a while and that's almost as hard to swallow as Gray's continued snubs.

When I walk through the door at a little after six, Addy and Kamryn are sitting on the couch, each holding a glass wine. "Hi." I drop my purse on the floor and take a seat between them. Laying my head back, I stare at the ceiling.

"Hi, sweetie. How are you?" Kam asks, rubbing my shoulder.

"I'm...dealing." I feel a bit better after my counseling session like I always do.

"You need to get changed," Addy announces.

"No. I'm too tired to go anywhere."

"Livia, you need to get out of this apartment. Besides, we're taking you somewhere fun. And dress warmly. We'll be outside." In October, the evenings in Illinois cool significantly.

I begin to protest again when she lays the guilt trip on thick. "You missed Kam's birthday last week. Think of this as a make-up."

"Wow. Harsh." Last week I was in the middle of a mental breakdown. "Okay." I give in because I know I won't win. Addy is one of the most tenacious people I know. And maybe getting out of here will help me take my mind off the fact that I haven't heard from Gray. That I may *never* hear from Gray.

Neither Kam nor Addy will tell me where we're going until we arrive. And by the time we reach Navy Pier, it's starting to get dark and the Ferris wheel is lit with bright lights. I have to sit in the car an extra couple of minutes, gaining my composure because the last time I looked down at Navy Pier and that carnival ride, I was in Gray's living room. I was happy.

Kam leans in the car, sympathy etched on her sad smile. "Are you okay, sweetie?"

I nod and wipe my eyes. If I could super glue my tear ducts shut, I would. I haven't cried this much in my entire life as I have in the past few weeks. What do you get when you mix together heartbreak with pregnancy hormones? A big, fucking hot mess with a capital H, that's what.

We take our time strolling down the pier, stopping at a couple of the little booths along the way. It's surprisingly busy for a Wednesday night in October. Then we're in front of Pier Park, in front of

331

the Ferris wheel and Kam and Addy leave me to buy tickets at the booth. I don't want to go, but I'm too numb to do anything but play along.

And then I see him, stepping out from behind a pillar. My breath hitches. I look at my friends and they watch me intently to make sure this is what I want. As if there's anything I want more.

My gaze swings back to Gray, who is now making his way toward me. Then he's in front of me, cupping my cheeks. My world narrows to just him. Everyone and everything else fade away. "What are you doing here?" I ask dumbly.

His eyes search mine and I'm awestruck at the love I see pouring from them. "Making sure our fairytale has a happy ending."

"Gray—" He eats the rest of my words with his lips, his mouth, his tongue.

"There isn't anyone else. There's *never* been anyone else," he whispers between kisses. "I love you so much, Livvy. So much," he mumbles against my mouth, kissing me over and over and over again. He hugs me tight and I feel his body tremble. Or maybe it's mine. We stand there, holding onto each other for dear life, as people mill around us. I don't know how long we're like that before he grabs my hand and takes me on my first Ferris wheel ride in Navy Pier.

There's so much to be said, so many questions we both have, but neither of us speaks. He holds me close as the ride takes us higher and higher, one hundred and fifty feet above the ground. My head rests on his shoulder. His free hand entwines with mine, his thumb drawing light circles on top. The view of Chicago from this height is incredible, but I can't enjoy it. All I can focus on is the feel of his hand in mine, and how his arm around me makes me feel like I'm finally home.

For the first time in nearly two weeks, I can breathe.

———————

The second we walk through his apartment door, Gray is all over me, the path to his bedroom littered with our clothes.

"Gray," I moan. His mouth and tongue are doing wicked things to my pussy and within only seconds, I'm ready to explode. I've been too long without this man touching me. "Right there, don't stop. Please don't..." The second he slides two fingers in and curls them precisely the right way, I climax, crying out his name. My hands hold him to me as I'm taken on the best ride I've ever been on—his mouth.

He crawls up my body, his lips taking mine like they own them. They do. He does. "Fuck, you taste sweet," he mutters against my mouth. He rolls us over, pulling me astride him. I palm my sensitive breasts. The low rumble coming from deep inside his chest makes me gush with desire.

"You are the sexiest thing I've ever seen. Ride me, angel. Hard," he demands. His hazel eyes glitter like gems in the glow of the lamp and I want to do nothing else but submit to his every whim. I position his cock and sink down, reveling in the sensation each inch brings to my extra sensitive nerve endings. My head falls back and we begin our sensual dance.

His hands direct every shift and roll of my hips and I follow his lead, letting him pleasure himself with my body. Within minutes, he's shouting my name and then I'm sprawled over him, our breathing shallow, our sweat-soaked bodies stuck together.

Gray positions us so that we're lying side-by-side. I can't look away from the man I love. The man I thought I would never have. The man I thought I didn't deserve. I'm still not sure I do, but I'm done questioning it. My soul weeps with pure joy to know that after everything that we've been put through he still wants me.

"There's no one else," he whispers. "What you saw last night was not what it looked like. I wasn't home. I didn't even know Lena was here. I swear I didn't touch her."

"Okay," I reply softly. I believe him.

"I'm so sorry, Livvy. For everything." Tears well in his eyes and mine. I realize we have a long night ahead of us. Of confessions and truths. I'm dreading telling him about the baby we lost. Sharing that type of news in a letter is cold and heartless and I wasn't about to do that to him. But now I'm bursting at the seams to share the joy of our new miracle. Tonight will be hard for both of us. We each have old skin to shed so we can start fresh. It will be unpleasant and uncomfortable and downright gut-wrenching, but necessary if we want to move forward. Which it appears we both do.

"Not more than I am," I finally whisper, feathering a finger down his cheek, catching a stray tear.

And then I begin.

Chapter 53

Livia

"You know how Alyse had been having issues after the accident," I started. When Alyse was eighteen, she had been in a terrible car accident. The driver didn't make it, and although Alyse wasn't nearly as injured as she could have been, she went into a deep depression, trying to kill herself twice. It was a difficult time for all of us.

"Yeah," he answered quietly. His right hand was linked with my left. His other hand stroked my hair.

"She was doing a lot better, of course, but that fear was always there that she'd slip back into that dark place. Dad called in a panic telling me I needed to get home right away, so naturally I thought it was Alyse. But when I got there, my dad was sitting in the middle of the living room on one of the dining room chairs surrounded by about half dozen men with guns."

I stop, trying to gain my composure, not wanting to continue, but knowing that I owed him at least this much. Gray had let me turn off the light so I could make my confessions under the shroud of darkened protection. The only way I'd be able to get the words out was if I didn't have to see how they'd gut him, but the moon shone bright tonight and I could see his face all too well once my eyes adjusted.

I wish I could snuff out its beams, just for the few precious minutes I need to purge my soul.

"It's okay if you don't want to talk about it, angel."

"No. There are things I need to tell you."

"You can stop anytime you want, alright?"

I take a deep breath and continue, but my voice is shaking uncontrollably. "I had no choice, Gray."

"I know, Livvy. It fucking guts me that you had to go through that and I didn't know. If he wasn't dead, I swear to you I would find him and kill him. I hired a detective to find you, but it was like you disappeared off the face of the earth. I'm so fucking sorry I didn't try harder."

"It's not your fault, Gray. Peter was very good at keeping things hidden, including me." He tries to pull me into him, but I resist. I needed the separation if I was going to get through this. "I don't think I can finish if I'm in your arms."

Giving my hand a squeeze, he replies, "Okay."

"A few weeks into my ordeal, I found out I was..." I stop, trying to swallow the bile that's creeping up my throat at the thought of telling him about the baby. "Jesus, this is harder than I thought it would be," I whisper.

"Take as much time as you need, angel."

"I found out I was...pregnant." He stiffened and his hold on my hand became almost painful. I could practically feel the rage rolling off of him.

"Jesus, Livvy. I'm not sure I can hear this."

Sitting up, he moved to get off the bed. I followed and tugged him back. I'm kneeling on the

337

soft mattress with him standing in front of me. Our outer shells are stark naked, and that's exactly how I feel inside having to tell him that a monster killed our baby.

Bare.

Raw.

Exposed.

This was the hardest thing I have ever had to do. Anguish rolled hotly down my face as I tried to purge the words from a place deep inside me that I've tried to bury for years. Cracking the lid on that compartment reopened that wound, making it as fresh as the day it happened.

"It was yours."

"Was?" he choked. His agony was mine. I felt it like it was a breathing entity that had us wrapped in its unbearable spell.

I could only nod. "When he found out, he beat me within an inch of my life. I'd be dead if it wasn't for Luke."

A string of low curses explodes before he pulls me into his arms, squeezing tightly, head buried in my long mane of hair. I feel his body shake and I know he's weeping, just like me. For an unknown period of time, we simply cling to each other for our very lives, like we'll irrevocably drift apart if we loosen our grips a single notch.

We both whisper *I'm sorry* over and over and over. It's not enough. No words in any language ever could be.

Next to losing my baby, it's the most gut-wrenching moment I've ever experienced, but equally freeing. My burden feels lighter, more bearable. I will never get over the malicious, intentional murder of our unborn child, but for the first time since it happened, I think I will actually be able to *really* deal with it because I'll have Gray. We'll have each other.

One secret down, one to go.

"There's something else."

"Livvy." It was an emotional plea, filled with anguish and pain, beseeching me to stop. He couldn't bear anymore, but I had to continue because if I didn't, I'd never get this next part out.

"After that, he had a procedure done that was supposed to render me sterile."

At that little bomb, before I could stop him, he pulled away, stalked across the room and slammed his fist repeatedly into the wall, roaring in both emotional and physical pain. I reached for the lamp, turning it on. When he turned back toward me, the look of pure, raw torture on his face was almost my complete undoing. I'd never seen someone in so much torment. Sliding down the wall, he put his face in his hands and openly sobbed.

"It didn't work," I tell him, but he can't hear me through his uncontrollable crying and mumbling. I climb off the bed and walk over to him on wobbly legs. When I'm close enough, he grabs my hips and wraps his arms tightly around my waist, burying his head in my belly. His tears cool my skin and cleanse my soul.

Threading my fingers through his hair, I call his name until his sobs subside enough he can hear me. "It didn't work, Gray. It didn't work."

His hold loosens and he pulls away, looking up my body. Confusion clouds his eyes, furrows his brows.

"It didn't work," I repeat. Because it's worth repeating. Over and over. I've repeated it a hundred times to myself since I found out I was pregnant, still not believing it's true.

"It didn't work?"

"No."

"I don't understand what you're saying, Livvy."

I take a long, deep breath. Here goes nothing. "I wasn't dehydrated from the flu. I didn't have the flu."

He swallows hard. "You didn't have the flu?"

"No. I was dehydrated from severe morning sickness."

"Morning sickness?"

I finally let a small smile touch my lips. The hardest part is now over. "Yes. I found out in the hospital that I'm pregnant."

"Pregnant?"

I almost laugh at how he's parroting everything I'm saying like if he hears it twice it will make it true. I kneel down, cupping his face. "Yes. Pregnant. With our baby."

"You're—sweet Jesus, you're pregnant?" The look of disbelief and shock are starting to concern me. Maybe he won't be as happy about this as I am. Maybe he's not ready for a family. Maybe telling him now was a bad—

I'm wrenched out of my thoughts when his lips crash to mine. Then his mouth is everywhere and he's laughing, but I can still feel his tears flow across my naked flesh. "You're pregnant? We're pregnant?" He grabs my face, looking deeply into my eyes. "*We're pregnant?*"

For as long as I live, I will never forget the love and adoration and pure joy I see in that one single moment in time. It's an unimaginable moment that I thought I would never have. That *we* would never have. It's suspended, frozen. I take a mental picture so I can replay it again and again and again. I can't possibly speak through my constricted airway, so I just nod.

The rest of the night is a blur.

We laugh.

We cry.

We make love.

We sleep.

We repeat.

Chapter 54

Gray

"Thanks for meeting me."

My twin nods, taking a seat beside me at the bar. He waves to the bartender to get him what I'm having and we both sit, face forward, the air thick with tension.

"Why am I here?" he finally asks, breaking the silence.

Until our lives took different paths, my twin was my best friend. We were inseparable. We were in the same sports. We liked the same girls, so it's no wonder we fell in love with the same woman. We sat together every day at lunch, with Ash and Conn, making our own little tight, impenetrable clique. Luke and I were cohorts at pulling dozens of pranks on our younger brothers. So when he started going down a path that I didn't want to follow, it crushed me. Ruined me. My best friend was lost. He abandoned me, just as I thought Livvy had. And that wound runs deep.

Still.

While Livvy and Luke have talked on the phone a couple of times, I know they haven't seen each other since the day he dropped off her letter in my office. I know that because she's spent every second with me. Livvy wants Luke in her life, which means he will be in mine. Although that pains me because I know how he feels about her, it also means I need to clear the air between us. I want my brother back. I've missed him. I just didn't realize how much.

But Livvy is right. I haven't been fair to Luke. I haven't heard his side of the story. We can't rebuild everything in a night, but we can start, if he's willing. This is important to Livvy, so it's important to me.

I swivel my barstool, so I'm facing him. "Thank you."

Turning his head, he asks, "For?"

For bringing her back to me. For keeping me from making the single biggest mistake of my life by walking away. For everything. "For saving Livvy."

He faces forward again, taking a large drink of his draft beer. He's silent for so long, I don't think he's going to respond, and suddenly I'm not sure this fragile reunion will work. Maybe things are too damaged between us.

"I should have done more," he finally quietly responds. Pain threads his voice and it hits me hard. Then he gives me a Reader's Digest version of his story and now I know Livvy's right. Luke may have started down the wrong path, but he wanted to turn around, go back. Turns out, I'm glad he didn't, because he saved my future wife and mother of my children. It's ironic how fate, or God, or whatever higher power you believe in, places people in and out of our lives at exactly the right time.

"I was out. I had worked out all the specifics and accompanying Peter on this pick up was my last job. I was done. Until we got there, I didn't know what we were doing. Then I saw her. Livia. And I knew I couldn't leave an innocent, vulnerable

343

woman all alone in a house with Satan's spawn and no protection. They would eat her alive. She'd be dead within a month. So I stayed and I plotted and I saved and I planned and I protected her as much as I could without drawing suspicion." He takes another sip, pausing to gather his thoughts.

"It took me three long, agonizing years to get her out."

"I thought she got out because that monster died?"

Luke turns his head, locking eyes with mine. They swirled with malice and hatred, but I knew it wasn't directed at me. Eventually he said, "She did." Only what I heard was, *I killed him. For her.*

Sitting quietly, we each finish our beers and order another. I reflect on his silent words, and how much someone has to love another person to kill for them. A fucking lot.

"Livvy's pregnant."

"I know," he responds flatly.

"I'm going to ask her to marry me." Yep. I'm marking. I need to make it clear that Livvy is mine. To everyone. Including my own flesh and blood.

"I know. I'm happy for you both. Truly."

"I'm sorry, Luke. For..." I leave my sentence hanging, but we both know what I mean. I'm sorry for so goddamn much.

"I didn't know about you, you know. Until recently." I heard him swallow thickly and felt his heartbreak as if it were my own. I knew all about that suffering, and it tore me apart that my brother had to accept that he'll never be able to have the woman he wants. "I tried not to fall in love with her.

344

I knew she loved someone else, was engaged to someone else, and I knew I'd never be *that* guy. For years, I was insanely jealous of him, but knowing that it's you..." His gaze pierces me, and I hang on every word to see how he finishes his sentence. "...almost makes it easier."

He stands and takes a long chug before setting his half empty mug down. Grabbing my shoulder, he squeezes hard. "It's always been you. You do deserve her, Gray." Then he walks away, leaving me there to rehash every word we spoke, and those we didn't.

Chapter 55

Livia

"Hey, do you have a minute?" Asher asks, knocking on the door. I look up from my mounds of paperwork to see the sheepish face of Gray's younger brother standing in my doorway.

"Yes, sure."

"Moving, huh?" He takes a couple of steps in, looking uncomfortable and I let him. It was a pretty shitty thing he did, having me fired when Gray didn't even know about it, but to some degree I get it. He was protecting his brother and I'd hurt Gray terribly before. Asher doesn't know the only way I'll ever leave Gray again is through death. Gray and I agreed that outside of Luke, myself and him, no one would know the circumstances of why I had disappeared. At least not now, maybe not ever. It's still too fresh, too painful.

"Today's actually my last day. Just finishing up a couple of things." I agreed to come back to work for Gray part-time just until I finished his little patent project, which we just wrapped up earlier this week. His new assistant, Georgia, started last week as well and I've spent the last few days training her. She's nice, experienced and is about fifty with three grandchildren, so it's a bonus that she's not some young hottie who's looking to get into my boyfriend's pants.

"Look, Livia, I wanted to personally apologize. What I did was wrong and you need to know that Gray didn't have anything to do with me delivering those severance papers. He just wanted you reassigned until he figured shit out. I took liberties I shouldn't have and for that, I'm sorry."

I study him for a couple seconds. "I understand, Asher."

Sitting down, he continues. "I need to get something off my chest, if that's alright."

"Okay." I brace myself for whatever he has to say.

"I love my family and I can't watch Gray go through losing you again, Livia. It nearly killed him before."

I look down and once again, guilt assails me. "I know," I respond quietly.

"If you tell me you're committed to him and you won't abandon him again, I'll believe you. I'll work on trusting you again."

I study Asher because somehow I feel like this is about more than just what happened between Gray and me. I feel like he has personal experience with this. I want to tell him about the baby, assure him that I'm not going anywhere, but we aren't going to tell anyone about the pregnancy until after my doctor's appointment tomorrow.

"I love Gray, Asher. I always have. I – I don't blame you for not trusting that I won't hurt him again. Hell, I'm sure I will, but you have my word I will never leave him."

He nods. "Fair enough." He rises to leave but stops before he walks out. "He was lost without you Livia."

Tears sting and all I can do is stare, biting my lip to keep the waterworks from falling. While I love the fact that I'm pregnant, I hate most of the effects the hormones have on my body.

Some days I'm one big ball of tears and snot.

Ten minutes later, I'm packing up the last of the papers into the cardboard box when the love of my life walks in. "Hey, angel. Packing up?"

"Yep, just got finished. I'll be walking Georgia through just a couple of things yet before I go, but she's catching on fast so I don't think I'll need to come back."

"Yes, she's great, actually." Walking around the desk, he pulls me to him. "Are you sure you won't reconsider staying? I'll miss not seeing your face every day."

Reaching up, I peck him on the lips. "You'll see me every day. It will give you incentive to get home to me faster at night."

"Hmmm...true." His mouth descends on mine and I'm instantly turned on. The one *upside* of the pregnancy hormones.

"I talked to our attorneys today about the patent. They're vetting our options," he whispers against my now kiss-swollen mouth.

"Good."

Just two days ago I discovered that one of the developers just happened to be HMT's former CFO's brother-in-law and had known about the acquisition of HMT by GRASCO Holdings. A year ago when they found out the CEO was looking to sell, they secretly filed the patent without anyone else knowing. They thought they'd done a good job at erasing all the evidence, but a few instant messages turned up in the mounds of paperwork I reviewed. Just a few sentences led to their demise. Wes was innocent, but I was betting he'd be gone within six months anyway.

"I think I'll have to find some more 'special projects' for you to work on. You did good, Livvy."

"Thanks, babe. We still on to see your mother next weekend?"

"Yep. She's going to go into meltdown when she finds out you're pregnant. You know that, right?"

I laugh. "Yes."

"Two thirty tomorrow right?"

"Two thirty. Are you still able to come?"

He cups my cheeks. "Wild horses couldn't keep me away from seeing my babies growing in your belly, Livvy."

"Babies? You think I'm having twins?"

"No, I don't think. I know."

Chapter 56

Gray

"Livia Kingsley?" a female voice calls from the open doorway. We stand and, hand in hand, dutifully follow our guide to one of the exam rooms. The nurse hands Livvy a gown and instructs her to take everything off, making sure the ties of the thin garment are in the back.

After she leaves, I stand and cross the small room. When I grab the bottom of Livvy's shirt and begin to drag it over her head, she asks breathlessly, "Gray, what are you doing?"

"Helping you disrobe." Our eyes lock and her bright smile slays me, as it always does. Once I have her in her bra and panties, I make her turn and I unhook the lacy material that keeps her full breasts and sensitive nipples from my view. My fingers follow the path down her arms as I push it to the floor.

Protesting, but not very hard, she mutters, "She said I could keep my bra on."

"It's obstructing my view," I breathe against her skin. I palm her round globes while I feather kisses along her shoulders and neck and she arches to give me better access. Her breathy moans make me want to unzip, bend her over the table and take her right here. I run my hands down her bare torso and slip my fingers under the waistband of her panties, which are now drenched with want and need. My name is a breathy entreaty, falling from her lips to my ears.

Kneeling, I palm her full cheeks before dragging her panties to the floor to join the rest of her clothes. I make sure my lips don't miss an inch of her thighs and ass as I slowly stand. Grabbing the robe, I guide her arms through the sleeves and tie it closed.

After she's seated on the exam table and thoroughly kissed, she quips, "That's probably the most exciting exam prep I've ever had." Her cheeks are flushed with desire and I'm hard as fucking stone.

Chuckling, I pull her close. Her arms circle my waist. We cling to each other, as we often do these days. "I wanted it to be memorable, angel."

"Mission accomplished."

For the past three weeks that we've been back together, other than work, we haven't spent one single second apart. The floodwaters that had threatened to wash away our very happiness have receded. Every day our relationship grows stronger and feels more secure. Permanent. I love this woman more than life itself. She's my everything.

The day after Livvy and I reconciled, I sent Addy a gift certificate for an all-expenses paid seven-day vacation to paradise for two. Maui. Extravagant? No. Not nearly enough for all of her help and faith, even when I didn't deserve it.

There are things that happened to Livvy that are hard to swallow and accept. She's opened up a little about her life, or lack thereof, with the fiend that kept her from me, and my soul aches for all that she's suffered. We've wept together a lot at the loss of our baby. That was a tough day, and I'm still struggling to accept how very different our life would have been had all of this not happened.

Livvy was right when she said I was also a victim in this. We've both suffered untold losses, but our love is strong. It's impenetrable and it's everlasting. Livvy suggested counseling for me, for us, and she continues to see her therapist separately. I started therapy last week and I think maybe talking about what happened with a disinterested third party may help me put a lot of this shit at least into perspective. I'm not sure it will ever be behind me, or us, because it happened. It's part of our lives and can't be forgotten. The events of our past shape our future, the people we become and the lives we live, whether we want them to or not.

There are so many things in my past that I would change if I could. But the one constant would be to have met this vivacious, beautiful woman at Rocky's Pizza in downtown Detroit on December 28, 2007.

My everything.

There's a cursory knock on the door right before it opens, and whom I assume is Livvy's doctor steps through. I release Livvy, move to her side, my hand palming her bare thigh.

"Hi, I'm Dr. Law." We exchange pleasantries and she moves around the room, readying for her exam. Finally, she stops and smiles. "Well, are you two ready to see your baby?"

Because of the history of multiples in my family and Livvy's severe morning sickness, they wanted her to come in at eight weeks for an ultrasound. The doctor takes what looks like a slim dildo, puts a condom on it, along with some gel and gently glides it between Livvy's legs, which are now resting in stirrups.

I smile to myself because I am quite sure the gel is unnecessary. And I have to admit, I've never been more jealous of a piece of medical equipment than I am right now.

"You okay, angel?" I ask softly, squeezing her hand.

"Yes."

We watch the monitor, anxiously waiting to see signs of life inside Livvy's womb. Then suddenly I see them. *Both* of them. Two clearly separate sacks that will protect our babies while they grow. They don't look like much of anything right now, but lima beans with budding hands and legs, but they couldn't be any more perfect to me.

I feel Livvy shake and when I look down, she's watching me watch the monitor, and water streams in rivulets down her face, into her hair. When she told me what that vile creature tried to do to her after he murdered our baby, I lost it. I have a hairline fracture in the top of my right hand from punching the wall. Now we're staring at a miracle that I prayed with everything in me would happen every time I was inside of her, even though I had no idea at the time she didn't think it ever could.

"Tell me you love me."

"I love you," she whispers.

I bring my lips to hers. "Not half as much as I love you, angel."

I can honestly say that I've never been happier than I am at this very moment. I stare at Livvy, my best friend, my very soul, the mother of my children, and I know that after the heartache we have both endured, we're right where we're supposed to be.

With each other.

Epilogue

Two weeks later...

Livia

"Angel, it's time to go." Gray's tugging on my hand before his mom stops us.

Gray and I came back to visit his mother for the weekend, in part because we wanted to tell her about the babies in person, but also because I've just missed her. When we told her, she spent all last night crying and hugging us. Then we thumbed through Gray's baby book, which was the first time I'd seen it. There were a lot of pictures of Luke, which I thoroughly enjoyed seeing too. Barb Colloway has no shortage of pictures of her boys.

"Oh, hang on dear. Just one minute," Barb says before rushing out of the room. Less than a minute later, she's back with a package wrapped in pastel *Congratulations* paper.

"What's this for?"

"For my firstborn's firstborns."

"Barb..." I look at Gray and he just shrugs his shoulders, smiling.

"Now, now. No tears. Go on, open it."

Sitting, I slowly tear off the thin recycled paper and open the package to reveal two of the most beautiful light blue handmade quilted baby blankets that I've ever seen. Intricate diamond patterns decorate the thick fabric and the trim is silky blue a couple of shades darker than the threaded material. I notice a couple of darker spots on the cloth, which I initially think are stains, but I quickly realize is wetness from my tears.

"They're beautiful, Barb. Where did you get these?"

"It was Gray's from when he was young. My grandmother made a quilt for each of the boys one year for Christmas and I had it repurposed into baby blankets, so it could be passed down to the next generation."

"But...we just told you yesterday. How...?"

She just winked. "Mother's intuition."

I hug her and let my happiness freely flow. "Thank you. Thank you so much."

"I'm glad you like them, dear."

"I love them."

I look up at Gray and I can hardly breathe with the love I feel for him. It's surreal. I still have to pinch myself some days wondering if I'm lost in a dream or if this life I'm now living is actually real. If it's a dream, I hope I never wake up. When he mouths *I love you*, I can't get help but go to him, wrapping myself in his embrace.

"Ready?"

"Do we have to go, Gray? Can't we stay here?" I ask softly. For some reason he's insistent we go out to dinner, even though we came home to see his mother.

"It's okay, Livia. You two go and have fun. I have plans anyway," Barb says, winked.

"Okay. Only if you're sure."

"Pshaw. You two have a good time. If I'm not here when you get home, I won't be late." I give her a quick kiss and hug and then we're on our way.

We're silent in the car, but it's a good silent. Gray's hand is threaded through my own and I'm replaying these last few weeks slowly, unable to help the smile that spreads.

"Have you talked to Asher?" I ask. He's still holding a grudge against Asher for firing me. I've been trying to convince him to let it go. Asher was just doing what family does. Protecting each other.

"Yes. We're cool." He picks up our entwined hands, kissing mine.

"What are you thinking about?" I ask.

His smile is blinding. "I'm thinking about how happy I am."

"Me too." Happy...and horny. I lean over the console, licking a path up his neck to his ear and grab his hardening cock, giving it a little squeeze. "Screw dinner. Take me somewhere and fuck me," I whisper against the shell of his ear.

He groans but stops my stroking hand with one of his own. "Food first, angel. You need to take care of my babies."

"Your loss," I pout.

Minutes later Gray pulls up outside of Rocky's Pizza and shuts off the car.

"Why are we here?" I ask, walking through the doors of the place I once worked. Where Gray and I first met. The memory of his proposal and telling me to suck him harder back in the employee lounge is one of my best and most used ones for the past several years.

357

"Can't a guy want to take his girl for the best pizza in town?"

"That's debatable," I laugh. I ate so much pizza all those years I worked here that I ended up almost hating it, but the smell wafting outside the minute we opened the door now actually has my stomach rumbling, which is a nice change from the nausea.

We take a seat and the waitress quickly brings us menus. I sit back against the cracked, red vinyl-covered booth and admire Gray, who is apparently very engrossed in figuring out what type of crust and toppings we're going to order.

I watch his mesmerizing eyes scan the list, wishing they were raking over me instead. I watch his lips move slightly and I remember the wicked things they were doing to me just hours ago in the bathroom of his mother's house. And I watch the brilliant smile break across his face when he feels my gaze, firing every neuron and cell inside my body.

His eyes rise to catch mine and he sets the menu down. "Do you realize this is the same exact place I was sitting when I first saw you?"

Suddenly all the oxygen seems to have left the room. I can barely breathe. I shake my head, not able to form words.

"You were so beautiful, Livvy. God, you literally took my breath away. I'd never wanted anything as much as I wanted you. On that day, do you know I told my brothers that I had just met my wife?"

358

My eyes mist. *No.* He never told me that. The restaurant is noisy, but all I can hear is Gray and the quiet, reverent words he speaks. Each one feels like another layer of love he's wrapping around my heart. He leans forward, taking my hands in his before he continues. "You breathe the very *life* into my soul, Livvy. I didn't even know I wasn't living until the day I laid eyes you. Without you, I've been lost, adrift, without purpose or meaning. With you...I'm finally whole. Christ, I can breathe again for the first time in years."

Then he slides from the booth and bends on one knee, pulling a ring from his pocket. When I see it, both hands fly to smother the sobs coming from deep within me. It's my original, custom-made engagement ring. The one I'd kept hidden all these years. And it's in his hands.

I regularly dreamed of the inscription he had etched inside just for me.

Everything.

Who knew one word could convey so much?

How does he have it? And I immediately know the answer to my own question. Addy.

"You're my everything, angel. I've waited eight years. I'm not waiting a minute longer to make you my wife. I love you so very much, Livia. Marry me. Please."

Then I'm on the floor with him, my mouth on his, whispering yes, yes, yes. History was repeating itself, but I knew this time would be different. We'd have our fairytale ending.

This time, we have our happily ever after.

~ The End ~

My musical inspiration for writing Forsaking Gray:

"Through The Ghost" by Shinedown
"Lie to Me (Denial)" by Red
"Torn to Pieces" by Pop Evil
"The Heart Wants What It Wants" by Selena Gomez
"Again" by Flyleaf
"All Falls Down" by Adelita's Way
"Take Me to Church" by Hozier
"Fully Alive" by Flyleaf
"All In" by Lifehouse
"Yours Again" by Red
"Fully Alive" by Flyleaf
"Beautiful" by Pop Evil
"Stars" by Sixx:A.M.
"Believe In Dreams" by Flyleaf

Other works by K.L. Kreig:

The Regent Vampire Lords series:

Surrendering
Belonging
Reawakening

Turn the page for a sneak peek at Undeniably Asher, the next book in the Colloway Brothers series. Release date winter 2015.

Undeniably Asher Excerpt

Alyse

It's almost noon and I steel myself for my next meeting, wondering what the hell Asher Colloway thinks he's trying to pull and why he didn't just put his name on my calendar instead of his holding company. Clearly he's trying to surprise me.

Well, the surprise is on him, because not only do I know it's him I'm meeting with, I know that he asked for client references, and I know he's called each and every one of them already. We're a small office and Heather keeps nothing from me, not to mention we like to give our clients a heads up when we know they'll be called by a potential client.

The thing is, I have no idea what he would possibly hire my small firm for, but since I'm desperate for revenue, I can't *not* take the meeting. I have more to think about now than just my pride. I have three employees and they're counting on me to feed and cloth themselves and their families. That's a heavy burden.

I thought about having Al sit in, but decided against it. I already know Asher and he knows me, so having another male in the room isn't really necessary. Besides, a little part of me is thrilled to spend a few hours alone with him, even if we are just discussing business. *Okay, a* big *part of me.*

I managed to close one deal earlier this week and am waiting to hear back from the other client, hopefully by the end of the day. That one doesn't look too promising, as we're a bit apart on pricing for our services. I have a small office and can't afford to be quite as flexible as other, larger firms that have more capital to work with. Another thing I did not take into consideration when I jumped into this dream of mine headfirst. *Ugh.*

My speakerphone squawks and Heather's voice floats through. Her normally quiet, soft demeanor has clearly been ratcheted up a few degrees, because she actually sounds excited and I can hear the smile in her voice. Yes, Asher Colloway will do that to a woman, at least any straight one. "Ms. Kingsley, your noon appointment is here."

Ms. Kingsley? Heather hasn't addressed me as Ms. Kingsley since our first interview and even at the end of that meeting she was calling me Alyse. I keep the laugh from my voice as I respond. "Thank you, Heather. Please send Mr. Colloway in." Once I disconnect I do chuckle, because Heather usually has me on speakerphone when she buzzes my appointments in, so Asher's little surprise has just been turned around. *Ha! Bo yaw!*

I'm still laughing when Asher opens my closed door, but the moment my eyes land on him, it dies. My gaze slowly travels down his insanely fit body and I realize that he's watching me watch him, but I don't care enough to stop.

He's absolutely breathtaking in his fitted charcoal suit and crisp white shirt, which he's left open at the throat, sans tie. And the tiny bit of chest hair I see peeking through against his golden skin makes me water in more than one place. I've never seen him in anything but jeans and henleys or polo shirts, but *hot damn* if he doesn't look even more mouthwatering when he's dressed up. My entire body feels warm and tingly, inside and out.

I gravitate toward men that have dark looks.

Dark hair.

Dark whiskers.

Dark eyes.

Dark personality.

And Asher Colloway fits that bill to a perfect "T". At a little over six feet, he's tall, at least for me since I hover around the five foot four mark, give or take half inch on a good day. All of the Colloway brothers could effortlessly grace the cover of a magazine, but Asher is different. He's a guy you could easily get lost in before your brain catches up with reminding you why you shouldn't. He has an aura about him that's nothing short of magical and when you look at him, a spell is woven that you can't escape. And you don't want to.

When I met him for the first time at seventeen, I thought he was the best thing since sliced bread. I even thought I was in love with him, but we were in very different places in our lives. And then I met Beck and I moved forward instead of looking back. Now, though...now, at twenty-nine, I can honestly say Asher *is* the sexiest man I have ever laid eyes on, hands down.

I want him. Desperately.

And desperation makes you do stupid, stupid things.

"Get your fill yet?" A smug smirk turns up one corner of his kissable mouth.

Damn him. I have absolutely no snarky comeback to that, because I've been openly ogling. I only hope I don't have drool dripping down my chin. I nonchalantly reach up to check, faking a cough.

"Why the secrecy?" I ask, changing subjects, not taking my eyes from him.

He closes the door before taking a seat in the chair across from my metal desk, throwing one foot onto the opposite knee. He steeples his fingers in front of his chin and the arrogant glint in his dark eyes makes me want to drop to my knees in front of him, unzip his pants and wipe it off.

"You knew it was me."

I knew Asher had taken over as CEO for his father's company - I *may* have asked Livia what the Colloway brothers were up to after she'd reunited with Gray. In preparation for this meeting when I researched GRASCO Holdings and found that CFC fell under them, at first I was irritated that Asher wanted to catch me cold. I never attend a client meeting without doing my homework first, especially since I'm fighting for the very existence of *ARK Consulting*. But then I quickly decided to turn the tables on the self-assured SOB.

Knowing that I would be meeting with Asher today, I've dressed particularly sexy in a short nude pencil skirt and a sheer royal blue blouse with a matching low-cut cami underneath. Definitely not how I would dress for a normal client meeting, but I went all out for Asher. I let a slow smile turn my lips as I sit back in my black vinyl chair and cross my legs.

Asher's eyes follow my leisurely movements and widen at the expanse of bare thigh I'm now showing. He may have even gotten a flash of the nude thong I'm wearing from his position. His heated eyes rise, snaring mine and I have to actually talk myself into breathing, trying to remain unaffected by the intense desire he clearly wants me to see. It's not working too well.

"It may surprise you to know that I do know how to use the Internet," I finally manage to bite sarcastically.

"You haven't changed a bit, Alyse."

"I beg to differ," I retort, knowing full well life has made me more cynical and closed off.

He rewards me with a small smile, which almost melts me on the spot. He's like the sun. Warm. Inviting. Only more deadly if you spend too much time in his presence. He's quiet for several beats, his eyes assessing me deliberately. "I like a woman with fire."

"Do you?" I cross my arms, unsure where this conversation is headed, but I feel like it's not about business anymore. I don't miss how his eyes linger too long on my now exposed cleavage.

"Yes." He uncrosses his leg and leans forward, elbows on spread knees, hands clasped. His want-filled gaze burns my cocky attitude to ashes. "It makes her complete submission all the sweeter."

A flash fire of heat scorches my lady parts. My mouth drops open temporarily before I think to close it. Asher is so good, so smooth and I am *waaaay* out of my league trying to trade barbs with him.

"What are you doing here, Asher?"

He leans back again, resuming a casual position, a slight smirk on his face. His eyes twinkle like stars and I find myself getting lost in them again. "Besides getting you wet?" he drawls roughly. Even though he's spot on, his assumption angers me and I open my mouth to protest when he interrupts. "You still with Popeye?"

It takes me a minute to figure out what he means. *Finn.* I stare at him in complete and utter shock for several moments. Then, I can't help it. I laugh. I've never been around a man that has as big of kahunas as Asher Colloway. He was always direct, but in the years since I've seen him, he's sharpened it considerably. It's refreshing and unsettling at the same time.

I shake my head, still chuckling, but he's stony silent and his desire has now clearly morphed into annoyance, which makes me laugh even harder. "And if I say yes?"

"Are you?"

I almost decide to lie just to see how he'll react, but anger isn't the type of response I want from Asher. I'm not really sure what I do want, but I know it's not that. "No."

As fast as his ire came, it went with my admission.

"Did you come here to question my relationship status? You could have just hopped on Facebook for that, saved yourself the drive." I've uncrossed my legs and now am leaning on my forearms, the coldness from the steel desk seeping into my exposed pores through the thin fabric. It's

November in Detroit and it's very cold, but I still can't regret my choice of wardrobe after seeing the appreciation in both Asher's eyes and slacks.

"Because it's not official until it's Facebook official, right?"

"Right," I drawl. "So, back to my original question. Why are you here?"

"I want to hire you."

I assumed when he was calling references that was his angle. I'm thrilled, but at the same time, disappointed. I need this job, but I also want Asher, even though that's not the best of ideas. And I can't have both.

Why?...a little voice whispers.

Because it's kind of faux pas to sleep with your clients, I tell that little slut.

"For?"

"There's someone embezzling within my company and I want them found and stopped and prosecuted." He pulls an envelope out of a folder that he'd set down on the edge of my desk earlier. "Our outside audit firm completed our annual audit and found a discrepancy in the books, but they aren't equipped to take it further. We need someone who has expertise in ferreting out things like this, whose techniques will hold up in a court of law. I know you've worked on cases before where your work has supported a legal case."

True. I live to bring down white-collar thieves. My dad was a thief; he just stole our childhood from my sister and I instead of a corporation or business. I think that's one of the reasons I went into this field to begin with. "Is this a past or ongoing issue?"

"I have reason to believe it's ongoing, but of course I can't be sure."

"Do you have any suspicions?"

"Yes. Unfortunately nothing solid, though."

I look down, unsure of how I should approach this. I don't want to talk myself out of a job, but I want to be up front as well. I don't doubt my ability in the slightest, but CFC would be, by far, the biggest client I've worked on and this project could possibly take months, given my small staff and dependent on how deep the embezzlement is buried. "You do know I haven't worked on a project for a company your size yet, correct?"

He nods, staying quiet.

"Okay. Let me look this over and work up a proposal and proposed timeline for your review. I can have it to you by mid-next week and then we can meet again, discuss any questions you might have. Negotiate terms."

"No."

My brows draw together in confusion. "No, what?"

"No. I told you I want to hire you. *You*. I've already done my research. I don't need to review anything."

I'm taken aback for a moment. "I could rob you blind. My fee may not even be competitive with the other firms you're considering."

"I'm already being robbed blind. And you won't. Whatever your fees, whatever your terms, I'll agree to them. I want the best, Alyse." He pauses before he adds, "And I hear that's you."

Huh? This is by far the weirdest client prospect meeting I've ever had. I have to wonder what the catch is, because this seems too good to be true. "Uh, oookay."

"I want you to start on Monday."

It's the Wednesday before Thanksgiving. I think for a minute, cataloging our current projects. I was planning to take this new client I just secured, but I can give that to Al as long as they agree. Tabitha still has at least two weeks on her current project, and I'll have to come in now on Friday to wrap up a few loose ends and do some paperwork. "Okay, that will work."

He's silent, studying me for a moment. "One more thing. And it's non-negotiable."

I smirk. "I'm not sleeping with you." *Even though right now I can think of nothing else but your hot, wet tongue worshiping every inch of me.*

Laughing, he leans forward, his forearms on my desk, his face mere inches from mine. I want to lean back, yet not at the same time, so I don't. Once again, Asher invades my personal space and I can't help the big breath I take, inhaling his manly, spicy scent. It's all I can do to keep my eyes from rolling back in my head.

He doesn't miss it either. I'm getting the distinct feeling he doesn't miss any of my bodily reactions to his inebriating presence. When he finally speaks his voice drops several octaves to panty-melting sexy. "Good. Because I'm looking forward to fucking you instead."

Holy balls. His blistering stare and egotistical words light a blaze deep within my belly. If I was wet before, I'm positively drenched now. And mute. Very, very mute. On account of the fact that my mouth is now bone dry and all thought has fled my desire-clouded brain.

His next words pull me out of the sexual haze he has enthralled us in. It's a place I could imagine myself staying. Forever. "I need you at headquarters during the audit. In Chicago."

I blink a few times to clear my fog, letting his words register. Being on-site during an audit is pretty standard, at least part of the time, but this will be a big audit and could take months. I bill for lodging and meal expenses, but the thought of spending months in a hotel and shuttling back and forth on the weekends to Detroit is less than appealing. On the other hand, it gets me closer to Livia. Hell, who am I kidding? I'd shuttle back and forth to San Francisco if there were a paying client there.

"You have offices here in Detroit, right?"

"Yes, but I need to keep this as quiet as possible. CFC is not all that big, so the fewer people that know about you, the better. I need you in Chicago. There's a secluded office available on my floor."

The thought of being near Asher daily does funny things to my insides. More than it should. More than I want. "That's going to be pretty costly for you," I murmur. *And me*, I think, in more ways than one.

372

He leans back slightly and I take a deep breath for the first time in long minutes without inhaling him. His unique fragrance is clouding my mind. And my judgment.

"I have another proposal."

I roll my eyes and lean back in my chair, but his magnetic pull makes it hard to do even that.

I am in so much trouble.

"I'm not staying with you, either."

"Why do you insist on ruining all my fun, Alyse?" he quips, winking.

I smile, but remain quiet. Even if he would be so bold to suggest it, he would have to know I'd never accept.

"Okay. If you won't stay with me, then we have an executive apartment that's not being used. It's fully furnished and close to the office. The building has a nice gym and a couple of restaurants. It's not terribly fancy, but it's better than a hotel."

"I – I don't know, Asher." I was hedging, but the second his proposal left his mouth, I'd already made up my mind. If I had a place that felt like my own, I could stay there most weekends instead of driving back to Detroit, where there was really nothing left for me, except bad memories and ghosts from my past that won't seem to let me out of their steely grip.

He gets comfortable again before continuing his sales pitch. "It's in the same building as Livia and Gray, so you'll also be close to your sister. I know you're helping with their shotgun wedding and wouldn't it be convenient to be able to hop in the elevator and pop in on her? Of course, I would probably call ahead first, because..."

He leaves his insinuation hanging and we both laugh, lightening the mood.

As I pretend to think about it for a couple of minutes, his intense gaze never leaves mine. I can feel him willing me into acquiescence and I almost break a smile, but that would be giving him too much and right now I need to hold parts of me back, because I can already tell Asher will demand everything from me. And then some. And I can feel certain girlie parts of me begging me to submit, submit, submit.

Seeing Asher again a couple of months ago triggered something inside me. Made me remember my girlish dreams when I was eighteen and in love with Beck. Dreams that have been too painful to remember, but now that I do, I want them desperately. And if I'm really honest, it made me remember what I felt when I almost gave myself to a young Asher Colloway.

I want bone-deep a family, happiness and a man that will worship me. I thought Beck was the man that would give me everything, but he's dead and apparently wasn't the man I thought he was at all.

Finn certainly wasn't that man.

And I don't think Asher Colloway can give me any of those things either. I'm not sure he can give *any* woman that.

Pleasure? *No doubt.*

A future? *Not likely.*

374

He's nearly thirty, never been married and is clearly a player and I just want more than that now. God knows I *deserve* more than that. As much as I'm attracted to him, sleeping with him is probably about the dumbest idea to ever cross my mind, yet my conviction not to needs a lot of reinforcement.

I re-focus on the reason we're having this discussion in the first place. Keeping my business afloat. "Okay. I accept your terms."

His smile blinds me, and all thoughts I just had about why I should stay away from this man floated out of the room on a cloud of pure lust.

Yep, my conviction needs a lot of work.

A. Lot.

Acknowledgements and Thanks!

I'm in a little in shock that I'm writing my thanks for my *fourth* novel. Seems surreal and not at all possible, but here I am, doing it anyway.

To my readers: If you're a fan of my paranormal works, then I **thank you** for trying out this contemporary read and I hope you've enjoyed it as much as the Regent Vampire Lords. The Colloway Brothers started screaming in my head not too far into writing the RVL series and had to take a break from my sexy lords to get these characters out so they'd stop talking to me and my God...did I fall in LOVE with every single brother!! (Yes, Amanda...I'm using *two* exclamation points).

If you like my book, ***please*** tell your friends, your neighbors, shout it from the rooftops. Hell, tell people you don't even like! The best thing you can do to support an author you love is word of mouth. Also consider joining **Kreig's Babes**, a private Facebook page where you can chat with fellow fans, make new friends and talk about books and anything else you feel like. They are a fab group of women! Oh, and we may occasionally have man-candy as well. ☺

To my girls, my betas: Tara, Kaitlyn, Beth, Sherri, Kate, Alaina, Sabrina, Zavara, Justine, Chrissy, Kelly, Sloan and Kayla...a million thanks will never be enough for your honesty and your valued opinions.

Since this was my first non-PNR book, I was a little unsure of myself, but your glowing feedback made me more confident. Special shout out to *Kate*, though. I equally love and hate your book reports, but your quirky comments make me LOL. So glad to have found you and your amazing insight which truly helped to shape this story. And Alaina, your honest feedback about plot holes made Gray and Livia's story the very best it could be. Thanks!

To my husband: Babe, you are my everything, my inspiration, my very heart. I can write about romance because I live it every day with you. Thanks for your undying support as my writing continues to consume me. You've become quite the little chef! ☺ You are my rock and I'm so very glad that you're proud of what I've been able to accomplish, because none of it would have been possible without you.

Thanks to my editor, Amanda at Progressive Edits. You are *so* much more than just an editor and marketing extraordinaire. You've become a guide, a friend and a mentor. Thanks for all you do for me, but most importantly, thanks for believing in me and pushing me to do things I *need* to do but don't really want to.

To my author and blogger friends: There are so many of you now (eeeek) that if I start naming everyone, I will inevitably forget and leave someone out and then I'll feel like a big pile of crap and beat myself up about it for weeks, so I won't name names, but if you're reading this, you know who are. Thanks for all the "likes", "shares" and blogging you do on my behalf. You have all helped this newbie more than you'll ever know and I'm so happy to have found a place where people share the same passion of books and reading and hot, sexy, alpha men as I do!

And finally a special thanks to Yocla Designs for the absolutely *A MA Z I N G* job you did on the book cover art! I adore your work, Clarissa.

About the Author

This is the hardest part...talking about myself.

I'm just a regular ol' Midwest girl who likes Game of Thrones and am obsessed with Modern Family and The Goldbergs. I run, I eat, I run, I eat. It's a vicious cycle. I love carbs, but there's love-hate relationship with my ass and thighs. Mostly hate. I like a good cocktail (oh hell...who am I kidding? I love *any* cocktail). I'm a huge creature of habit, but I'll tell you I'm flexible. I read every single day and if I don't get a chance...watch the hell out, I'm a raving bitch. My iPad and me: BFFs. I'm direct and I make no apologies for it. I swear too much. I love alternative music and in my next life I want to be a bad-ass female rocker. I hate, hate, hate spiders, telemarketers, liver, acne, winter and loose hairs that fall down my shirt (don't ask, it's a thing).

I have a great job (no...truly it is) outside of writing. My kids and my husband are my entire world and I'd never have made it this far without them. My soul mate husband of nearly twenty-eight years provides unwavering support and my two grown children know the types of books I write and they don't judge their mom anyway (and my daughter is a beta reader even...yes, that can be awkward... very).

Although Forsaking Gray is the fourth full-length novel that I have published in less than a year, I still consider myself a virgin author. I'm <u>sincerely</u> humbled by each and every like on my FB page or sign-up for my newsletter or outreach from someone who has read and loved my books. I still can't get over the great support and reviews for my Regent Vampire Lords series from bloggers and my "fans". I've made more friends in the last year than I've made in my life and I'm a pretty affable person. It's surreal. I'm pretty sure it always will be.

In short, I am blessed...and I know it.

If you enjoyed this book, <u>please</u> consider leaving a review on Goodreads, Amazon, Barnes and Noble, or the many various other on-line places you can purchase ebooks. Even one or two sentences or simply rating the book is helpful for other readers. If you're anything like me, you rely on reader reviews to help make your determination on purchasing a great book in the vast sea of many great ones available. Many THANKS!

If you'd like to keep up on my newest releases, please sign up for my newsletter at klkreig.com. I promise no spamming.

Finally, if you would like to learn more about K.L. Kreig or message her, visit her at the following places:

Facebook: https://www.facebook.com/pages/KL-Kreig/808927362462053?ref=hl

Kreig's Babes private FB page: https://www.facebook.com/groups/646655825434751/

Website: http://klkreig.com

Goodreads: https://www.goodreads.com/author/show/9845429.K_L_Kreig

Email: klkreig@gmail.com

Twitter: https://twitter.com/klkreig

TSU: http://www.tsu.co/klkreig